MW01224529

Making Amends

A Novel

By

D. J. Callaghan

 FriesenPress

Suite 300 - 990 Fort St
Victoria, BC, V8V 3K2
Canada

www.friesenpress.com

ISBN
978-1-5255-7651-5 (Hardcover)
978-1-5255-7652-2 (Paperback)
978-1-5255-7653-9 (eBook)

1. FICTION, ROMANCE, PARANORMAL

Distributed to the trade by The Ingram Book Company

Making Amends

Chapter 1 – Jenna 1

Chapter 2 – The Best-Laid Plans 13

Chapter 3 – Mackenzie 23

Chapter 4 – Afterlife 39

Chapter 5 – Born Again 53

Chapter 6 – The Muse 65

Chapter 7 – Abduction Foiled 79

Chapter 8 – Therapy 93

Chapter 9 – Danny 107

Chapter 10 – The Art of Forgiveness 119

Chapter 11 – Letting Go 131

Chapter 12 – Second Chances 143

Chapter 13 – Trucker Joe 155

Chapter 14 – Karma's a Bitch 167

Chapter 15 – True Story 179

Chapter 16 – Can't Win Them All 191

Chapter 17 – The Kid 203

Chapter 18 – Jenna and the Paramedic 213

Chapter 19 – Secrets Revealed 225

Chapter 20 – Baby Makes Five 237

Chapter 21 – Graduation Day 249

Chapter 1

Jenna

January 9, 2016

Jenna sat in the little coffee shop a few blocks from her home trying desperately to calm her fury. She racked her brain in an attempt to fully understand what was causing such a volcano of emotions. She loved Danny but sometimes she just couldn't stand to be around him and even after sixteen years they still hadn't been able to find a way to work together. His condescending attitude always managed to rub her the wrong way.

They had been to counselling several times to learn how to communicate with one another, and they did really well—in the psychologist's office. But left on their own they just didn't seem to be able to work things out like reasonable adults. With a weary sigh, she wondered why she even kept trying. He simply seemed unwilling to change, to hear her, to respect her ideas.

She stared off into space. People came and went, going about their business, chatting, laughing, but all it was to her was background noise, no different than the distant sound of traffic on the freeway or a clock ticking. She was so engrossed in her own thoughts that she didn't notice Danny standing there until he cleared his throat.

"Can I sit down with you?" he asked as he shifted his weight from foot to foot, obviously unsure of the reception that awaited him.

Jen sighed again and gestured to the seat opposite her. "I'm not sure what good it's going to do but it's still a free country."

"Wow! What an overwhelmingly warm reception! I can't imagine how I could possibly refuse it." Sarcasm dripped from his every word as he proceeded to sit down.

"Look Danny, I'm just tired. Tired of fighting. Tired of struggling. Why can't we seem to find a way to interact without making each other crazy? Why do you always have to be right? Why can't you, just once, try to see things from my perspective?"

With a snort he replied, "Funny you should say that because I'm feeling exactly the same way. Why do you always have to fight me on every front? Why can't you just trust me once in a while?" He paused, a look of sadness and defeat on his handsome face, a face she knew almost as well as her own. She could close her eyes and see each individual eyelash that framed his sleepy blue eyes, the little points on his ears. She could feel the soft skin on his chin just above his goatee. She still remembered the first time she met him, how taken she had been with this gentle giant.

At 5"9", she didn't feel small very often but as her brother introduced his friend and co-worker to her at one of his many backyard barbecues, she found she was forced to look an awfully long way up. And when his huge hand enveloped hers, she felt something she hadn't felt in a long time: safe.

She was looking at him so intently she almost missed his next sentence. The noises around her died out completely as her senses narrowed, focusing intently on the words he was saying.

"Jenna, I think we need a trial separation." He paused a moment looking down at the table then back up at her. "I just don't want to live like this anymore."

She felt a chill move through her body. She knew she was at a defining moment in her life; a seismic shift was about to occur. She was on a collision course with fate and there was nothing she could do to stop it. She wanted to plead, to argue, placate, cajole. The problem was, she knew he was right. They were both just so set in their own way, they were clearly unable to see one another's viewpoint. Maybe some distance would make things clearer.

"I think maybe you're right, Danny." She had a hard time getting the words over the lump in her throat.

She had no idea how long they sat just looking at each other. They both knew this move was extreme, but they also knew they needed do something extreme to reset their relationship, even though both were fully aware that this could be the end for them.

"I love you so very much, Jenna." Danny was the one to break the silence.

"I know, Danny, and I love you, but we're both old enough to know that love does not conquer all," Jenna said as she stood up and threw her bag over her shoulder, suddenly unable to sit there a moment longer. "If you just give me a couple of hours, I'll pack some things and go."

Following her lead, he got up too, saying, "No need. You can stay in the house until we figure things out. I'm already packed. I'll go out to the cabin. It's harder for you to leave with your studio in the house." They'd built the studio when Danny got tired of sacrificing the kitchen table to Jenna's latest project. Since then, her paintings had become so popular she had been able to make it her full-time job.

Suddenly, Jenna couldn't breathe. Panic washed over her. She didn't want to be in the house without him. It was *their* house! She didn't care about the studio. She could paint anywhere. As fear threatened to over-whelm her, another thought converged on her already shattered senses.

"How long, Danny?"

"What do you mean?"

"How long are we going to do this trial separation before we decide to either give up completely or try again?"

"I don't know, Jenna," he sighed. "As long as it takes." With that, he turned and headed for the door.

It was only a short walk from the coffee shop to their house but to Jenna it felt like forever. She walked with her shoulders slumped, feet dragging, head down. Like a woman carrying the weight of the world on her shoulders, or one who had aged twenty years in the blink of an eye. She had suspected this day would come. Things between them had been a struggle for most of their sixteen-year marriage, but she honestly believed if they kept trying they would find a way.

Tears behind her eyes fought for release, but she refused to give in. She refused to be that crazy lady walking down the street muttering to herself with tears streaming down her face. Only when she was safe behind closed doors would she allow them to flow.

As she made her way home she was painfully aware of the acuteness of her senses. Everything around her felt so bright, so painfully sharp. The sky was brighter blue then it had any right be, the sun glinting off the fresh, white snow was blinding, and the sounds of the children playing in the neighbourhood playground that usually made her smile sounded sharp and shrill, grating on her nerves until she was sure she would scream. Finally, she reached her gate. She stopped and took it all in: her fence, her yard, her front porch—*their* fence, *their* yard, *their* front porch.

They built this house, she and Danny together. It had been a labour of love, every nail, every board, every shingle. They picked out flooring, paint colours, appliances. Arguing, laughing, and loving. But the arguments overshadowed everything else. It seemed before they could get down to any real decisions they had to have a knockdown, drag-out fight. Finding a compromise was always a bloody battle, but once the war was over they would get back on track. Until then the power struggle was epic. She understood Danny's decision to leave. If she were honest she would have to admit that if he hadn't, she eventually would have. They were both exhausted; maybe this would give them a chance to clear their heads.

Taking a deep breath, she braced herself for the onslaught of joy that would greet her when she opened the door. The one thing she could always count on was their two crazy poodles being happy to see her. One black as night named Choco and the other an apricot named Cara would inundate her from both sides, jousting for position and attention. They would jump up on their hind legs, making themselves almost as tall as she was, their entire bodies wiggling with sheer and utter ecstasy. They would bury their fuzzy puppy noses on each side of her neck, giving it a good licking. They would dance like that for a while until they were calm enough to let her put her things down and take her shoes off, then they would nose through her things to see if there were any hidden treats or new puppy toys.

But this time, when she opened the door there was nothing. She was met with a deafening silence. *Of course,* she thought. Danny would never leave Choco behind, and where Choco went so did Cara. Choco was so closely bonded with Danny he would lose his fuzzy poodle mind if Danny left for any length of time and even though Cara was her dog, Cara was never without Choco.

Sadness descended on her like a snowfall in winter, chilling her to the bone as she sat on the bench in the foyer, slowly taking off her hat, scarf, mitts, and coat. Then she just sat staring into space, unable to comprehend this turn of events or what to do next. She understood too well that, even though he used the words "trial separation," this could very well be the end of their marriage. Not many people came back from trial separations, and for all their fighting she could honestly not imagine her life without him.

She gave her head a firm shake and reminded herself that this was not the first time she had had to deal with difficulty and, odds were, it probably would not be the last. She found it ironic that now that she was safe within the confines of her house, the tears she so desperately tried to stave off were gone. There was nothing left but a numb, empty feeling. For this she was grateful. Now she just had to get on with the business of the day. At least that's what she told herself.

Forcing herself up off the bench, she hung her outside clothes in the entry closet and stepped into her house slippers. They were old and worn, very much the way she felt. Then she decided her first order of business would be to get rid of this suffocating silence. Heading to her library, she searched through her playlist and turned on the surround sound. This was definitely one battle she was glad she lost. Danny was right, she loved the sound of music as it filled every corner of the house.

Next, she headed for the bedroom. This was ground zero. They had just bought new bedroom furnishings, a battle all in itself, but when they finally got them home each had a set idea in mind as to how they should be arranged. Jenna was a creature of habit and when she found a layout she liked she never wanted to change it. She wanted the new pieces to go in the spaces vacated by the old furniture. Danny, on the other hand, loved to switch things up, always looking for better ways to do things. And so the war began. It ended with Jenna stomping out of the house in a fit of temper and Danny standing there looking lost.

She smiled a small, sad smile. Danny had set up the entire room, even hanging the drapes and making the bed, exactly the way she wanted it. *Funny*, she thought to herself. *It doesn't feel like much of a victory.* The tears that had previously eluded her suddenly came rushing to the surface as she sat down on the bed and cried.

Post Separation - Week 1

After her initial crying spell, Jenna did her best to go about her business as usual. She forced herself to get up at her usual time and move through her daily routine. But now there were gaps in that routine that she felt as acutely as a physical blow and whenever she got to one of them it took her breath away, leaving her gasping for air.

Normally, she would wait for the dogs to get up and loom over her with the message that it was time for them to be fed and let out for their morning pee. They were incredibly accurate alarm clocks, waking her faithfully at 6 a.m., sharp. Her coffee maker was set to an automatic timer so the smell of coffee, one her favourite, would greet her as she made her way downstairs with both pups hot on her heels threatening to trip her.

Once their needs were taken care of, she would make two breakfast smoothies, pour two cups of coffee, then turn on the morning news. By this time, Danny was usually just out of the shower and getting dressed. She would wait for him with a smile on her face as he bounced down the stairs and every morning without fail he would greet her with a "Good morning, beautiful wife," and she would reply, turning her face up for a kiss, "Good morning, lover."

Once Danny was off to work and breakfast was cleaned up, Jenna would head upstairs, put on her workout clothes, and go to the gym they had built in the little sunroom where, during the winter months, she would do a five-to-eight-kilometre run—depending on the day—on her trusty old treadmill. Then she would grab a quick shower, brush her teeth, braid her freshly washed, waist-length chestnut hair, slip on a pair of leggings and a long T-shirt, and head for her office.

Selling prints of her original artwork was where Jenna made most of her income, so every morning she would check her email and print any new orders that had come in. To keep her work from becoming too commercial, she only sold a set number of prints from each original. Because of this practice, she often had to send out emails to people who wanted prints that were sold out. For the most part, she was able to satisfy those customers with recommended prints of other original pieces at a discount.

It had taken a lot of years and hard work to get her name out in the art world and finally be able to earn a comfortable living doing what she loved, but it had definitely been worth the effort.

Once her online orders were printed and neatly stacked in a pile, Jenna would then move on to her finances, her attention to detail and need for order made her a meticulous bookkeeper and her accountant's favourite client. She made up for all the other customers who thought a shoebox full of receipts, bank statements, and deposit slips were a functional set of books.

By 9 a.m., Monday through to Friday, she was in her studio, orders in hand and ready for the fun part of the job. First, she would pull the prints, attach the orders to each one, and set them on her big workbench for packaging later in the day. Then she would sit at her easel where she currently had a commissioned piece waiting to be started. Between the orders, the odd commission, and her gallery showings, she was kept busy enough that she could lose an entire day if she wasn't careful, so she'd gotten into the habit of setting a timer to let her know when to stop for lunch, get the orders packaged for postal pickup, and get started on dinner.

When her children were still at home, Jenna had made sure to keep her evenings and weekends for them. Now, even though that they were grown and gone, she stayed in the same routine. She was very militant about her habits. Keeping everything on schedule gave her a sense of security she never had in the chaotic household in which she grew up.

Now, with Danny and the pups gone, she often found herself standing, staring into space, unsure of what she was supposed to do next. She tried to soldier on and find a new routine but she just couldn't seem to get into her groove. Each morning, for that first week, she found herself waking confused. It always took a few minutes before she realized that it wasn't the dogs that woke her, but the smell of coffee as it was still set for its usual time. She would reach her leg out, searching for Danny and find nothing but cold sheets and emptiness. Then came the body blow, the terrible sense of loss. She would slowly roll out of bed and make her way down the stairs.

It took three days before she stopped making two smoothies and then, in a fit of rage, throwing them both in the sink. She was not sure when she stopped waiting for Danny to come down the stairs, or home from work, or when she stopped opening the door to let Choco and Cara back in only to realize she'd never let them out in the first place.

With iron determination those first few days, Jenna would wrestle herself into her workout clothes and trudge down to her treadmill, but by the end of the week she couldn't find the energy or desire to go through the motions and even though she still kept up with her online orders, when she went into her studio she found she was unable to paint a thing. She felt that pressure acutely as she sat staring at the blank 36-by-36-inch canvas on her easel. The deadline for this commissioned piece was looming. The time allotted should have been more than enough for her to finish, but she would sit in front of the canvas for hours, willing herself to do something, anything. *Just start,* she would urge herself. *Inspiration will come. You just have to start!* But no matter how hard she tried, she was unable to put brush to canvas. By week two, she covered the blank canvas with a sheet so she didn't have to keep looking at her abject failure and she gave up.

Post Separation - Week 2

Two weeks had passed. Jenna hadn't heard a word from Danny. Her first action each day was to check her phone in case she'd missed his call. Her voice mail was always full but none of the calls were from Danny. She carried it with her everywhere she went, continuously checking that her ringtone was turned as high as it would go. Her heart broke a little more with every day that passed. She knew she could reach out to him, but she told herself he was the one who'd left her, so he should be the one to make the first move. She couldn't face the rejection of knowing she meant so little to him that he could leave her so completely.

Her iron resolve was failing her. She still got out of bed in the morning and did her morning ablutions. But she couldn't face getting on her treadmill and running like a rat on a wheel. It was hard, under normal circumstances for her to keep her spirits up during the dark, dismal winter days of January in Northern Alberta, but this separation felt like a lead weight around her neck threatening to drown her. She was desperately lonely.

Even though she was unable to paint, she tried to keep busy filling her on-line orders, maintaining her finances, tidying her house, cleaning out closets. She even went out to shop for groceries . . . once. But it seemed as though everywhere she looked there were couples chatting and laughing together as they picked up their grocery items. As she watched them she was acutely aware of how alone she truly was, how much she missed Danny, how much she'd lost. This painful reminder made her vow to order her groceries on line from that point on. She would have them delivered and not have to face this agony again.

On her way home from the terrible grocery trip, she made a pit stop at the local liquor store. She and Danny enjoyed the occasional glass of wine in the evening, if they went out for a nice dinner or during social settings, but Jenna religiously kept it to no more than two glasses a couple of times a week. She'd grown up in an alcoholic household. Her dad, not able to deal with her mother's death in a horrific car accident when Jenna was just twelve, used booze to drown his sorrows. He made some unfortunate choices while under the influence, choices through which Jenna would spend a lifetime trying to find her way. She swore she wouldn't repeat this cycle.

Thankfully, the liquor store was empty so Jenna could pick a couple of nice bottles of Sauvignon Blanc to enjoy in the evening while losing herself in mindless television without happy couples, everywhere she looked, as painful reminders. She still kept it to two glasses per evening. But whereas before it was one or two evenings a week, it was now part of her nightly routine.

Each morning she would wake with a deep sense of shame and promise herself this would be the day she would get her life back on track. Each evening when the loneliness overwhelmed her she would give in, telling herself she would do better tomorrow, completing the vicious circle.

Post Separation - Week 3

Three weeks went by and there had still been no word from Danny. Jenna was getting up later and later, some days not at all. She had battled what she referred to as *black days* for most of her adult life, but she'd worked hard to put strategies in place to keep them to minimum. The strategies were failing and she didn't have any energy left to fight. She had given up waiting for Danny to call and resigned herself to the fact that her marriage was, indeed, over. That resignation took the last of her will to fight.

Her house was a disaster, littered with take-out food containers, wine bottles, dirty dishes, and dust bunnies. Even though she didn't bother to get dressed most mornings, she still kept up her personal hygiene. But after her shower, instead of putting on clean clothes, she would slip into a pair of flannel pajamas.

Her days were filled with daytime television, wine, and takeout she ordered online. Her two-glass-a-day rule had gone by the wayside when she found wine numbed the pain, for a while a least. For the first time in her life, she felt she understood her father's disease. She desperately wished she could tell him but he'd passed away several years before with neither of his children able to forgive him his human frailties.

She didn't open the mail, piled high in front of her door. She simply pushed it out of the way with her foot when delivery people arrived with her groceries and wine. She was a prisoner of her own making; her home, her refuge, had become her prison.

Post Separation - Week 4

By week four not only was Jenna still self-imprisoned, she was barely able to get out of bed. The black days had become an endless void that held her firmly in its grip. She had stopped eating completely and was now subsisting on coffee and wine. Each morning she would wander down the stairs like the wraith she now resembled, grab a coffee, sit in the cozy window seat by her front window, and watch people coming and going about their days while she waited for the delivery man to come with a fresh supply of groceries.

These "groceries" were wine, coffee, and milk (for her coffee). He usually came between 9 and 11 a.m. If it was close to 11, she could pour herself a glass of wine as soon as the door was closed, but if it was earlier she made herself wait; after all, she wasn't an alcoholic. Then she would head back up the stairs, crawl into her bed, turn on the TV, and drink wine until she fell back to sleep.

There was very little resemblance left of the well-kept woman she had been less than a month before. Her long, dark hair, not having seen a brush in a week, was a matted mess. Her healthy, glowing skin had turned sallow and yellow from the lack of food and fresh air and the effects of the alcohol. Her once strong and athletic figure was now skeletal and emaciated, nothing more than a withered shell. She didn't care. She refused to look in a mirror. She couldn't bear to see the wreck she'd become. She hadn't cried a tear since that first day. She was just a mass of pain and sadness.

Chapter 2

The Best-Laid Plans

February 9, 2016

When Jenna woke that morning, head pounding from too much wine and too little food, exactly one month from the day Danny left, she knew things had to be different. Every morning for the past week she had awoken overwhelmed with shame. Shame at the train wreck she had become. She'd gone over all of her failures with pinpoint accuracy and flogged herself mercilessly for each one, real and imagined. She knew she was to blame for Danny's leaving. She was just surprised it had taken him so long. After all, everyone left her eventually. She missed everything about him and time had not made it better. If anything, she missed him more with every passing day.

Jenna had always found it peculiar that some people seemed to move through this life rarely touched by tragedy or loss, while others suffered both with terrible frequency. By the time she was thirty, she'd lost both parents, her grandparents, her first husband, Sam, her brother, Mackenzie (Mac), and too many friends to count.

After Mac's death, she started having reccurring nightmares where she could see the people she'd lost in her mind's eye like so many toy soldiers marching blindly toward a cliff. She would scream at them to stop but they were deaf to her cries. She would have to watch each one, as they came to the cliff's edge, walk right over and tumble headlong into the abyss.

But Danny was different. He told her he would never leave her. If someone as patient as he was couldn't bear to stay with her, no one could.

This day, one month after the end of her marriage, with crystal clarity, Jenna made her decision. She got out of bed, went to her office and sat down at her computer. She had three letters to write. The first one was to Danny. She wrote:

Dear Danny,

I'm so sorry for all I've put you through. I know I came into this marriage with more baggage then any one man should have to unpack. I just want you to know my years with you have been more than I could have hoped for. You made me want to be so much better but I simply could not live up to the standards I set for myself. I've come to realize some people are just not able to figure out how to live in this world and find peace. Unfortunately, I am one of those people.

There are no words in the English language to describe how much I love you. Please understand, you hold no blame for my decisions. Please reach out to Brenna and Brandon. They will need you now more than ever.

Eternally yours,

Jenna

Jenna took the letter off the printer, folded it, and placed in an envelope with Danny's name carefully written across the front. She placed it on the only clear spot on her desk and moved onto the next two letters. These were even more difficult because she was writing them to her children. How do you explain to your children your choice to leave them? Yes, they were adults and, yes, her son, Brandon, wasn't even speaking to her. But they were still her children. She was all they had had for two years after their father, her first husband, Sam, died in Afghanistan. The children had only been two and five that terrible day the officers came to her door so their memory of him consisted mostly of photos and the stories she told about their father, her hero.

Her hands shook as she sat at the keyboard trying to figure out what she could possibly say that would make her decision make sense to them. She desperately wanted a glass of wine but she didn't want her last words to her children to be drunken ramblings. With a deep sigh, she started to type:

Dear Brenna,

I know you can't possibly understand how I could make a conscious choice to leave you. Please understand just how much I love you. You have been such a blessing to me as I've watched you grow and blossom into the incredible woman you are today. Despite all the trauma and tragedy you've faced you have met it with strength, dignity, and grace.

You've been an incredible support for me throughout the years, when life threatened to drown me. But, my darling girl, you should never have had to be, if I had been the mother you deserved and not just one more thing for you to overcome.

I find myself in a black, endless pit once more. This time, however, I'm not able to see the light at the end of the tunnel. I'm afraid I am finally without hope and I refuse to weigh you down again with my disease.

You will mourn me, but I believe you will move on and I hope someday I will become a memory you can cherish.

With all my love,

Mom

Jenna was very careful to leave the situation between her and Danny out. She didn't want Brenna to blame him because even though he wasn't her biological father, he was the only one she'd ever known.

Next came the most difficult letter of them all, the one to her son Brandon, her first born. She was almost twenty-one when she'd discovered she was pregnant and had just finished her Qualification Level 5 (QL5) as a medical technician (med tech) with the Canadian Forces (CF). She had been dating Sam for almost three years, which was its own cosmic joke, since when they met she hated him on sight. He was the sergeant in command (IC) of her section in basic training.

She was seventeen when the recruiters came to her high school for career day. She had been working hard to finish school. It was her only hope of escaping a home life that had become unbearable. Her dad was drunk all the time and now that her little brother, Mackenzie, had quit school and taken off to work on the big dairy farm down the road, she didn't have a buffer anymore. She was all alone with her dad and his perverse friends who kept putting their hands on her and trying to back her into corners.

She only had a month to go before graduation and still hadn't figured out what she wanted to do next as she wandered through the gymnasium, passing booth after booth.

University was out of the question. She knew she'd never be able to afford it and she refused to owe the kind of money she would need to borrow in student loans. The other booths were mostly oil companies or secretarial schools—yuk! Then she came across the army recruiters' booth.

Two very fit and attractive young people were standing straight and tall in their cad-pad uniforms, hands behind their backs, feet slightly apart, engaged in conversation with many of the boys in her graduating class. What stood out most to her was that one of them was a young woman. The female recruiter spotted Jenna taking an interest and disengaged herself from the group to approach her. "We could use more women in the forces. Are you interested?"

"Actually, I am," Jenna said, surprising herself. She didn't know a lot about her country's military so it had never been a consideration, but as she watched the video showing young soldiers powering through the obstacle courses, teammates supporting teammates, excitement began to stir in her.

The next thing she knew, she was sitting at a desk going through all the different careers on offer. The recruiter explained that if Jenna was interested she would pick three careers and fill out the application forms. Once her application was processed, they would schedule her for an aptitude test, a complete medical, and a physical fitness test. If she passed all of these they would place her in one of the three trades she picked, depending on her aptitude and the trade that needed people the most. Then she would be flown to Saint-Jean-sur-Richelieu, Quebec, to start basic training on the army's dime.

Training usually took about a year and half providing there were no injuries or obstacles. She would be paid as an untrained private, housed and fed during that time until her first posting. The idea of being 4,000 miles away from her dad was the only prompting she needed. She filled out the application on the spot.

She passed all the tests with flying colours and was beyond excited to be offered med tech as her trade, her first choice. She also opted to go army because it just seemed so bad ass.

Her last month of school, the bus trip to Edmonton and her flight to Quebec were all a blur, but getting off the bus at St. Jean with all the other new recruits was etched in her memory. The bus pulled up in front of one of many brown brick buildings. Three military personnel stood waiting as it came to a complete stop and the door opened.

One of the soldiers marched onto the bus, a big brawny man with a bad attitude. "All right, you little piss ants! Grab you kit and get your asses off this bus and get formed up single file on the sidewalk. I'm Sgt. Kaufmann and I will be your worst nightmare for the next twelve weeks."

True to his word, he was.

He was also her Sam.

Basic training was a nightmare and she wanted to quit every single day but she just had nowhere else to go, so she pushed through and finally the twelve weeks were over and she'd made it, graduating top candidate of her course. Sgt. Kaufmann seemed to make it his personal mission to make her life as difficult as he possibly could. When she finished basic she swore if she never saw him again it would be too soon.

The universe had different plans.

Sam was tired of being stuck in the training cell. He had put in for a re-muster and, all through Jenna's course, was eagerly waiting for it to go through.

Making it through basic had given her a confidence she never had before so the second part of Jenna's training was much easier. It was soldier qualification (SQ) and she loved it. Loved the weapons training, loved the drill, and loved leopard crawling through the long grass at the Land Forces Central Area Training Centre in Meaford, Ontario. It was physically grueling but her coursemates had become her family. She made connections that would last a lifetime. They trained together, ate together, slept in the same barracks, and partied together during the short leave periods they were given.

Soldier qualification went by quickly, then came the final part of her training before she was given her first posting, her trade training. She remembered her excitement as she got back on that green and white army bus and headed for the Canadian Forces Health Services Training Centre in Borden, Ontario. She was housed in the barracks referred to as the Nunnery. She never did find out why it was called that.

She got there around noon on a Sunday. They were scheduled to be at the training centre at 5 p.m. to get further direction. When she walked into the drill hall of the training centre, she spotted him. Her stomach lurched as she scooted behind her course mates, hoping he wouldn't see her. *What is* he *doing here?* she thought to herself.

Unfortunately, he did see her and walked toward her. With a deep sigh, Jenna straightened her stance and looked directly at him. She was confused when she saw he was wearing Corporal (Cpl) epaulets and that his beret no longer sported the infantry cap badge she'd come to despise. It was a med tech cap badge. Sgt. Kaufmann was now Cpl Kaufmann. He had re-mustered to med tech. He was her course mate. *You've got to be fucking kidding!* Jenna fumed.

He greeted her with a "Hey there, Doyle, good to see you made it through." She snorted, "Yeh, no thanks to you."

"Actually, I think you'll find it *is* thanks to me, at least in part."

"Oh? How is that? All you did was pick on me."

"Actually, Doyle, I made you top candidate."

"Seriously! You're going to take credit for my hard work!"

"You're only as good as your instructor, Doyle. A course never fails. It's the instructor who fails. The same goes for the reverse."

Jenna felt the fury she'd managed to contain all through basic rise to the surface. "You pompous, arrogant fuck!" She growled. Even though he was, technically, a rank above her, as course mates they were equals and she didn't have to hold her tongue. But as she took a breath to proceed in letting him know exactly what she thought of his teaching methods, he interrupted using her first name.

"Jenna, I'm sorry. I've been in the army now for more than six years and in the training cell for two of those. In all that time no one ever affected me the way you did. When I first looked into those startling eyes I couldn't think straight. I had to get my head in the game, so I told myself you were just a cream puff and wouldn't last a week. But you proved me wrong. You were more than just a pretty face. You proved to be an outstanding soldier. You handled everything I could possibly throw at you and more."

Jenna stood stunned. It sounded so strange to hear him say her name, since one of the first things they were told in basic was that the army didn't issue them a first name, and even stranger to hear his admission. But before she could utter a word, someone yelled "ROOM!" and everyone came to attention as the course staff entered the drill hall, barking orders.

The rest, as they say, is history.

Afghanistan was heating up and both she and Sam put in for their first tour. It was during her medical workup that they discovered she was pregnant. They planned to get married after the tour was over, with their tour allowance, but now that she had to stay back, Sam insisted they get married before he left. He wanted his baby to have his name and to know Jenna and the baby would be taken care of with no complications. Since he wouldn't be back before the baby was born, Jenna agreed.

Although Jenna had experienced love before, nothing could have prepared her for the enormity of the love between a mother and her child. Brandon was her first experience with love of that magnitude. She shared in all of his firsts with wonder and joy beyond measure, each milestone imprinted on her heart.

He had always been a handful, but by the time he was fourteen, she could see the signs of depression and anxiety only because she knew them so well, having suffered them for many years herself. She tried to get him to talk to her, sent him to psychologist after psychologist, but he had shut down completely and wouldn't let anyone in. Her heart broke as she watched him struggle, every attempt to reach him failing miserably.

She'd had such a strong bond with Brandon during the first ten years of his life. Brandon was only five when his father was killed in the Afghanistan conflict and before that, Sam was either on tour or training for tour, so the children never really had a chance to know him. He was a very peripheral figure in their lives. She was, for all intents and purposes, a single mother until Danny came along. Brandon was seven and Brenna four.

By sixteen, Brandon was completely out of control. He was failing high school, drinking heavily, and doing drugs. He would disappear for days, then weeks, and finally he didn't come home at all. She spent hours scouring the streets for him, desperate to find him one minute and terrified she would the next. Terrified she'd find him dead behind a dumpster or in a ditch somewhere. She'd managed to find her way through the tragedies that rocked her world in the past, but Jenna knew beyond a shadow of a doubt that losing her son would destroy her. So when the police came to her door with her scrawny, filthy teenage boy, she did the only thing she had left to do. She loaded him in her car and took him to rehab.

As angry as he was, Brandon did well in rehab. He was able to detox from the drugs and alcohol and come home three months later. But he was not the same. He was polite and did all that was asked of him, but he avoided them all like the plague. When he was offered a job on the oil rigs up north, he jumped at the chance. As soon as he graduated high school, bags already packed and waiting, he got into his old truck and left home. For the first few years he continued to fulfill his familial obligations, showing up for birthdays and family holidays, but by the time he was twenty-two, he stopped coming home completely. If they wanted to see him they had to go to him. He was still polite and respectful, but kept himself at arm's length, never letting his mother or sister get too close. Jenna's heart shattered.

Now it was time to write his letter:

Dear Brandon,

The first thing I want to say to you is I love you and there is nothing on heaven or earth that can change that fact. No matter where I am, I will love you. I am so sorry for the mistakes I've made that caused you pain and I know when you get this letter, I will have been the cause of even more pain for you. All I can say is, I am so incredibly proud of you for all you managed to overcome and accomplish and I am ashamed that I have failed you yet again. I find it ironic that, thousands of years of bad parental decisions notwithstanding, humanity still thinks instincts will provide us the parenting skills we need to do the most important job in the world, raising our future.

My beautiful boy, you didn't come with an instruction manual and I didn't have good examples to follow, but I did the best I knew to do, honestly trying to do what was best for you. Sadly, it was just one more aspect of my life where I failed.

Having said all this, I want you to know that my actions ARE NOT YOUR FAULT! I simply refuse to be a burden to you and your sister and seem to have come to the end of my ability to face another day. But before I go into that good night, I want you know how very much I love you and how sorry I am for the hurt I've caused.

With all my love,

Mom

The final letter completed, Jenna took both of them off the printer, folded them in the same manner as the one for Danny, stuffed them into envelopes, and sat them on the hall table where they could be easily seen. Just as she was setting them down, the doorbell rang with her "grocery" order. Usually, she just let them put the order on the porch and leave, but this time she ran to the door. She needed to cancel her orders, and this would save her an extra task.

The deliveryman was already down the steps when she called out to him. The shocked look on his face as he took in her disheveled appearance spoke volumes about how far down she'd gone and reinforced her belief that she was irredeemable. She mumbled the instructions and quickly closed the door when he nodded his understanding.

With her wine, a wine glass (after all, she wasn't that far gone), and photo albums under her arm, she made her way up the stairs to her bedroom and crawled under the covers. Propping herself up with pillows, she poured her first glass of wine, glanced at her nightstand to ensure her bottle of Clonazepam was still where she'd left it, and began going through her photos. As she journeyed down memory lane, from her baby pictures to her current life, the tears she hadn't been able to cry since the day Danny left found their way to the surface and she cried.

She cried for what seemed like hours, her body quaking with the enormity of the pain. She cried so hard her stomach heaved. Finally empty of all emotion, she poured another glass of wine, staring blankly at the painting on her bedroom wall. Then she poured another and another and another and another. One bottle down.

Head swimming with the effects of the alcohol, she opened her second bottle and continued pouring the wine down her throat, one glass at a time. Now she was on her last glass. Despite the intensity of her intoxication, her resolve was still firmly in place as she fumbled for the bottle of pills.

She was able to get the bottle open and the handful of pills into her mouth with a great deal of difficulty, knocking empty wine bottles off the night stand in the process. Then she took her last glass of wine and gulped it down in its entirety. She washed down the pills and waited for the final release.

Chapter 3

Mackenzie

July 7, 2011

Mac was nine years old the day his mother, Anna, died. He always said it was the day he lost both his parents. Previous to that day, they had been a very normal, middle-class family.

His mother taught third grade in the small Alberta town in which they'd grown up and his dad owned the only gas station/convenience store.

His parents worked hard, but always seemed to have time for him and Jenna. After dinner every night, once chores were done, they would all sit around the big kitchen table, their mom grading papers, Jenna and Mac doing their homework, and Dad doing the crosswords in the local newspaper.

If the weather was nice, sometimes his parents would come out to their big backyard and toss the football around. If the weather was bad, they would play board games or charades. Often, his dad would pick up his old second-hand Gibson guitar, his mom would accompany him on the piano, and Jenna and Mac would sing old songs that were popular long before they were born but they knew word for word.

There always seemed to be an extra person or two around the dinner table as neighbours and friends were welcomed like family and there was always room for an extra plate.

Their home was filled with love, laughter and fun. It was an idyllic childhood.

For all the time his parents spent with him and Jenna, they always kept Thursday evenings for themselves.

Mac's parents had a standing reservation at the only nice restaurant in town. In Mac's memory, they never missed a Thursday. His parents would go for dinner and dancing, but since the next day was still technically a work day, they were always home by 10 p.m.

Mrs. Swanson, the middle-aged lady from across the street, babysat until Jenna was old enough.

Once Jenna and Mac were off to school, Anna would get busy making homemade pizzas and one of their favourite desserts, like dark chocolate cake with white butter cream icing or chocolate chunk cookies with walnuts.

She would wrap the pizzas in cellophane and pop them in the fridge unbaked until the kids were ready to eat. That way, they always got fresh, hot pizza. Everyone looked forward to Thursdays!

November 8, 1983, was no different. Jenna was twelve and had been babysitting her little brother for just about year. It was the first snowfall of the season and Mac and Jenna were laughing and trying to have a snow-ball fight but the snow was too cold to stick so they were just throwing cold powder at one another. Mom and Dad came out of the house dressed in their Sunday best and smelling like a mixture of Dad's aftershave and Mom's perfume.

They stopped horsing around in the snow and ran up to their parents for the customary hugs, cheek kisses, and last-minute directions. Blissfully unaware that the next few hours would be the last of these carefree moments, Mom waved from the passenger window while Dad maneuvered the old navy blue Buick down the drive and headed out of their neighbourhood.

Mac and Jenna were sound asleep on the sofa when the doorbell rang. They both startled awake in confusion. Their parents wouldn't ring their own doorbell and they were strictly instructed to never open the door to strangers.

Jenna went to the door and peeked through the peephole while nine-year-old Mac stood on the ready at the other side with his baseball bat in his hands, poised to swing should the situation warrant it.

Mac's heart was already in his throat when Jenna said in a confused voice, "It's the police?"

Mac felt a chill seep through every pore in his scalp and fill his entire body. With trepidation, he lowered the bat and came over to his sister as she opened the door to the end of their world.

Two young officers stood awkwardly on the top step. When Jenna opened the door, the first one took off his hat; his blonde hair shone under the porch lights. "Is this the home of John and Anna Doyle?" he asked.

Jenna's voice cracked when she answered, "Yes."

"Is there an adult with you?"

"No, I'm twelve, I'm old enough to babysit my brother." Under the fear was a note of defiance.

The officer cleared his throat. "I'm sorry, but your parents have been in a car accident. Is there someone we can call who can be with you kids right now?"

"In emergencies, we're supposed to call Mrs. Swanson. She lives right there." Jenna's voice registered the panic Mac was feeling as she pointed to the house directly across from them. "Are my parents OK?" she asked.

Mac could see the internal battle being waged behind the blonde officer's eyes. At least he was looking at them. The other officer kept his eyes conspicuously downcast, his hat now also in his hands.

They weren't told that their mother was dead and their father in critical condition until the second officer roused Mrs. Swanson and filled her in. She rushed over in her housecoat and slippers and wrapped both children tightly in her soft warmth while the officers broke the news.

A carload of drunk teens had run a red light and hit their parents' car broadside. Their mother was killed instantly, she never knew what hit her. At least that's what the police officer kept repeating as though that would somehow make their mother's loss easier to endure.

John Doyle was never the same. He suffered a severe concussion, ruptured spleen, and a multitude of broken bones and was in the hospital for two months on heavy pain medications.

The ruptured spleen was removed and his brain and bones healed, but his heart never recovered. He just couldn't get over the guilt of being in the driver's seat when the car hit the passenger side of the car, the side where his beautiful wife sat, head back, blue eyes shining as she laughed at one of his corny jokes.

He found the painkillers not only helped with the physical pain but also numbed the emotional pain, so by the time he left the hospital he had significant dependency. When he could no longer get prescription meds, he turned to alcohol and spent the rest of his life slowly following the wife he loved so much he didn't know how to live without her.

Jenna didn't have the privilege of mourning her mother properly. She had to step up and try to fill her shoes as much as a twelve-year-old possibly could. Mac still needed a parent and Jenna was it.

By the time Mac was thirteen and Jenna was sixteen, their dad had managed to drink away their home and business, along with that every semblance of the life they had shared and the family they had once been when their mother was alive.

They moved into an old, rundown shack on the edge of town and lived on social assistance and whatever money Jenna brought home working nights and weekends at a local diner. She was careful not to let her dad know how much money she made. She knew he would just drink it away and it was the only thing that kept them in food and school supplies and Jenna was determined they would both finish school.

Their dad had a new group of friends. Friends he met at the local bar and often found their way home with him, reluctant for the party to end. These so-called friends would help themselves to the few things of value they had left but when one of them tried to help themselves to Jenna one night while she was sleeping, Mac beat him to within an inch of his life with his trusty old baseball bat, the only thing he'd kept from a life he couldn't bear to remember.

Mac was fourteen and he was a very angry young man, angry at his weak drunk of a father, angry at the teachers who were continuously trying to engage him in his classes, even angry at Jenna for being so responsible and devoted to their dad after all he'd put them through. So when Mr. Richmond, who owned the big dairy farm down the road, picked him up on the side of an old dirt road and offered him a job, he jumped at the chance and didn't look back.

Ed Richmond wasn't normally in the habit of picking up skinny kids with ripped jeans and holes in their sneakers, but in a town of 150 people, everyone knew everyone, and even though it wasn't his usual practice to pay attention to town gossip he'd seen Mac's family disintegrate with his own eyes and it tugged at his heart strings. So without giving it a moment's thought, seeing an opportunity to offer a hand up, Ed stopped and threw Mac a life preserver that came complete with room and board.

Mac was relieved when Jenna finally graduated high school and joined the army. He had no regrets about leaving his dad to his own devices; he felt no responsibility toward him whatsoever but he worried about Jenna. She had always been there for him doing her best to make sure he ate well and got to school, and even though he resented it at the time, he knew she did it out of love and couldn't hold that against her.

When he started receiving letters filled with her lowest lows and greatest successes he found it cathartic to respond in kind. Even though they were thousands of miles away, they had never been closer.

He was nineteen when he met Olivia, Mr. Richmond's niece, for the first time.

She was seventeen, with sun-bleached blonde hair, big brown eyes, and legs that went on forever. She had just finished high school and was working for her uncle until university started in the fall.

Mr. Richmond introduced them and told Mac it was his job to show her the ropes, but Mac wondered who was going to truly get schooled when she bounced past him to the barn, long, jaunty ponytail slapping him in the face on her way by.

She was the most beautiful girl Mac had ever laid eyes on and he honestly would have been happy just to be in her presence. He certainly didn't expect that she would contribute much to the hard manual labour that was required on a dairy farm—or any farm, for that matter.

It wasn't long, however before he realized just how seriously he had underestimated her. Her energy and cheerful disposition seemed endless as she worked shoulder to shoulder with him, proving her metal.

By the end of the summer he was hopelessly and helplessly in love. The thought of her leaving to go to university gutted him. Unfortunately, she didn't seem to feel the same way. She refused every attempt he made to get her to go out with him. She had a goal in mind and wasn't about to let anything as frivolous as a relationship get in the way.

So Mac did the only thing he could think of: he applied for every job he was remotely qualified for in the city and was beyond excited when he was offered a position as a grounds maintenance worker for the city itself.

When he gave Mr. Richmond his notice, he asked that it be kept just between them. He didn't want Olivia to get the feeling he was stalking her. He wanted to get settled first and then take things slowly. He knew he had to get it right because she was the puzzle piece that had been missing in his life.

For the first time in a very long time, things seemed to fall into place for Mac.

Mac was over the moon to find that Olivia had feelings for him too and to learn how much it had meant to her that he would go to such efforts just to explore the possibility of a relationship with her.

It wasn't long before she moved in with him. She told herself it was to save money on rent, but they both knew better. On her twentieth birthday, Mac proposed and they were married the following summer.

Olivia graduated nursing school with honours and was able to get a job at the Northwest Health Care Centre as a trauma nurse. And Mac, despite only having a Grade 10 education, worked his way up into a management position with the city. They found the perfect fixer-upper in a nice quiet neighbourhood and by all appearances were the epitome of the perfect middle-class couple.

The only dark cloud that hung over their relationship was Olivia's desire to have children and Mac's refusal to even entertain the idea. He was terrified of being like his father and, in his mind, believed Olivia was all he would ever need.

After four years of marriage he finally relented, afraid his unwavering stance would cost him his wife. His little pink-faced daughter was born a year later and Mac lost his heart once more. He was as devoted and loving a father as he was a husband.

But for each milestone Mac reached and each success he achieved, he always seemed to be waiting for the other shoe to drop. He could never allow himself to enjoy it because he lived in constant fear of losing it, of something terrible happening to Olivia or Mackayla, of losing his job or his house.

As every new fear raised its ugly head and was compounded by old, unacknowledged trauma from his childhood, Mac was driven to work harder and harder. If he was moving he wasn't thinking and if he wasn't thinking he wasn't feeling, so he worked long hours at his job and then came home and worked longer hours on their home or yard or whatever other project he could think up, anything to keep him distracted.

He was so driven it worried Olivia. He could no longer hide from her the toll the years of stress were taking on his mind and body. She often wanted to mention her concerns to Jenna, with whom she had become very close over the years, but Jenna had shouldered all Mac and Jenna's familial obligations since Mac cut himself off from his father. Olivia didn't want to upset her, so she kept her own counsel until the night she found Mac in the backyard, stark naked, staring off into space.

It was after midnight and she had just gotten home from an evening shift when she noticed the back door was wide open. Her first instinct was to run upstairs and check on Mackayla, who was sound asleep in her bed. Olivia then went to her room and found it empty.

Heading back downstairs, she softly called out to Mac, careful not to wake their daughter. As she headed out the back door she could see him standing there, silent and still.

When she got to him, she reached out to touch his arm only to have him jerk it away and give a startled yell. He'd been sleep walking and her touched jarred him awake. It took several minutes to bring him out of his panicked, disoriented state and get him in the house and back to bed. This became such a regular occurrence and, finally out of desperation, she approached Jenna at a family barbecue with her concerns.

"Is there anyone at the hospital you could get him to talk to?" Jenna asked.

"He refuses to talk me, let alone a stranger. He just keeps changing the subject. I just don't know what to do anymore. Even Mackayla is starting to notice her daddy is not acting like himself." Frustration and fear were clear in Olivia's voice.

"Let me see if Danny can talk to him," Jenna suggested.

Danny and Mac had been friends since the first day Mac started at the city. They were partnered together and Danny's laid-back, openly friendly personality complemented Mac's drive and intensity. They were a great team and became close friends.

When Jenna met Danny at one of Olivia and Mac's summer barbecues, she was immediately drawn to his easy, kind demeanour. He was like a cool glass of water on a hot day.

Sam had been gone for a year and although she still mourned his death every day, another emotion was starting to emerge. Loneliness.

She missed having a companion, someone to share her day-to-day struggles, cares and concerns with, so when Danny worked up the courage to ask her out, she surprised herself by saying "sure." They were married a year later.

"Maybe?" Olivia sounded doubtful. "Anything is worth a try."

"Sure," Jenna agreed.

Danny was hesitant to approach Mac, saying, "Just give him some time and space. That's how guys work things out. He knows I'm here if he needs to talk."

Mac couldn't talk to Danny or anyone else because he firmly believed this was simply a weakness of character and he didn't want his friend to see how weak he was. He just had to toughen up, dig in, and push forward and it would pass.

Unfortunately, Mac was headed for a freefall and the people who loved him the most could only stand by and watch.

Mac saw the way Olivia and Jenna looked at him with worry on their faces. He wasn't sleeping anymore. Every night just as he was drifting off he would be startled awake, never knowing where he might find himself.

After the night in the yard, he stopped going to bed in the buff, making sure he had pyjama bottoms on so he didn't accidentally flash his neighbours or, worse, traumatize his daughter.

His job was starting to suffer from his lack of sleep. Panic plagued him because his job was suffering. Depression was eating at his mind like a parasitic insect because of the lack of sleep and the panic. It was a terrifying merry-go-round that, for the life of him, he just couldn't find a way off. Finally out of desperation, he made an appointment with their family doctor.

"I just don't know what's wrong with me," Mac told the doctor.

"Mac, no one is invincible. It sounds to me like you've been carrying a lot of weight around for a very long time. I think we should put you on some anti-anxiety and antidepressant medications, but I'd also like you to refer you to a psychiatrist for monitoring."

As the doctor wrote out his prescriptions and referral, Mac expressed his lack of enthusiasm about seeing a psychiatrist. "I just need to get my head back in the game, doc. I don't need some stranger digging around in it."

"Mac, it's really important that these medications be monitored. That's what psychiatrists are trained to do. Please promise me you will go to this appointment."

As the doctor handed Mac the papers, Mac assured him he would do as instructed and left the office with no intention of following through. As soon as he was out of sight of the doctor, he crumpled the referral into a ball and tossed it in the nearest waste basket.

The anti-anxiety medication worked immediately. It dulled his senses and slowed down his racing thoughts. *Wow, this is amazing!* he thought to himself as he gave himself over to its full effects. He'd lived so many years on the edge of a razor blade that this new sensation was a balm to his tattered psyche—like finding an oasis after wandering the desert for an eternity.

He wasn't nearly as happy with the effects of the antidepressants. All he noticed were the side effects and they were not nearly as pleasant a sensation, so after a couple of days, he stopped using them. The doctor advised him that the side effects were temporary and it would be a few weeks before he got the full effects of the medication, but Mac was tired of suffering.

Mac also discovered that he could get a full night's sleep if he took the anti-anxiety meds with a beer. It knocked him right out and voila! No night terrors.

Life was great!

Until he discovered he was almost out of medication.

He knew his refusal to follow through on the doctor's orders meant he couldn't go back to him so he thought he'd try the medicentre on a few blocks away.

To his amazement, it was relatively easy to get his meds refilled.

The next time, however, was not so easy. So when he needed another refill, he simply found another medicentre across the city.

But then a new problem arose. The pharmacist they'd been going to for years was starting to look at Mac with suspicion. Now Mac wasn't just shopping doctors, he was shopping pharmacies.

Mac knew he was heading down a slippery slope, and that little voice in the back of his mind kept showing him images of his dad's descent into drug addiction and alcoholism. Every night when he went to bed he swore the next day would be the day he would stop using. Every morning he awoke examining the events of the day before. As he did, shame would slowly and agonizingly fill every cell. Unable to face it, he would reach for the pills. It had become a vicious cycle. The hate he felt for his dad all these years was now turned on himself and the shame of knowing he had become what he so despised left him desperate to numb. The pills numbed.

He was so immersed in the mental illness/self-medication process he failed to notice his family.

He was so high all the time now. He was barely able to go to work. He could neither take care of the maintenance of the house and yard nor help Olivia with the day-to-day running of their household.

Where he was once an active partner, now he was a liability, not that she let herself think that way. She did her absolute best to step up and do what needed to be done because she desperately believed this would pass and the Mac she married would come back to her. But she was exhausted and terrified.

Mackayla was almost seven by then, and missed her dad. They had been best friends. Inseparable. This stranger that inhabited his body scared her and she avoided him as much as she possibly could. Once a happy, well-adjusted child, she'd become withdrawn and anxious and spent most of her time in her room or out in the old tree house they'd built together. She was still polite and helped Olivia as much as she could to fill in the gap her dad left, but the impact of his disease was glaringly obvious to anyone who cared to notice.

Jenna noticed.

She was always very careful with her baby brother. She had a decent idea of the level of pain he kept buried throughout the years. She dealt with her own fall-out from the Chernobyl of their childhood. But she had never been able to write their dad off the way Mac could. Being three years older, she had had more of the awesome father John had been than Mac had. When Mac needed him in those formidable years between childhood and manhood, John wasn't available and now Mac was repeating the cycle.

After two years of watching Mac's descent, Jenna couldn't stay quiet anymore. She'd watched her dad die of cirrhosis of the liver at sixty. She'd taken care of his funeral, she'd paid the bills he left behind and never asked Mac for a thing because she knew he would refuse and that's just what she had always done, taken care of things, taken care of Mac.

When Olivia called and asked her to come over, Jenna had a sense of foreboding. She sat in silence as Olivia described the past two years, but even though Olivia pulled no punches, Jen was not prepared for the man that walked through the door.

She hadn't seen Mac in months. She and Danny had just bought the cabin and when she wasn't working on her art they were out restoring it for year-round use. Time had gotten away from her and before she knew it, three months had passed.

The stranger in front of her gave her a goofy grin and a little wave as he kicked off his boots. Giving his wife a kiss on the cheek, he made his way to the fridge, grabbed a beer, and sat down at the breakfast nook. "What's up, Jen? Long time no see," he said with a slight slur.

"I don't know, Mac, what the fuck is up?" She was too stunned to hide the shock and fear she felt at his appearance. He was disheveled and obviously under the influence of something. She could only guess what it was.

"What's your problem?" he snapped, emphasizing the word *your*. He was angry and confused by her tone. Jen never talked to him like that.

"You just got home from work and you're already high! You're lucky you haven't been arrested for driving under the influence, Mac!"

"Fuck off already, Jen!" Mac slid off the stool and stalked out of the kitchen to plop down in his recliner in front of the television.

Jen followed him and grabbed the remote from his hand before he could tune her out. "What are you doing to yourself, brother? You need help before you lose everything just like dad did!"

The mention of their father sent Mac over the edge. He launched out of the chair and grabbed Jen's wrist. "Mind your own gawd damn business, Jen. No one asked you to save me!"

Olivia stepped between them, grabbing Mac's hand and pulling if off Jen's arm. It was totally out of character for Mac to put his hands on his sister or anyone in anger. It suddenly occurred to her that she no longer knew this man in front of her. Sadness overwhelmed her as she realized she couldn't keep lying to herself. There was a very real possibility that the man she'd married was never coming back.

Turning to Jenna, she said, "I'm sorry for all of this, Jen, but I think you should probably go for now. I'll give you a call later."

Jenna looked at her brother and then at his wife struggling to keep the tears at bay and asked, "Are you sure you want to be alone with him?"

"I'll be fine," Olivia assured her.

Turning back to her brother, Jenna said, "if you can't get it together for yourself, maybe you should think about what you're doing to your family before it's too late." With that, she turned and quietly walked out the door.

Mac sat back down in his chair, turned on the television, and tuned out, the look of defeat and sadness on Olivia's face not even registering.

Shaking her head, Olivia turned and left the room. Quietly she went upstairs and packed a bag with some of Mac's clothes. She put it in the spare room and went about her evening routine.

After dinner, she cleared up the dishes, helped Mackayla with her homework, then sent her off for a bath and bed.

Mac didn't join them for dinner. The only time he got up out of his chair was to grab another beer. Six cans in and he was sound asleep where he would probably stay until the wee hours of the morning.

Olivia grabbed a note pad and pen from the office and headed upstairs. She kissed Mackayla good night then went into the spare room. There, she put together a carefully written note telling Mac how much she loved him but that until he got the help he so desperately needed, he couldn't be in the house with her and MacKayla. She had let things go long enough.

Carefully, she carted the bag she'd packed down the stairs and placed in front of the door with the note tucked in the straps where Mac couldn't miss it.

With that completed, Olivia went back up to the room she and Mac shared, washed her face, brushed her teeth, and changed into a clean pair of pajamas. She grabbed the novel she was reading and went back into the spare room, locked the door, and crawled into bed.

She must have reread the same paragraph a hundred times. She knew the book wasn't the problem she just couldn't focus her mind. She was filled with uncertainty. Was she doing the right thing she wondered. Finally giving up on the book, she shut off the bedside lamp and slid down into the guest bed, closed her eyes and willed sleep to come.

Around 3 a.m., she heard Mac come up the stairs and stop by the closed guest room door. She heard the door knob rattle. Finding it locked, he made his way to their room where he swallowed a pill and fell onto the bed fully clothed. Within minutes, Olivia could hear his snores coming through the walls.

Olivia wasn't sure what time she finally fell asleep but she didn't hear Mac get up that morning nor did she hear him leave for work. But when she got up, the bag, the note, and Mac were all gone. The enormity of her actions took her breath away and she suddenly had a sense that this would not end well. Before she could examine this feeling, Mackayla came into the kitchen looking for breakfast.

Mac had felt sick when he got up that morning and found the packed bag by the door. He'd unfolded the note and although the words Olivia used were very careful not to say their relationship was over, that was what Mac read between the lines. The thing he feared the most had come to pass. He was losing his family.

He hadn't taken a pill that morning. Every time he'd reached for the bottle, Jen's words had come back and sounded over and over in his head. He'd refused to believe he was anything like his dad. After all, he still had a job and a house and Olivia would calm down—eventually. At least that's what he told himself.

When he got to his office and booted up his computer, he found an urgent email in his inbox from the city supervisor. His heart started thudding in his chest as he made his way to the supervisor's office.

"Hey, Dave," he said trying to keep his voice steady and wishing he had taken that pill. "You wanted to see me."

"Yes," Dave stood up in greeting. "Shut the door and take a seat please, Mac."

Mac did what he was instructed.

Once he was seated, he asked, "What's this about?"

"Well, Mac, you've been with the city for almost twelve years now, correct?"

"I have."

"Up until about two years ago, you were one of our shining stars. What happened?" Dave pinned his gaze directly on Mac, making his squirm.

"I don't know what you mean?"

"Well, Mac, let me spell it out for you. Over the past two years it's been noted, that on a number of occasions, you've come to work under the influence. The past six months your absences have exceeded that of your entire career here. You have been given verbal warnings and written warnings, and numerous opportunities to access our employee assistance program, which you have systematically refused. I'm afraid there is nothing more we can do for you. You've put us in a position where the only course of action left to us is to terminate your employment." That said, Dave handed Mac a letter of termination. "You will be paid a small severance and you've accumulated some vacation pay on your final cheque. I am truly sorry, Mac."

In stunned silence, Mac took the termination letter and left the supervisor's office. He was only thirty-five years old, but he moved like an eighty-year-old. Truth be told, he felt like an eighty-year-old.

Climbing back into his car, he shut the door and just sat in the parking lot looking at the man in rearview mirror. He had no idea how long he sat there staring at the stranger looking back at him, desperately trying to process what had happened to his life. He went over failure after failure, feeling the weight of it suffocating him. Then his old friend shame came to visit. Finally, came the hard, cold realization, an understanding so profound he couldn't believe he was never able to see it before. He was finally able to understand with crystal cruel clarity why his dad had done the things he had done because Mac had become him.

Mac also came to realize that not everyone caught a break in this life. His tortured mind convinced him that he was one of those people and the only thing he had to look forward to was more of the same.

He felt the weight of his failings as a husband, a father, and a brother and he was tired. Tired of having to live with the damage he'd done to the people he loved most in this world.

He could see now what he hadn't been able to see before. Olivia struggling to keep up their marriage and their family intact, Mackayla becoming more and more withdrawn and anxious, and the fear in Jen's face as she tried to talk sense to him.

He became acutely aware of the impact of his selfishness and he made a choice to end it.

He may have slipped into the same destructive behaviours as his father, but he would not draw them out for years and years. He would stop this now. He would make it look like an accident to spare his family the trauma of living with his suicide.

Decision made, he took his car out to an old secondary highway. He intended to get it up to speed then drive into a tree or power pole, but when he saw the semi he made a split-second choice to drive right through the stop sign aiming for the trailer the driver was pulling.

A nano second before his car slid under the trailer Mac felt the impact of his decision and a deep and powerful regret was the only emotion present as he ended his own life.

Chapter 4

Afterlife

As Mac's soul left his body and he was able to see the scene of the accident he left behind, it surprised him he could still feel emotion. The feelings were different because he no longer had a body to be impacted by them, but he felt regret on a soul level. Somehow, it made the emotion sharper, more acute, purer.

As he examined this new state of being, he discovered the one thing he expected to feel but didn't: fear. He would learn that fear was synonymous with being "alive." It was a body sensation necessary for life to continue to exist. Fear kept people alive.

"Fascinating, isn't it?" A voice came from behind him.

Mac turned to see an angel just over his right shoulder. *Ah, OK*, he thought. *So that Sunday school story was true.*

"All stories have some basis in fact, Mackenzie."

"Who are you?" Mac asked trying to come to terms with a conversation happening inside his mind as opposed to verbally.

"No body, no words, Mackenzie," the angel answered the unasked question. "I'm Daniel, your guardian angel. We've been together since the moment of your conception, Mac."

"Really? Judging by my life and subsequent death, you weren't very good at your job."

The sarcasm wasn't lost on Daniel. "Oh, my friend, you have so much to learn but for now we have one more stop before we go home."

"Home?"

"Be patient, my friend. All your questions will be answered in due time."

The next thing Mac knew they were moving with the wind and clouds, then they were over Mac's house.

Jenna's car was parked behind Olivia's in the driveway. A police car was slowing down, stopping in front of his house. He felt a sadness so profound he ached as he realized he hadn't saved his family from trauma, he'd simply changed the trajectory of it.

He watched the police walk up the stone sidewalk to the front door. He watched Olivia open the door, Jenna standing behind her.

He heard the words "suicide by semi." He heard Olivia scream, loud and agonizing, one single sound that reverberated throughout the world. He saw Jenna slowly sink to her knees. He had just become one more thing she had to survive. God help him.

"He will." Daniel was in his head again.

"Who will?" Mac asked.

"God will help you." Daniel replied. "And, brother, you need it."

With that, they were moving through the clouds again, sailing on the wind.

Mac's next awareness was standing before his dad. Mac searched his new state for any of the old anger, animosity, and hatred he'd carried with him for the past twenty-five years but it was gone, it didn't exist here. The only emotion Mac felt was love in its purest form.

John stood, arms wide, to embrace his son. Mac walked into them. Devoid of earthly bodies, it was more a merging of energy, a recognition of connection.

When their energy separated again, Mac noticed his mother wasn't there to meet him. Sadness again.

"Don't be sad, Mac." His dad, in his mind again. "Your mother had very little to make amends for so she was reincarnated almost seven years ago. Do you want to see where she is now?"

"Yes!" Mac thought emphatically.

No sooner did he think it then the clouds parted and Mac saw his daughter getting off the school bus in front of their house.

"You mean all this time . . ."

"Yes, Mac, she was with you. She is your daughter in this incarnation."

Mac wept. All the years he'd spent missing his mom and she had been right there with him all that time.

"Why are *you* still here?" Mac asked his dad.

"Well, Mac, you have to clear your slate, so to speak, before you can be reincarnated as a pure soul. And as you well know, I, too, have a lot of clearing to do. Part of it was to be here for you when you arrived. Because I bear much of the burden for how you arrived, it's my job to help you work through it."

"How do I do that?" Mac asked.

"That's what you'll learn while you're on this plane, son. But first you have to fully understand the consequences of your choices."

That said, Mac noticed Daniel had disappeared and been replaced by a new angel.

"Where did Daniel go?"

"His job was to be with you from inception to death. Once he escorted you to the afterlife, his job was done. He's gone on to his next assignment."

"Who are you?"

"I'm Raphael. I'm the angel of healing and it's time for your first lesson."

"What's my first lesson?"

"Taking a look at your life from beginning to end."

Mac's mind cleared and, much like a video, his life unfolded before him.

He saw the moment his cells came together and began to knit themselves into his human form. He saw the moment his essence filled that form. He saw his birth, his childhood, his adolescence.

As he watched, he also noticed how many times Daniel stood behind him, supporting him when life was too hard for Mac to stand on his own two feet. He noticed Daniel give him a nudge, moving him out of the path of a moving car. He saw Daniel wrap him in his wings when Mac's mother died. He saw Daniel fill him with the strength of two men when Mac stepped in to defend his sister.

It was Daniel who moved Olivia's resume to the bottom of the pile when she would have gone to work for Starbucks instead of her uncle. It was Daniel who supported an exhausted new father night after night, while he rocked his tiny daughter. It was Daniel who gave that same father the strength to go to work the next morning and it was Daniel who sat in the car beside Mac, holding his hand, when Mac made his exit.

Daniel had been with Mac his entire life.

"So you see, Mackenzie, even at your loneliest, you've never been alone." Raphael brought Mac's focus back to the present. "I know you have a lot of questions and they will be answered in good time, but it's time to meet Zadkiel. He rules the heavens and will show you how to work out your karma."

"Is that angel speak for hell?" Mac asked. Having been raised in the church while his mom was alive, he fully expected to be met with fire and brimstone for the mortal sin of suicide. But he soon learned hell was not a dimension but a human creation.

"No, Mac, hell was invented by humans to instill fear in people. It was the most effective way ever created to make men do the bidding of self-proclaimed agents of God, to control the masses and condone atrocities committed in God's name. I know this is all very daunting, but please understand you will not have to work through it alone. There is an angel assigned to every situation and you will always be supported with love and compassion."

And so Mac met the archangel who was God's right hand.

They didn't appear to have moved at all as an ocean landscape unfolded around them. Mac could feel the spray of the water as it slapped against the rocky cliffs, he could smell the ocean breeze and taste the salt on his tongue. He found it exhilarating, if not a bit overwhelming, to experience all these senses without the confines of a body.

In the time it took for him to take it all in, another angel appeared, sitting on a rock watching the waves crash against the shore. Mac assumed it must be Zadkiel.

"Welcome, Mackenzie." He heard the words in his mind like his own inner voice yet distinctly different. "Have a seat," Zadkiel said, and indicated the rock beside him.

They sat in silence while the landscape slowly changed again. Mac found himself still seated but now he was on a plain, black chair with a chrome frame like you might find in a doctor's waiting room or an auditorium. Zadkiel was still beside him. They were in a cold industrial room now with stainless steel all around them. In front of them was a gurney with what appeared to be a body under a sheet. Standing beside the gurney facing them was a middle-aged woman in a lab coat, who Mac guessed was a coroner, a police officer, and two other women Mac recognized as Olivia and Jenna.

Jenna, with her distinct military stance, had her arm around Olivia, holding her steady as the coroner moved the sheet off the face on the gurney. The coroner was very careful not to move the sheet any further than Mac's chin.

Mac was surprised to see his own face bearing little of the trauma of the mangled mess he'd left on the highway.

He heard a sound that could have been mistaken for the wail of the banshee and it broke his heart to know it came from his beautiful wife as she was forced to come to terms with the fact that this wasn't just a bad dream she would wake up from.

Mac could see Jenna was all that was keeping Olivia upright, the effort clearly showing on her face. But where his Olivia was sobbing inconsolably, Jenna was stoic and dry eyed; where the ocean of tears Olivia cried seemed to diminish her, Jenna stood taller and stronger, refusing to bend.

"She was always the strong one," Mac said to the angel beside him

"Look again, Mackenzie," Zadkiel instructed. "Look past the outside shell."

"How do I do that?"

"By looking with your heart, not your eyes."

As Mac concentrated on the two women, their outer shells slowly faded away, leaving their souls bared. He could see to their essence and the marks life had left on them. Olivia had only a few marks but they were so deeply etched Mac knew they would change the very core of her.

Jenna's essence was very different. Underneath the cool, calm surface, she looked like Mary Shelley's Frankenstein monster. Her essence was so warped and twisted he was amazed she was still able to function at all. She was covered in old scars but it was the newest wound that struck him the hardest because he knew he was the one who had put it there. He felt the weight of it. It was too heavy to bear.

Zadkiel put his hand on Mac's shoulder and Mac noticed the weight instantly became easier to carry. It still felt impossibly heavy, but it no longer threatened to crush him.

"This is only a small fraction of impact of your actions, Mackenzie. Every incarnation has important lessons that need to be learned before you can move on to the next one. You made the decision to cease your existence before you could finish your lessons. Those lessons still need to be learned."

"How do I do that?"

"I'm afraid you will be earthbound until you've learned what you were meant to learn. Then you'll be called upon to make amends. Only then can you be reincarnated."

As Zadkiel was talking, another angel appeared beside him. "As in life, Mackenzie, you don't have to do this alone." He nodded to the new angel. "This is Dina. He will be with you helping you as you learn what you need to. While you're here, you'll be able to travel anywhere on earth. You'll be able to visit one of your loved ones or all of them but they won't be able to see you." With that, Zadkiel disappeared.

Time was different for Mac in his non-living state. He was able to move backward and forward freely, which enabled him to get a full understanding of the destruction he had left in his wake. True to Zadkiel's words, though, he was never left to do it on his own. Dina was with him, giving him what he needed when he needed it.

At first, he spent his time with his family. He stood behind them at his funeral, supporting Jenna as she supported Olivia and Makayla. He wrapped his arms around Mackayla as she sat sobbing beside her mother. He did his best to absorb their pain, but it was like trying to stuff a mountain into a marble bag; it was just too big to contain.

It surprised him to see how many people filled the church, how many lives he'd touched, family and friends he'd lost contact with during the years, store clerks, co-workers, neighbours. For each living person there was a guardian angel and loved ones who, like Mac, had passed without fulfilling their living obligations. The church looked like it would explode at the seams.

Despite all those in attendance, Mac's gaze kept going to one, lone man standing at the very back of the church. Mac could see the same fresh wound marring the man's soul as his wife and sister carried.

Mac turned to Dina and asked, "who is that?"

"That's the driver of the truck you hit. When the time is right, you will have some work to do there, my friend."

Mac nodded in understanding.

Time passed in the blink of an eye for Mac. At first, he watched over his entire family, trying to be a comfort to all of them at the same time but as time went by, he found himself drawn more to Olivia and Makayla.

It turned out Jenna had a whole host of people with her. After his funeral, Mac found her surrounded by her guardian angel, Sam, her first husband, their dad, and an entire unit of men and women she'd served with who had died by suicide or on the battlefield.

True to his word, John also spent a lot of time with Mac, working with Dina to show him how to maneuver the world in his new form.

Jenna also had Danny, who desperately wanted to be there for her. It saddened Mac to see her so effectively and efficiently shut Danny out of her grief. After his funeral, she systematically removed Mac from existence, taking any photos of him off the walls. Christmas gifts, anniversary gifts, birthday gifts he'd given her throughout the years, all taken out of cupboards or drawers and placed in the box with the photos. On top lay his funeral notice. Carefully, she taped up the box and placed it in the furthest corner under the stairs. Stacking other boxes all around it, she shut out any memory of him.

If Olivia or Mackayla brought him up in conversation, she would smile politely and pretend to listen but internally she was checking the walls she erected to ensure her that they were still firmly in place, allowing nothing to get in. If Danny or anyone else tried to mention Mac, she shut them down firmly and politely.

Unfortunately, while she was shutting out the pain of his memory, she was also shutting out the love, comfort, and support that would have helped her heal, so she was left with an open wound oozing and festering that would, in time, cause an unbreachable divide between her and Danny.

This saddened Mac because he saw how good Danny was for Jenna. How much he loved her and wanted to be everything she needed and so much more.

Mac could see that, as deeply as Jenna had loved Sam, Sam was never meant to be more to her in this life than the father of her children, but Danny was her soulmate, the yin to her yang. Apart they were half of the equation; together, they made a whole. They had been together for eternities, balancing and complementing one another through the ages.

Mac also discovered that his daughter was sensitive to his presence. As she lay sobbing night after night he would often sit by her bed, stroking her hair. More than once she would reach up and place her hand where his had been. He would bring her things, like coins, or feathers. She would gather them all and put them in an old shoebox that held pictures of them together before he let mental illness separate them and ultimately destroy him.

Olivia wasn't quite so sensitive, but Mac found he could talk to her in her dreams. He would lay beside her in their bed and whisper in her ear how much he loved her as he held her tightly. She would wake up with a small smile and tears streaming down her face, her heart heavy with the loneliness of his loss.

As the years went by, Mac tried everything he could to get his wife and daughter past their grief, but where Jenna refused to acknowledge hers, Olivia and Mackayla were stuck in theirs, each one's grief feeding the other's, neither able to move past it.

Eventually, Mac had to expand his circle because he was there to finish his life's lessons, as well as make amends. As much as he wanted to, he couldn't spend all his time with his family. He knew it was time to make a visit to the man at the back of the church. Dina told him his name was Joseph Burns, but that his family and friends called him Joe.

Mac stood outside Joe's house. It was located in a very nice neighbourhood and looked as though it had once been a well-kept, welcoming family home. Now the lawn was overgrown and the mailbox was knocked over. Mac suspected it had been hit by the car in the drive with the big dent in the rear fender. The paint around the doors and windows was chipped and peeling.

Inside, Mac found Joe slumped over the kitchen table nursing a cup of coffee. Dirty dishes covered the counters and filled the sinks, dust bunnies turned into dust pterodactyls and a trail of dirty laundry that looked like it was trying to make a getaway covered the floor. Needing to know how this man had made this journey to the land of complete dysfunction, Mac asked Dina to take him to the start of his decline. It didn't surprise him to find himself sitting in the passenger seat of Joe's truck.

Joe was on his way home to see his family after being on the road for three days and Mac could feel his excitement. As Joe talked to his wife on the Bluetooth, he told her he was only ten kilometres away and couldn't wait to hold her in his arms.

Mac could hear the squeals of the excited children in the background. Daddy was coming home.

Then Mac heard Joe yell, "Oh my God! He's not going to stop! He's not going to stop! Oh my God!"

On the other end of the phone, Joe's wife heard it all, her husband's frantic words, the impact, the metal bending and crumpling. "Joe!" she screamed over and over until he told in her in a strange, distant voice that he would have to call her back. He hung up and left her hanging on the other end of the phone not knowing what terrible thing had just happened to her husband.

It took Joe a half a kilometre to get his truck stopped. He looked at the undercarriage of his trailer at the twisted metal that was once Mac's car in shock and disbelief. It looked like an awful abstract painting. Finally gathering his wits about him, he called 911. As the 911 dispatcher asked him the status of the occupants of the other car, he spotted something lying a few feet from the wreckage. It took his mind a moment to translate the image. When Mac's car slid under the trailer it had peeled the roof off like a sardine can. Mac's body remained in the car. His head lay on the pavement looking up at the sky.

In that moment, Mac understood why the coroner had been so careful to keep the sheet at neck level.

Joe ran to the ditch and gave into violent vomiting as he sank to his knees with the 911 operator's insistent voice sounding in the silence. This is where the first responders found him.

Joe never came home to his wife and family. A shadow did.

Joe could never get that image out his head. Night after night, the nightmares would come. Soon, he wasn't even going to bed. His wife would find him sitting in front of the television at all hours. He couldn't bring himself to get back into a truck, so consequently lost his truck and his job.

Within six months, he was completely unable to leave the house. He was consumed with anxiety. His wife desperately tried to get him help but every time he tried to go past the front door he would have a full-blown panic attack that would cause him to claw his way back inside and stand quaking on the other side of the door.

By the time a year had passed, Joe was only getting worse and it was having such an impact on their small children that Joe's wife finally moved out of the house. She told him she would do anything she could to help him but the children needed stability and she couldn't keep exposing them to Joe's insanity.

"It never even occurred to me that my actions would destroy this man's life," Mac said as the responsibility of the damage he had done to an innocent stranger sat like a lead weight on his shoulders. "How do I fix this?" Mac asked in desperation.

Dina's answer was cryptic, as it often was. All he would say was, "You'll know when the time is right."

Mac knew better then to press so with a heavy heart he moved on.

He found in his new state that he could travel the world in the blink of an eye. He had a lot to learn so he spent a lot of time in classrooms and universities, exploring historical landmarks. He studied the governments of the world, sat in business meetings with the most powerful people, witnessed humanity's worst atrocities but also found, in the most unlikely of places, the absolute best in humanity. He learned that no matter how bad things looked, there was always a small shining star that illuminated the darkest corners. He found the most unusual heroes and incredible strength in the frailest of the frail. But through all his lessons, what made him the saddest was when he studied the religions of the world.

In life, he had never been a particularly religious man, but now that he understood there really were other planes of existence and entities like those described in the Bible, he was hungry to learn more.

He visited the temples, synagogues, and churches of the world religions. He visited holy shrines, the Dalai Lama, and every manner of guru, priest, or holy man that the suffering, lost, thirsty masses flocked to for answers and comfort. What he found was that for every one honestly, deeply spiritual person, three demonic entities soaked up the energy of the desperate and fed, like gluttons, off it. In most cases these entities were in positions of leadership and power, often referred to as Godly and charismatic.

These entities weren't the demons of the Bible or folklore. They were humans who had learned to feed off the fear and suffering of others for their own gain. Mac met the first one at a tent revival in Mississippi, also the scene of his most powerful lesson. This demon was a preacher serving a generous buffet of fear in the form of fire and brimstone to several hundred self-proclaimed righteous people.

Initially Mac didn't recognize his soul as human. It was warped and twisted like Jenna's, but the energy that made up Jenna's was green, signifying someone who was ruled by her heart, someone whose energy source was mother earth. This man's energy was red and angry. Mac could see him syphoning light from his parishioners and when he was done, a small, withered seed was left deeply planted in the congregation's root, tendrils starting to sprout and grow.

"The seeds of discord," Dina told him. "If this seed gets rooted too deeply, good people can be moved to do unimaginable things, all in the name of God."

Mac learned this was a phenomenom that plagued every single religious group known to man. But there was always a handful of people who seemed to be immune. Mac could see that these people were strongly connected to the pure energy of the universe. A strong beam of light could be clearly seen running through these individuals, connecting them with the heavens.

Mac also noticed many of these people were not people of means. As a matter of fact, many of them were on the streets, living hand to mouth, many were the ones society called crazy or mentally defective. Which was not to say that there were no bright souls, as Mac came to call them, with money and means but they were very few and far between. Most of the bright souls, however, were the people shunned by polite society, the people others thought were odd or peculiar, and they were peculiar because they could see on a level the general population could not. Some of them could even see angels and those, like Mac, who had passed on.

As Mac traversed the world, he was made aware of all he had missed by being so locked inside his own world. One of the biggest things was what was happening to his sister. While he was going down the rabbit hole of depression and trauma, his sister had been fighting tooth and nail to keep from falling into a hole of her own.

Seven years had passed now. Mac was with Jenna at the restaurant when Danny told her he was leaving. Even though Jenna showed nothing outwardly, Mac could see the new wound. The one his death left had never really healed, so this new wound was threatening to tear it wide open and Mac wasn't sure if Jenna could find her way through it, so he stayed with her.

As he watched her descent into hell, he begged Dina to let him help her. He yelled at his father, asking him how he could stand by and watch her suffer. He lamented to Sam. He even tried reaching Zadkiel to intercede on her behalf. They all just kept telling him to wait; it would all work out according to God's plan.

Then as she swallowed the pills and chased them with wine, Zadkiel finally made an appearance.

"It's time for you to start making amends, Mackenzie."

In desperation, Mac screamed at the golden angel standing before him. "How!"

"You have to get the pills out of her system before they start to dissolve. Use your initiative, Mac."

Not knowing what else to do, Mac pulled back his arm, fist clenched, and punched his sister in the stomach as hard as he could. Fully expecting his fist to pass right through her, he was utterly amazed to have made solid contact.

Alone in her room, Jenna doubled over and fell from her bed. Her stomach cramping viciously, she crawled to the bathroom and barely made it to the toilet. She began to heave up the contents of her stomach. Stomach empty, she lay down on the cold bathroom floor and passed out.

As Sam knelt by Jenna and moved the sweaty hair from her brow, Mac turned to the head angel and asked, "How was I able to do that and why didn't anyone else help her?"

"Because, Mackenzie, as you can now see, the wound you left on her is the one she cannot heal. It's that unhealed wound that brought her to this place. When she wakes, she'll be able to see you—all of us, actually. Your job is to help her heal so she can live out the life intended for her. Her job will be to help you fix the lives your actions destroyed." The angel was starting to disappear. "Oh, and Mackenzie, it will surprise you to find out just how many lives there are."

When Mac turned back to Jenna, he was surprised to find only him and Sam in the room.

"Why are you the only one left with me?" Mac asked Sam, suddenly realizing this was the first time they'd spoken in the seven years he roamed the earth.

Sam unfurled his wings and said, "because I'm her guardian angel. I'm here to help you help her."

Chapter 5

Born Again

Jenna woke up shivering on her bathroom floor. The first thing she noticed was the stench of vomit combined with her unwashed body. Her next awareness was the disgusting taste in her pasty mouth. *Oh my God, that's gross!* she thought as she slowly moved into a cross-legged seated position. Her head pounded as she tried to figure out the events of the previous day.

Head hanging, eyes closed, she was soon visited by her old friend, shame. Next came helplessness, then defeat. *What took you guys so long?* she thought as the emotions washed over her.

Silently, Mac came into the room and knelt down in front of her. He gently said, "You know I couldn't let you do that, sis."

Slowly, slowly, Jenna opened her eyes and looked up through her greasy, stringy wall of hair. Seeing her long-dead brother kneeling in front of her sent her into fits of screaming. She scrambled backward until her back hit the bathroom wall.

With nowhere else to go, Jenna closed her eyes, her mind scrambling to make sense of what she'd seen, her heart beating in hyperdrive.

OK, she thought to herself. *There is one of several possibilities going on here. Either I've finally lost my mind and I'm seeing things, I'm DTing and I'm seeing things, or I'm dead.*

Taking a deep breath, Jenna opened her eyes again; this time, she not only saw Mac, still kneeling in front of her, but she also saw Sam standing behind him.

"Yup, I'm dead," she whispered to herself. "But why am I still stuck in this nasty body with a dirty hangover? Ah crap! I'm in hell, that's why." She answered her own question.

Reaching up, she moved her hair away from her face. Keeping her eyes fixed on Mac and Sam, she slowly slid up the wall into a standing position, reactivating the construction zone in her head.

Heart still pounding, she inched her way past Mac and Sam and moved toward her bed as though she were surrounded by half-starved tigers. She crawled back under the covers settling on the idea that this must be some sort of very realistic nightmare. Pulling the covers over her head, she willed herself to go back to sleep.

After a few minutes of deep breathing exercises, she was able to get her heart rate back to normal and eventually drifted off to sleep.

Once she was asleep, Sam lay down on the bed behind her and wrapped her in his arms.

With a soft sigh, she settled further into the bed and slept soundly for the first time in months.

Mac quietly left the room and headed down the stairs.

Jenna woke several hours later with a soft smile on her lips and her mind clear. She rolled over, yawned, and stretched, going over the strange events of the night.

Sam had left the bed when he felt her start to wake so she would have no idea that he'd ever been there, holding her, comforting her, sending peace to her shattered psyche.

Lifting the covers, Jenna caught a whiff of herself and grimaced. "Oh my God, I stink!" she said to herself as she got out of bed and headed for the bathroom. There, she stopped to look in the mirror.

She didn't recognize the face that looked back at her. "Who are you?" She whispered as she touched the glass.

Her dark hair hung to her waist in greasy, matted ropes. She could see a yellow tinge in the whites of her dark-ringed, bloodshot eyes. Her cheeks were concave and her chin too sharp from all the weight she'd lost over the past weeks.

Turning away from the mirror, she moved to her tub, turned on the water, set the temperature, added some of her favourite bath foam, and stripped out of her nasty night clothes. While the tub filled, she brushed her teeth thoroughly, using a liberal amount of mouthwash when toothpaste didn't quite cut it. Then she

sank into the warm, soapy water and let out a deep sigh.

Once the tub was filled, she sat back and let her mind wander over the events that had led her to this place in time. How had things gotten so out of hand? Never in her wildest dreams would she have believed she could have ended up like this. Had she really tried to commit suicide or was it just part of that bizarre dream? And seeing Mac and Sam? She hadn't thought of them in years, hadn't let herself think of them, why now? Giving her a head a careful shake, she closed her eyes and let the hot, sudsy water work its magic as it soothed her emaciated body and tired spirit.

Jen shampooed her hair twice and conditioned it generously. The scent of her hair products was much more pleasant than that of sweat and vomit. A good hour had passed when she finally pulled herself out of the tub, fingers and toes like withered grapes. As she dried herself off she caught a glimpse of her naked body in the mirror. Refusing to look at the wreckage, she quickly looked away, grabbed her bathrobe and wide-tooth comb, and sat down on the side on her bed.

Gently, she attempted to work the comb through her matted hair. It didn't take long for her arm to tire. She gave up and pulled it into three strands, grimacing as she heard the strands snapping, she plaited it into a long braid down her back.

Finishing that, she went in search of some clean clothes, and was surprised to find a clean pair of leggings and a long top. She finished her ablutions and headed down the stairs to her kitchen feeling better then she had in a long time.

She grimaced again when she saw the state of her house. Digging her coffee pot out of the disaster, she washed a mug and started brewing a cup of coffee, taking in the tantalizing smell as it dripped into her cup. Coffee finished, she opened her fridge to get some milk but found a science experiment gone very, very wrong.

She closed the fridge door and scratched her head. She wondered where the milk was from yesterday's order. She noticed it sitting on her cluttered counter were she'd left it, too preoccupied to put it away. She grabbed the milk, opened it, and gave it cautious sniff. Satisfied it hadn't spoiled overnight, she topped up her coffee and started toward the living room to enjoy it.

As she rounded the corner and headed for the sofa, Mac and Sam, who were already sitting there deep in conversation, turned in perfect synchronicity and got to their feet.

Taking in his sister's freshly scrubbed person, Mac said, "Well, it's a good start, sis, but we have a long way to go."

Jen stood frozen for several seconds, coffee cup falling from her limp fingers and shattering on the floor, spraying coffee all over the room like crime scene spatter. Shaking her head, she clasped her hand over her mouth and turned and ran down the hall and out the front door, slamming it behind her.

Body shaking, heart stuttering, mind racing, she sat down on her front step with a small thud. "What the fuck!" She struggled to calm the earthquake going on inside her mind and body. "This cannot be real! This cannot be real! This cannot be real!" she repeated to herself like a mantra.

In the house, Mac looked at Sam and asked, "How am I supposed to help her when I scare her half to death every time she sees me?"

"Give me a few minutes," Sam said as he headed to the door.

Quietly, Sam moved to sit beside Jen, gently placing his hand on her shoulder. As her guardian angel, he was able to take some of her fear and soothe her shattered nerves. "Hey, beautiful lady, I know this is a lot to take in, but let me assure you it is real."

"How? How can it be real, Sam? This shit just doesn't happen to normal people! Seriously, Sam, WHAT THE FUCK! You left us eighteen years ago. How can you be sitting here beside me? I buried you, for God's sake!" She choked back a sob.

Drawing her tight up against his side, Sam explained. "You're right, Jen, in this life I died in Afghanistan, but I never left you. I've lived many times before and this was my last incarnation. Once a spirit has lived out their incarnations, the next evolution is to become a guardian angel and I was blessed to be assigned to you."

"OK, so supposing I could buy that explanation, what's up with Mac? Am I such a handful I need two guardian angels?"

Sam laughed, "Well you are definitely a handful, but no, Mac's been given a rather rare opportunity. His suicide did a lot of damage to a lot of people, you being one of those people. He was sent back to keep you from making the same mistake."

"So it really was suicide? I desperately wanted to believe it was a just a terrible accident, that the police were wrong. I didn't want to think he could just leave us like that." Jenna was crying freely now.

Sam noticed her neighbours looking at her with suspicion as they walked down the sidewalk, some with pets, others just out for stroll, all of them cutting a wide swath and quickening their steps past the crazy lady talking to herself.

"I think we should go inside, Jen," he suggested.

Reluctantly, Jen got up off the step and turned to the door. She walked back into her house with Sam trailing her. She sighed. Her beautiful home was in a shambles. Looking at it just made her tired.

She headed for the living room where Mac had taken refuge again, pacing the floor. Sam placed his hand on her shoulder to help her deal with the fear and emotions of seeing her dead brother.

As she stared at her brother standing just a few feet away from her, looking just like the Mac she remembered before he gave into the mental illness, the tears she'd managed to get under control started again this time in torrents, emotions tearing at her like a category 5 hurricane.

She ran at him, screaming at him, hitting him with seven years of pent-up grief. "How could you do that?" she screamed. "How could you leave me after all we've been through together! How could you leave Olivia and Mackayla? Do you know what you did to them?"

Mac wrapped Jen up in his arms and let her pain and fury run its course before leading her to the sofa. Sitting, he pulled her down with him. Sam sat on the other side of her, resting a hand on her shoulder again.

"I can't tell you how sorry I am at the devastation I've caused so many people by my actions," he started. "But as far as how I could do it, I think you of all people can answer that question, no?" He asked with one eyebrow raised in question. "You just attempted to do the very same thing."

That said, Mac reached over, grabbed the box of tissue on the side table, and handed it to a sniffling Jenna. She took a handful and sat silently looking at the tissues in her hand as she took in his words, giving them the weight they required. He was right. Even after all the pain his suicide caused she had very nearly done the same thing.

"There's one small difference, Mac. You had a family that loved you madly and needed you desperately! I have no one." Looking up into his clear blue eyes she asked, "how long do you honestly think it would have taken for someone to find my body? Days? Weeks? Months? Danny hasn't contacted me in weeks, Brandon hasn't spoken more than a few words to me in years. Brenna and Olivia have completely given up on me. Even my dogs are gone." She hiccupped before continuing. "You had everything to live for, I have nothing."

"Sadly, Jen, only part of what you just said is true. I did have everything to live for. So do you. Unfortunately, you're so caught in your own pain right now you can't think straight. That's partially why I've been allowed to be here with you right now."

"What's the other part, Mac?"

"Once we get you back on your feet, I need your help, Jen."

It was her turn to look at him with one brow raised. "Oh, do tell," she said with a mix of sarcasm and suspicion.

"I have a lot of people to help and you're one of a very few people who can see me. I'm going to need you to be my man on the ground, so to speak." He gave her that little grin she remembered so well from when he was a little boy trying to get her involved in one of his schemes. "But first we have to get you back to full fighting order, sis, and that's going to take some doing."

Sinking to the sofa, she looked up at Mac and Sam, shaking her head, still struggling to comprehend it all. "How am I supposed to help you when I've run my own life into the crapper? I wouldn't even know where to start to sort it all out." Her face showed exhaustion at just the thought of the effort it would take to get back on her feet, let alone helping her dead brother clean up the mess he'd left behind.

"Well, sis, that's why we're here. This will all look a lot easier when we get some proper food into your body. When was the last time you ate?"

Searching her memory bank, Jen found she honestly couldn't remember the last time she put anything of substance in her stomach. She shrugged her shoulders in reply, suddenly feeling the effects of the lack of solid food and too many days on a liquid diet.

"Well, how about we go do an inventory of your kitchen and make a list. Then we'll go to the grocery store and get you some food—yes?" Jen nodded her agreement.

As she struggled to get back off the sofa, Mac took one arm and Sam the other. With their support, Jen was able to clear the rotting food out her fridge and sort her pantry. She made a long grocery list.

She would never be able to carry it all so she would have to drive to grocery store. This knowledge gave her a lot of anxiety because it had been weeks since she'd driven or left her house at all.

Sensing her fear, Sam, who had been working with Mac to put all the garbage strewn around her kitchen into garbage bags, came over to her and put his hand on her shoulder again. The fear immediately dissipated.

"It's OK, babe, we're in this together. We won't let you do this alone."

Another torrential downpour threatened Jen as she said, "I've missed you so much, Sam! It was so hard living without you."

"I know, Jen, but you got through that. You can get through this. And just remember, I've *always* been there. Now let's get you out the door."

Mac tied up the huge garbage bag filled with old food containers, rotting food from the counters and fridge, and a variety of grocery bags and store flyers. He carried it with him as they all filed out of the kitchen into the garage.

At the rear of the trio, Jen grabbed her purse and the keys off the bench by the door, still shaking her head as her "life-challenged" bodyguards fought over who got the front seat.

While Jen opened the garage door and Mac took the garbage out to the bin, Sam jumped into the passenger side with an impish grin. Jen had to laugh when she saw the look on her brother's face.

As she slid into the driver's seat of her dark red Grand Cherokee, and pressed the ignition button, she took a minute to enjoy the feeling of the leather seat as it molded to her. Backing out of her drive into the street, her stomach growled ferociously, twisting with hunger.

"I think we'd better get you breakfast before we do anything," Sam commented.

All in agreement they headed for the McDonald's in the same shopping centre as Jenna's grocery store. Jen parked halfway between the two stores and they all piled out of the car, Sam and Mac opening and closing the passenger doors.

Unfortunately, they didn't take into consideration that Sam and Mac were invisible to everyone else until they heard loud gasp from a lady a few cars away loading her purchases into her own car.

Taking in the confused look on Jenna's face, Mac told her she was the only one who could see them. Jenna, quick on her feet, waved at the lady and said, "It's a brand new car with all automatic doors. Stupid thing seems to have a glitch. I'll have to take it back into the dealership."

Since the human brain always seems to need to accept what makes the most sense, and even though no such car existed, the lady didn't question Jenna's explanation but just gave her a little embarrassed grin and continued on her way.

Safely inside the McDonald's, Jenna stopped at the computerized self-order board and began making her selections. Sam and Mac did the same.

Sam and Mac found seats at the very back of the restaurant in a reasonably concealed corner, away from prying eyes, while Jenna waited for their orders. If the clerk was surprised by the anorexic-looking woman who came in alone but picked up enough food to feed three, he didn't show it, much to Jenna's extreme relief.

Setting the food on the table her celestial sentries had chosen, Jenna sat down and tucked into it with a gusto.

"Oh my God! This is sooooo good! I forgot how good solid food was," she moaned.

While she was eating her Egg McMuffin, Sam and Mac were stealthily eating theirs, careful not to be seen. The last thing Jenna needed was some trashy magazine following her around haranguing her about ghosts or aliens or whatever explanation they would come up with.

A thought suddenly dawned on Jenna as she watched them eat.

"Hey, I thought spirits or angels or whatever the hell you two are didn't need to eat?"

"We don't *need* to eat. Even though we can enjoy food while we're here, there's no physical requirement for it," Sam replied.

"But where does the food go?" she pondered more to herself than to them. "Wait! Don't answer that!" she said quickly, holding her hand up to stop Sam who was already preparing an answer, realizing she didn't really want to know. "Let's just enjoy the food."

As Jenna watched the antics of the two goofy ghosts sitting across from her, she couldn't help but laugh. They had always gotten along like brothers in life; apparently, their relationship hadn't changed in the afterlife. They were just like she remembered them; it was as if she'd gone back in time. God, how she'd missed them. She didn't even care that people were looking at her like she was an escapee from the psych ward. It just felt good to feel good.

Finally, full and content, Jenna got up, her celestial sentries following suit. She dumped the tray of food wrappers and paper cups into the garbage bin, placed the tray on top, and they headed to the grocery store where the antics continued.

Jenna wheeled her cart down the aisles selecting the food on her list and trying to ignore Tweedle Dee and Tweedle Dumber as they excitedly jumped up and down, motioning to all manner of garbage food, from cupcakes to potato chips.

"Good God, you two are worse than shopping with teenagers," she sighed under her breath as she gave in and put a box of Twinkies into her cart.

Finally content that she had everything on her list, she wheeled up to the checkout. As the cashier who had been checking Jenna's groceries for years did a double take, not quite able to hide his surprise at her appearance, Jenna's new lighter mood dimmed.

When she went to pay and card after card was declined, she could feel the anxiety overwhelming her again. She was almost ready to burst into tears and flee from the store when one of the cards finally worked.

Sam's hand on her shoulder gave her the strength she needed to keep her composure while her groceries were being bagged and they made their way out of the store. As she opened the doors so Sam and Mac could get into the car, with the secondary task of loading her groceries, she looked up and across the parking lot at the liquor store.

She wanted a drink so badly she could already taste it, feel it running down her throat, settling in her stomach, its warmth and comfort spreading through her body. Giving her head a shake, she dug deep inside searching for that small bit of steel that still dwelled at the core of her and she got in her car, backed it out of its parking spot, and headed for home.

The gentle voice of Sam beside her said, "Jen, I am so proud of you."

"Why didn't you help me?" she asked him.

"Because you needed to know you could do it yourself. Plus, who says I didn't?" He gave her that naughty boy grin.

Pulling up to her house, she spotted Brenna's car in the driveway. Her heart lightened again at the prospect of seeing her daughter. She'd missed her so much.

Quickly parking in the garage, conscious of her heavenly hosts and the fact that Brenna wouldn't be able to see or hear them, Jenna gathered a load of groceries and ran them into the house. She set them in the pantry just off the garage and called out to her daughter. "I'll be right there, sweetheart, I just have to grab another load or two of groceries."

Since they couldn't help without the threat of attracting attention, Sam and Mac went into the house ahead of Jen, Sam to see his daughter and Mac to see his niece.

Jenna ran back and forth a couple more times, carrying as many bags as she safely could, as fast as she could. On her last trip, she closed her car door with a bump of her hip. She was so excited to see Brenna she just dropped the bags on the pantry floor without unpacking them and went in search of her.

Finding Brenna had cleared her usual spot at the breakfast nook, Jenna ran up to her and apologized for the disaster zone her house had become. She was just about to give her daughter a hug from behind when she noticed Sam's face. He was standing in front of Brenna on the other side of the nook. He gave his head a little warning shake. Mac was looking at a something on the counter in front of Brenna, something Brenna was staring at so intently she hadn't moved a muscle at her mother's entrance.

Jenna moved around the nook to see what was the cause of such interest, then let out a gasp. In front of Brenna was the letter Jenna had written to her.

The pain in Brenna's eyes when she finally looked up at her mother made Jenna's heart constrict. The shock on Brenna's face when she realized how sick her mother really was caused her heart to shatter.

Chapter 6

The Muse

"What's going on, Mom?" Brenna asked, tears running down her face as she took in her mother's sallow skin stretched tightly over her bony frame.

Her mother had always been beautiful to her, with her smoky grey eyes and long dark hair. When Brenna was a little girl she thought her mom was a princess out of a storybook. Her strong, athletic build seemed to mirror her inner strength. Until this moment, Brenna honestly believed her mother was the strongest woman in the world, that there was nothing she couldn't do or handle.

Brenna had watched her do the seemingly impossible without breaking stride. This frail, broken woman who wrote the letter in front of her was a stranger that Brenna couldn't reconcile with the no nonsense, get-er-done, head-down-ass up mother she knew.

"What happened to you? Where's Danny? Oh my God, Mom! Seriously! What the fuck is this, Mom!? A suicide note!" Brenna shot questions rapid fire at her mother, her voice raising to a shout, all the while waving the letter at her.

Jenna felt sick at the pain she'd caused her daughter. She reached across the counter and took the letter out of her hands and placed it on the counter. Then she took Brenna's hands in hers. "I'm so sorry, baby, I know I have a lot of explaining to do."

Then Jenna let go of her daughter's hands and made her way around the nook to take a stool beside her. She knew Brenna deserved an explanation but for the life of her, she couldn't figure out what had happened, how had she allowed things to get so out of hand.

"First," she said, "Danny and I been living apart for the past few weeks." She was struggling to sort the events out in her own mind as she began her explaination. Oddly, the fact that she could now also see Brenna's guardian angel, Arielle, with her hand resting on Brenna's shoulder, barely registered as she spoke. "I suppose the stress of that brought up other things I've never dealt with and it caused a system overload." She looked at Mac and Sam. They nodded their support and urged her to continue. "I guess I needed . . ." she paused, "No—I *need*—help, Brenna. I just didn't want to put more on you or Olivia and didn't know where else to turn." Jenna finished the sentence and looked down at her hands.

Brenna got up from her stool and hugged her mother tightly. "Mom, I'm stronger then I look. After all, I am your daughter." Smiling through her tears, she stepped back. "I can't believe you ever doubted how much I need you. With all the people I have had to learn to live without, how could you expect me to live without you? You lived without your own mother, how could you ask me to live without mine?" She delivered her words ever so gently but they hit with impact of a rocket-propelled missile. "I depend on you to break trail for me, Mom. You're the one who puts up the sign posts that I follow. You're who I strive to be. Is suicide really the example you want to set?"

Seeing that her words had had the desired effect, Brenna got up grabbed her letter and headed to the office to get the other two. She then went over to the shredder, looked at her mother pointedly, and shredded all three. "Now, there will be no more of that, right, Mom!?"

Hand on her heart, looking solemnly at her daughter, Jenna promised. She was so proud of her strong, fierce daughter she thought her heart would explode.

"Come on, Mom, let's get this house in order. Then we can figure out the next step." With that said, Brenna headed to pantry where the groceries were waiting, freezer items melting on the floor, and began putting things away.

Together, they stripped the towels and bedding, gathered mountains of dirty clothes off the floors and sorted it all into piles, then started a huge load of laundry. After putting fresh sheets on Jenna's bed, Brenna grabbed new towels from the linen closet and went through the house replacing the dirty ones while Jenna gathered up all the wine bottles, wine glasses, dirty dishes and refuse, making several trips up and down the stairs. Before long, her bedroom was tidied with all evidence of the night before erased.

Heading into the ensuite with a mop bucket and a bottle Mr. Clean, Jenna ignored the faint smell of vomit that still lingered—the only evidence left of her suicide attempt—and started scrubbing toilet, tub, sink, and floor.

While she did that, Brenna dusted and cleaned the other rooms on the main floor, and ran the vacuum over the floors and stairs.

By the time they'd finished the upper floor, they realized it was well past lunch and they were famished.

Jenna opened a can of tomato soup, dumped it into a pot, and put it on the stove to heat. Then she started constructing grilled cheese sandwiches, Brenna's favourite meal when she was a little girl.

Sitting side by side at the breakfast nook, mother and daughter ate their late lunch with shoulders touching, both needing that contact, as the celestial threesome watched, satisfaction on their faces.

Lunch finished, both women got up and started clearing the debris in the kitchen. They ran load after load of dishes through the dishwasher and while they washed, Jenna tucked into the office while Brenna dusted and tidied the living room.

Jenna cringed as she took in the stacks of unopened mail—overdue credit card bills and unpaid utilities. *No wonder all my cards were declined at the grocery store*, she thought to herself.

Once she got the office organized and cleaned, she sat down to see the state of her bank account, read emails, listen to phone messages, and prioritize bills.

She was relieved to see the household account shared by her and Danny had a healthy balance; at least she could get all the utilities paid up to date. Danny's pay was still being deposited but he wasn't using much to live on.

Keeping her grocery and gas budget in mind, Jenna used the remainder of the funds to put a payment on each overdue credit card. This task done, she breathed a small sigh and moved onto her emails.

She cringed when she noted several from Susan Feldman, the director of The Westend Health Care Centre. The first couple of emails were polite, simply asking when they could get a status report on the painting they'd commissioned, the one that was supposed to be close to completion.

By the third unanswered email the tone had changed significantly, becoming quite concerned; by number five they were threatening legal action.

Jenna responded by apologizing profusely, saying she had been very, very ill and unable to access her emails (not technically a lie) and that she would do everything she could to get the commissioned piece done on time. Then she apologized again. Once the email was sent she sat thinking: shit! shit! shit!" She only had two weeks left to finish the piece.

"Oh, well, one crisis at time," she whispered to herself, leaving the office. She headed for her studio. The canvas she needed to have completed in two weeks was blank. Panic threatened to overwhelm her again.

Sam placed his hand on her shoulder and Mac whispered in her ear, "Just breathe, sis. You're not alone."

She turned off the light in her studio and left the room, deciding she would cross that bridge after a good night's sleep, and closed the door behind her.

She went into the kitchen and joined Brenna, who was already assembling a prepared salad and slicing cold chicken to add to it.

Jenna fought her craving for a glass of wine and put the kettle on for tea. She pulled two mugs from the cupboard. This time, they sat on the sofa in the living room to eat their light dinner to the sound of the TV droning in the background. Jenna, more exhausted then she had ever been before but feeling happier than she could remember, sat looking at her beautiful daughter.

Mac headed off to check on Olivia and Mackayla as the two guardian angels sat with their charges.

"This is going to take some getting used to," Jenna mused as she thought about the number of times they'd startled her throughout the day. She still wasn't convinced she wasn't either dreaming or crazy, but she'd decided just running with it took less energy than fighting it.

Around 9 p.m., Brenna yawned and stretched. As she got up from the sofa, she turned to mother. "I hope you don't mind, but I'm going to crash in the spare suite tonight." It wasn't a question. There was no way Brenna was leaving her mother alone.

Jenna smiled and said that would be wonderful and got up as well. She followed Brenna up the stairs, shutting off lights on the way. When they reached the top, Jenna hugged her daughter tightly and said, "I really don't know what I'd have done without you today. I love you so much, baby!"

Brenna relaxed into her mother's arms, hugging her back just as tightly. "I love you too, Mom. See you in the morning."

Both women headed in opposite directions to settle for the night.

Brenna crawled into the guest bed, propping herself up with pillows, and sent a text to her partner, Ethan. She had been keeping him appraised of the situation throughout the day, so he wasn't surprised when she let him know she would be staying with her mother until she was sure she could be safely left alone.

In the other room, Jenna was so exhausted she literally fell into bed and crashed, but she wasn't asleep more than a few minutes when she shot upright and bolted from the room, eyes wild, completely unaware until she hit the cold hard wood of the first floor. She was so disoriented when she came to she didn't know who she was, where she was, or how she'd gotten there. As she opened her mouth to scream, she felt a gentle hand on her shoulder.

Sam guided her to the bottom step where she slowly sat as information trickled into her befuddled brain. She let out a stuttering sigh.

Brenna was laying in the guest bed reading a book when she heard her mother's flight from her room and down the stairs. Dropping the book, she scrambled out of bed and ran toward the sound. Seeing her mother sitting on the step with a panicked look on her face, Brenna plopped down beside her and asked, deeply concerned, "What's going on, Mom? Are you OK?"

As Jenna took a few deep breaths in an attempt to calm herself, she said, "It's been a long time since that's happened."

"What happened, exactly?"

"I'm not really sure. I've tried to explain these episodes to several doctors but the best explanation they could give me is night terrors," she told her daughter as the internal quaking finally eased up. "I started having them just after Sam died."

"Really?" Brenna was surprised. "I've had no idea. How did you hide it from us for so long?"

"I always went to bed when you both were sound asleep when you were little and when you were old enough, you shared the basement so I was able to get myself under control before I disturbed you both."

"Do you know what causes them?"

"As near as I've been able to figure out, extreme stress seems to bring them on. Anyway, enough of this." She patted her daughter's knee. "Let's go to bed, kiddo. We've both had a crazy day."

She got up off the step, offered Brenna a hand, and they both headed back up the stairs to take another stab at getting some sleep, neither of them very successfully.

The night terror triggered long, dormant nightmares for Jenna, who tossed and turned, crying and moaning in her sleep as Sam lay beside her, soothing and comforting her through the worst of them.

Brenna lay awake listening to the sounds coming from her mother's room, wondering how she had lived this long with no idea how much her mother was suffering. Both women were completely wiped, faces drawn with black bags under their eyes by the time morning came. So when Jenna told her daughter she was going for a run, Brenna looked at her like she'd lost her mind.

"You're kidding, right?"

"Nope, I need to get back into a routine and that's the best place to start. Wanna come?"

"I didn't bring any workout clothes or shoes," Brenna answered, thinking she was out of the woods.

"No worries, I have extra clothes and a pair of sneakers that will fit."

Reluctantly, Brenna agreed. The two women suited up, looking more like sisters than mother and daughter, and headed down the sidewalk toward Jenna's favourite running path. After about three kilometres, both of them were winded and had slowed down to a walk, Jenna because she had let herself get out of shape and Brenna because she wasn't a runner.

As they walked, Brenna took the opportunity to ask the questions that had been weighing on her mind since the day before. She'd been mulling an idea around all morning and was hoping she could fit it into the conversation at some point.

"So, Mom," she asked slowly, "what exactly happened? How long have you and Danny been separated? Obviously, you weren't going to tell us. Didn't you think we had a right to know?"

Jenna took a deep breath. "We decided on a trial separation. I think we were both just tired. Or maybe it was just me. I don't really know. I just know he left and if he hadn't, I would have." As she spoke, she was watching Mac listening intently as he strolled in the slush-covered grass of the berm beside her. Sam was taking up the rear with Arielle, Brenna's guardian angel.

"I'm not sure when we stopped trying, or maybe I should say, when *I* stopped trying. I just know we were having more bad times then good times together and that's never a good sign."

"Have you ever thought about counselling?" Brenna asked, carefully opening up the subject she'd been mulling over during the night.

Jenna didn't answer right away. She just stopped on the sidewalk a few feet from the house and turned to look at her daughter.

If the celestial trio had any breath to hold they would have, as everyone waited to see how this suggestion would be received. When Jenna didn't answer, Brenna carried on.

"Mom, I think you need to and I think you need to address the drinking while you're at it. When I took the garbage out I saw all your empties. Mom, I think you have a problem." She said this as quickly as she could, before her courage failed her.

Brenna's shoulder's sagged as tears started down her mother's face.

"I'm sorry, Mom, I didn't mean to hurt you. I knew it was too soon to bring it up. Please don't cry, Mom! Please." Brenna hugged her mom, desperately wishing she could take the words back.

Jenna pulled away, wiped her face, and patted her daughter on the back. "Let's get into the house before I give the neighbours any more fodder for gossip," she said.

Once inside, Jenna kicked off her sneakers and headed for the kitchen to put on a pot of coffee, her first of the day. Then she turned to her daughter, who sat in her spot at the breakfast nook, head down and looking miserable. Jenna went over to her and kissed the top of her head. She sat beside her to wait for the coffee to perk.

"I'm sorry, honey. Please don't feel bad. You're absolutely right. I need help. I'm just embarrassed that I did the exact same thing my father did and my brother did. I turned to alcohol when I swore I would never put my family through that. I just feel like a hypocrite and a failure is all. When I woke up yesterday I knew I couldn't carry everything alone anymore."

Brenna got up and poured them both a coffee. She put milk in her mother's cup and cream and sugar in hers. She sat the mugs down on the nook in front of them and took up her spot again.

"Mom, you're not a failure, you're human. And to tell the truth, it's a relief to finally have evidence of that."

Jenna looked at Brenna, her eyebrows canted.

"Do you know how hard it is to live in the shadow of Superwoman? Good God, Mom, you never broke stride, in all these years. Tragedy after tragedy and you never so much as flinched, just did what needed to be done making the rest of us feel weak and inadequate in our human frailty. You set an impossible standard."

Jenna sat quietly as she processed her daughter's words. Mac high-fived Sam because Brenna had just said what Jenna needed to hear in a way only Brenna could.

While Jenna sat without words, Brenna finished her coffee and got up to make them both some breakfast.

Jenna was still processing as she mindlessly dug into the scrambled eggs and toast her daughter placed in front of her. She sipped her now cold coffee between bites.

Done eating, they both got up, cleared the dishes, and headed toward the stairs to shower. At the bottom of the stairs Jenna turned to take Brenna's hand and, breaking her silence, said, "I am so blessed to have you, baby. I honestly don't know what I'd do without you. You don't have to live up to anyone, you are truly spectacular just the way you are. Now let's get showered and call Aunt Olivia to see if she knows a good therapist."

She stripped out of her sweaty clothes in the laundry room that opened to Jenna's walk-in closet/dressing room and threw them into the washer but didn't start it, waiting until she had Brenna's clothes to add to the load. Then she headed through the dressing area, grabbed a fresh pair of leggings, a jersey knit tunic, and underwear. In her ensuite she got the tub running and added her favourite bubble bath.

While the tub filled she brushed her teeth and hair and put the latter in a high bun to keep it from getting wet. It had taken her forever to get a brush through it the previous night so she made a mental note to make a hair appointment, one more thing on her list of things to do today.

She'd never been one to make standing hair appointments—it was just too much of a commitment to be a slave to her hair. While in the army, she'd learned the easiest thing was to keep it long enough to put in a bun. It kept her hair neat enough to avoid being a target for a dress and deportment jacking and took very little time.

After leaving the army, she still found it the easiest way to wear her hair, but she had always made sure it was trimmed and healthy looking. The past few weeks of self-abuse had done a number on it though. Now it looked as damaged and broken as she felt.

Although she allowed herself a bit of a soak, she didn't linger too long in the bath. She had a lot to do. Normally, she would just have had a quick shower, but her mind and body had craved the hot, sudsy embrace, so she'd given in to it.

So much had happened in such a short time, she found her mind was reeling, and even though she could still see and interact with Mac and Sam and now Arielle, she still wasn't entirely sure she hadn't completely lost her mind. The jury was out on that front. It was one of the reasons she was open to the idea of seeing a therapist.

She also had to get started on her commission. If she put in some long days and didn't get caught up in her usual nit picking, it would still be possible to finish it in time. But time was definitely something she couldn't afford to waste.

Reluctantly, she lifted herself out of the bath, pulled the drain, and toweled off. As she moisturized her freshly scrubbed face, she noticed that yesterday's regular meals and the act of putting her world back together had done wonders for her complexion. She still bore the evidence of her troubled night with the dark circles under her eyes, but her face had lost its sallow, sunken look.

"It's a start," she said to her reflection in the mirror.

She dressed and left the room to find Mac and Sam reclining on her bed, watching a hockey game. Her heart gave a little squeeze as she watched them sitting there the same in death as they had been in life. They'd had such a short time with Sam but Mac had a serious case of hero worship and soon became the little brother Sam never had. Jenna remembered slight twinges of jealousy she'd feel when she and Sam would get home from weeks in the field because it was Sam Mac always called first.

Brenna was in and out of the shower, dressed and on her cell when Jenna came out of her bedroom. She had taken the opportunity to contact Olivia and fill her in on what had been happening in Jenna's world. She had been careful to leave out the suicide note.

Olivia said she knew of some very good therapists and would make some calls. She would pop over to the house after her shift with the details. She needed to see for herself that Jenna was on the road to recovery. Jenna had been her rock through Mac's death and it broke Olivia's heart to find out Jenna needed her and she hadn't been there.

Disconnecting with Olivia, Brenna sent a quick text to Ethan telling him she was going to stay with her mother another day and see how things went. He texted back asking if she needed him to bring her anything. It was reading week so she didn't have any classes to attend but she'd hoped to work on some of her university assignments to get a a jump on things for a change. It didn't seem to matter how much time she gave herself, she always seemed to be scrambling at the last minute.

She paused, weighing whether she should get him to bring her computer bag with her laptop and assignments, then decided against it. One more day wouldn't make much of a difference and Ethan had his own studies to work on so she said, "No, I think it can wait another day. If I feel like I need to stay longer, I'll just run home and get what I need. Thanks, though. I love you."

"I love you, too, babe. I'm here if you need me." She smiled, knowing it was true. He had always been there for her, just like Danny had always been there for her mom. That thought caused the smile to leave her face as she wondered what was going to happen between them. She knew that was one area only they could figure out, but it stressed her out. Danny may not be her biological dad, but he was her dad nonetheless, and the idea of losing him made her a little nauseous. Shaking her head, she decided: one bridge at a time!

Jenna was in her office opening mail and answering emails when Brenna came down the stairs. This time, she was relieved to find an email from Susan saying she was sorry to hear that Jenna had been sick and glad that she was on the mend. She requested that Jenna keep her apprised of the situation in case an extension was required. Susan's kindness choked Jenna up as she hurried through her administration so she could get into the gallery and earn it. Besides, she really needed the money for the finished painting.

When she'd checked her bank account she'd found that Danny had made a substantial withdrawal the previous day. He had every right to it—most of what was in the account was his pay anyway, and he had been careful to ensure there was enough for the bills that automatically came out—but it didn't leave much for her necessities or groceries. With the overdue payments from the bills she'd let get away on her, she would need to dip into her savings to make ends meet.

Other than the account activity, Danny still kept himself scarce. He hadn't called, emailed, texted, nothing, and it still cut to the quick. But Jenna squared her shoulders, shut down her computer, fixed herself a cup of coffee, and went into her gallery, passing Brenna who was perusing cookbooks and planning the next two meals of the day.

Cooking was Brenna's passion. Jenna had always told her she was wasting her time in law school when cooking was obviously what she loved. Brenna had just shrugged and said cooking didn't afford a very comfortable lifestyle.

Jenna sat down in front of her canvas once more with determination. She loaded her palate with all her main colours, picked up her three-inch wash brush, and tried to imagine what to create for the family room of a hospital.

Anxiety was turning the coffee sour in her stomach as she sat, unable to move beyond the brush in her hand. After several minutes, anxiety turned to panic. "Fuck! Fuck! Fuck!" she swore and threw the brush down on the cabinet that butted up against her easel to hold her brushes, paints, and supplies.

"What's the matter, Mom?" Brenna asked, and her voice caused Jenna to jump. She hadn't heard her come into the room and sit quietly in the corner with her cookbook like she used to as a little girl.

As Jenna looked at her daughter, she saw Sam playing lovingly with her hair, Arielle standing behind her, her hand resting lovingly on her shoulder, and Mac kneeling beside her looking at the cookbook and making happy faces at recipes he liked and scrunching up his face at the ones he didn't.

"Don't move!" she said to her daughter, excitement in her voice. She had found her muse. She knew exactly what she wanted to paint. She picked up her sketch pad and a pencil and started scribbling like a woman possessed. When she was painting from her imagination, she didn't need to sketch things, they just seemed to flow, but when she had live subjects, she needed to get it down as quickly as she could before anyone moved or the light shifted.

Brenna was used to being a subject for her mother, so she just sighed very carefully and did her best to sit, statue still, until her mother told her it was OK to move.

The celestial trio were not as accommodating, however, especially Mac, who kept trying to get Brenna to turn the page of the cookbook. More than once Jenna had to give him the death stare. Of course, Brenna had no idea she was surrounded by other-worldly beings and thought her mother was glaring at her. She would return her glares with one of her own.

Through it all though, it only took a little better than an hour for Jenna to get the sketch down to a place she could start to paint from. She let Brenna relax then and began the process of transferring the sketch to the canvas. Brenna left the studio to start lunch so her mother could stay "in the zone," keeping well out of Jenna's line of sight so as not to risk getting sucked into being her model again.

Jenna worked through the day and well into the evening, only stopping long enough to wolf down the food Brenna brought her. She was so enraptured with her work she didn't hear Olivia come in at all.

Olivia only stopped long enough to get an update on Jenna. Seeing her working feverishly in her studio, Olivia didn't want to disturb her so she left Brenna with information on a therapist she had worked with and held in high regard. Giving her niece a hug, she told Brenna to call her if she needed anything else and asked that she be kept updated.

Brenna hugged her back and promised she would, then dialed the number her aunt had provided and set up an appointment for her mother. She didn't want to risk Jenna getting cold feet.

It was shortly after 10 that night when Jenna gave her painting one last brush stroke and got up off her stool, straightened out the kinks, and took a step back to look at her work. She was extremely pleased. It wasn't done yet but the bulk of it was. Just a little shading here and touch-up there and she could call it complete.

Once again, she had failed to hear Brenna come in until she let out a small gasp.

"Oh my God, Mom, it's incredible!" she breathed. "Where on earth did you ever come up with an idea like that?"

"Trust me, Brenna," her mother replied, "if I told you, you would never believe me."

Still staring at the painting of her with her dad, hand in her hair, Uncle Mac kneeling beside her and someone she didn't recognize standing behind her, she asked, "who is that?"

"She's your guardian angel, Bren."

Brenna looked at her mother with an odd expression on her face. Just when she thought her mom was at a turning point, she suddenly wasn't so sure. There was something about the angel in the painting that bothered her, something she couldn't put her finger on, and she was worried by the way her mom said "guardian angel" with such certainty.

Chapter 7

Abduction Foiled

"**M**om," Brenna started, "Aunt Olivia stopped by while you were working."

"Oh." Jenna was busy cleaning her easel and brushes, putting things away for the night. "How come?"

"I called her to let her know what was happening and to see if she knew of a good therapist."

Jenna stopped what she was doing to look at her daughter. "And? What all did you tell her?"

"Don't worry, Mom, I just told her you and Danny were taking a break and you were going through a rough patch. That's all, I promise." Brenna handed her mother the piece of paper with the therapist's name and address and the appointment information. "I took the liberty of making you an appointment. As luck would have it, she had a cancellation this Thursday."

"Thanks, baby." Jenna took the paper, slid it into her pocket, and continued with her clean-up. Once she was done, she turned to take one last look at her hard work. She felt an enormous sense of having accomplished something really special. Turning off the lights and shutting the glass doors that separated her studio from the rest of house, she headed off to bed with Brenna and the celestial trio trailing behind her.

She slept the sleep of innocence. When she woke, she was amazed at how wonderful she felt. *So this is how it feels to get a good night's sleep*, she thought to herself. *This is fabulous!*

She quickly changed out of her pajamas and into her running gear and bounced down the stairs with a new lease on life.

Brenna, staring blurry eyed into a large cup of coffee, declined her invitation to go for a run. It didn't appear that she had had as good a night's sleep. Jenna dropped a kiss on her bedhead and bounced out the door and down the street, Mac and Sam on either side.

She found the first three kilometres much easier today so she pushed on, hitting her wall at her five-kilometre loop. Satisfied with that she settled into a brisk walk to cool down. As they approached her house, her pace slowed. Mac ran ahead and walked backward to face her. She had just opened her mouth to warn him that he was in a collision course with a neighbour walking his dog when the neighbour passed right through him. The dog barked furiously and the man shivered.

"I will never get used to that," she said with a little shiver of her own, then asked, "What's up, Mac?"

"I know you're just getting your world back in order, sis, but I need your help."

At her front step now, she sat down and looked up at Mac, who stayed standing in front of her.

"OK, what do you need? A cheeseburger? A taco? Some KFC?" she teased.

She stopped abruptly, getting an uncomfortable feeling in the pit of her stomach when she saw the look on his face. She took his hand and said, "I'm sorry, Mac. What's going on?"

"My daughter's in trouble and I need your help," he started. "I've been watching over her and Olivia since I died and Mackayla has had a really hard time."

"No kidding!" Jenna said, her voice thick with sarcasm. "I hadn't noticed."

Mac held up his hand. "I'm sorry. I didn't mean to insinuate that you were unaware of her pain, but you have to admit, you haven't exactly been available yourself these days."

Jenna had the good grace to blush at Mac's gentle reminder of her own actions. "Point taken. So, what's happening that has you so worried?"

"Well, as you know, Mackayla doesn't leave her room much these days. She spends most of her time on her laptop." Mac paused. "The other day I was curious to see what she was working on so I took a look. It turns out she hasn't been doing homework but has been chatting with a girl she met on line. This girl has managed to get very close to Mackayla and is trying to set up a meeting with her."

Jenna's face registered her concerns. "Does Olivia know about this?"

"No, you know how cagey teenagers can be. Mackayla makes sure her history is cleared every night after their conversation so there's no trace of it when Olivia checks up on her."

"Shit!"

"That's not the worst of it. This girl has managed to talk my level-headed daughter into meeting up with her tonight after school and because Olivia's working evenings this week, she won't be home to notice if Mackayla doesn't come home on time. Mackayla has always been so responsible Olivia has never had to worry. What's worse, this girl is actually a decoy working for a local pimp. They make friends with pretty, lonely girls and the next thing you know, they're strung out on drugs and turning tricks."

As Mac relayed the story, rage slowly filled Jenna. "No worries, Mac. I think it's time for Mackayla and Auntie to get together. It's been far too long. I'll call Olivia and let her know I'm picking her up after school."

"That will work today, but what about tomorrow or the next day? These guys have nothing but time. We need a more permanent fix, Jen."

Frustration getting the better of her, Jenna snapped. "Well, what's your brilliant idea, Mac? You're the guy with the inside information. I'm open to suggestions."

"I don't have any, Jen," Mac replied, miserably. "I just know I'm the guy that made this mess and I need to fix it and you're the only person who can help me."

Feeling bad about her outburst, she reached out to Mac again and said, "Don't worry, brother, we'll figure this out if I have to stalk Mackayla until she's forty."

Getting up off the step, Jenna headed into the house to find Brenna watching her out the window with a seriously concerned look on her face. She'd been watching her mom talking to thin air and seemingly reaching out to people who weren't there.

Jenna's heart gave a little thump, but she decided to bluff her way through it by untying her shoes and heading up the stairs to change out of her sweaty running clothes. Halfway up, Brenna asked, "Who were you talking to, Mom?"

Thinking quickly, Jenna pulled her ear buds out of her ears and held up her cell phone. "I was on the phone with the hospital. They called to see about my progress on their painting." Jenna sprinted the rest of the way up the stairs leaving Brenna to ponder this explanation over. Brenna followed behind her at a much slower pace, mulling over the little oddities she'd been noticing in her mother lately, things like the way she often looked past Brenna as though there was something only she could see, and this new habit of talking to herself. These just weren't characteristics common to Jenna. Beyond that was her constant referral to angels.

For as long as Brenna could remember, Jenna had never talked about God or Jesus, other than in fits of swearing, and she certainly never talked about angels. Now she was painting them, along with two people Jenna had done everything in her power to erase from her memory.

She could hear the water running in her mother's ensuite as she entered the guest bathroom. She started brushing her teeth thoughtfully. She knew she needed to get back to her life; it was already Wednesday and half of the week that she'd planned to use to get a jump start on her studies was gone. But she was still doubtful of her mother's well-being. On the one hand, Jenna certainly seemed to have snapped out her terrible depression, not that she would have allowed anyone to see the worst of that, but on the other, Brenna had an unsettling feeling that something was going on behind the scenes to which she wasn't privy, and it bothered her.

Giving herself a mental shake, she spit the last of the toothpaste into the sink and rinsed it down the drain. Then she hopped in the shower herself. She lathered her body in shower gel and, as she stood under the warm, soothing spray, she continued to wrestle with the decision of whether she should stay or go. She decided she would put the question to Jenna and watch her reaction. She hoped that would make the answer clearer.

Brenna felt relieved at having finally come up with a plan of action. She stepped out of the shower and dried off, throwing the wet towel on a pile on the floor to gather up after she dressed in the clothes she'd been wearing for two days. They were clean, as she had laundered them the day before, but she would be glad to get back to her own apartment and a choice of clothes.

She rinsed her toothbrush thoroughly, dried it, slipped it into the plastic holder, and then put it back in her purse. Next, Brenna stripped the bed linens, grabbed the wet towel on the way to the laundry, and threw them all in the wash. She grabbed fresh towels and bedding from the linen closet, remade the bed, wiped down the bathroom, rehung the clean towel, grabbed her purse, and headed back down the stairs to talk to her mom.

While Brenna had been busy doing this, Jenna had been wracking her brain as to the best course of action to prevent her niece from putting herself in a terrible situation. She went through her morning routine on autopilot as she quietly discussed idea after idea with Mac, dismissing one after the other until she settled on the simplest one.

Right from the day Mackayla was born, she and Jenna had a special bond. As an infant, Mackayla could often only be calmed by Jenna when she fussed. It didn't seem to matter how much time passed between visits, Mackayla always remembered her aunt. As Mackayla got older, she thought her aunt was a hero for serving her country, and when Jenna retired from the army and became a successful artist, it only served to increase her niece's admiration as both things seemed very romantic to a young girl. She would talk to Jenna about things she couldn't share with her mom and Jenna was always careful to keep her confidences, so Jenna hoped if she could catch her after school before Mackayla caught the bus to the mall, maybe, just maybe, her niece would confide in her again.

Mac thought this was as good a plan as any. He would keep an eye on his daughter throughout the day to make sure she didn't duck out of school early. So when Jenna was sure Mackayla was off to school, she called Olivia to ask if she would mind Jenna picking Mackayla up from school.

Olivia agreed wholeheartedly. Since her conversation with Brenna, she'd been very worried about her sister-in-law. It gave her a sense of relief that Jenna was not only willing to leave the house but that she wanted to spend time with Mackayla. Olivia was so worried about Mackayla's withdrawal, and Jenna and Mackayla had always been like two peas in a pod. She hoped spending time together would do them both good.

Operation Save Mackayla was a go.

When Jenna came down the stairs she found her daughter pacing back and forth in the kitchen in front of the coffeemaker as the dark brown nectar slowly filled the pot.

"What's up, little pup?" Jenna asked.

Brenna stopped mid-pace and grabbed two cups from the cupboard just as the coffeemaker spit out the last of the coffee. She filled two mugs and handed one to her mother she said, "Mom? I was wondering if you needed me to stay a bit longer or if I should head home this morning." She watched Jenna closely for any tells that might give away anxiety at the idea of her leaving.

Jenna just smiled, kissed her daughter's head, and said, "Baby, you have been such a blessing, I honestly don't know what I would have done without you these past two days. But it's time for you to get back to your life and back to your boy." That's how Jenna referred to Ethan and it always made Brenna smile.

"Are you sure, Mom?"

"Of course. I'm getting stronger every day and I promise I will go to my appointment tomorrow." She sat on the stool at the breakfast nook and continued, "To tell the truth, darling girl, I'm looking forward to it."

Relieved, Brenna said, "Promise you'll text me tonight and after your appointment tomorrow?"

Hand on her heart, Jenna smiled. "I promise."

The two women ate a cold breakfast in companionable silence and after helping Jenna clean up the dishes, Brenna headed for the door. Jenna following behind her and gave her a huge warm hug.

"I love you so much, baby!"

"I love you too, Mom."

Once Brenna was gone, Jenna set her alarm to one hour before Mackayla's school let out. She wanted to be sure to give herself plenty of time to get across the city. Then she headed for her studio. Mac flitted in and out but Sam was with her constantly as she worked on the finer details of her painting.

Now that she was finally in a place where she could talk to Sam freely, she took the opportunity to ask her burning questions. She had so many she didn't know where to start, so she started with the one that had tortured her for years.

"What happened out there, Sam?

"Well," Sam started. "It was a routine patrol, if there is such a thing in a war zone. I was the medic assigned to the 2nd Princess Patricia's Canadian Light Infantry when we came under fire. There were more of us and we were much better armed, so it didn't take long to suppress the enemy.

While we were disarming the enemy and checking for any signs of life, I came across a man who was still alive but seriously injured. As I knelt beside him to administer first aid, I failed to ensure that I could see both hands. It was a fatal mistake. He had a grenade in his hand that was covered by his jacket. He'd pulled the pin while we were distracted with the others and when I tried to help him, he let go of the spoon. Of course the grenade went off and blew us both up."

Jenna had stopped painting and was listening intently to Sam's story. All they had been told was that he had been killed in combat. She swiped angrily at the tears running down her face.

She had always regretted not getting an opportunity to go on a tour. It felt like training to be a pilot but never getting out of the flight simulator.

"Did you suffer, Sam?" she asked quietly.

"Honestly, no. My body was in shock. I didn't know what hit me."

"Is it true what they say, no matter how hardened a soldier is, when they are dying, they always cry out for their mothers?"

"Yes. If you think about it, we start life in our mother's womb, fed by her body. It only stands to reason that when your life is ending, she is the one you reach out to. But that's not to say I didn't think of you and our children, and want to hold you all one more time."

Jenna nodded her understanding.

"So is it because you died trying to save the enemy that you got guardian angel status?" she asked.

"Yes and no. I've lived through many incarnations and learned many things. This was my last one, but even after life we never stop learning and growing. Part of that growth is to be a guardian angel."

"Wait! wait! wait!" Jenna put up her hand. "I don't know much about this stuff, but aren't humans assigned a guardian angel at birth who stays with them their entire life?"

Sam responded, "That's true in some cases, but not all. Some people are born with special gifts and as they grow into those gifts, their needs change; as such, they require different guardian angels. You're one of those people."

Overwhelmed by it all, Jenna just shook her head and turned back to her painting. "I don't understand any of this, but I'm really glad you're here, Sam."

She worked in silence, stopping only to have lunch, until Mac popped back in minutes before her alarm sounded. Quickly cleaning up her painting supplies, she washed her hands, checked her face for paint streaks, grabbed her bag, and headed to the garage. She stopped at her car, took a deep breath, and looked over at Mac, who already had the passenger door open.

"What happens if this doesn't work? Can you guys put a word in upstairs for a successful mission?"

"Already done," was Mac's reply. "Let's saddle up and head on out."

The drive to her niece's school was uneventful. The roads were relatively quiet since rush hour wouldn't start for another hour or so. Jen arrived thirty minutes early so was able to park just in front of the bus stop. Mackayla should see her before she got to the stop and vice versa. Jenna should be able to cut her off at the pass, so to speak.

Fifteen minutes later, parents started arriving to pick up their little darlings, and fifteen minutes after that, the school's main doors flew open and out poured masses of teenage energy, the kids pushing and shoving each other in a rush to get that first breath of fresh air after a long day of dry, dusty textbooks and even drier, dustier teachers.

Jenna got out of her Cherokee, dialed 911 on her cell phone, careful not to hit the dial button, slid it into the kangaroo pocket of her tunic, then leaned against the passenger door, legs crossed in a seemingly casual manner, watching the crowds carefully for her niece. Even if there was chance she might miss the vibrant redhead, her ace in the hole, super sleuth ghost dad was on the case. He whispered excitedly in Jenna's ear when he saw his daughter exit the school.

It hurt Jenna to see her niece come out solo, head down, trying not to attract attention. She looked so small and alone. She gave the crowds of noisy teenagers a wide berth, avoiding their jostling and clowning as she made a beeline for the bus stop. She wouldn't have noticed her aunt standing there against her cherry red Cherokee if Jenna hadn't called out to her.

"Auntie Jen!" Mackayla burst out and ran to her. When she reached her, she gave her a boisterous hug and asked, "What are you doing here?"

Laughing at her niece's obvious happiness over seeing her, she said, "I was in the neighbourhood and asked your mom if it was OK to take you out for a bite. I haven't seen you in forever."

A little frown played on Mackayla's face, clearly torn between wanting to spend time with her favourite aunt and her previously made commitment.

"What do ya say?" Jenna asked, as she opened the passenger door. All the while, Mackayla's guardian angel was whispering encouragement in her ear.

After what felt like forever, Mackayla made a decision and told her aunt that she had made arrangements to meet a friend at the mall. She left out the part that it was someone she'd been chatting with online and she that had never actually met her.

"Well, why don't you let me give you a lift since I have to go that way anyway and I could use the opportunity to pick up some art supplies at DeSerres."

Mackayla hated taking the city bus at this time of day. It was always so full of school kids and it was standing room only. She was happy to accept the ride her aunt offered. Plus, it would give her some time to catch up with one of the only people she trusted to talk too.

They chatted nonstop during the twenty-minute trip. Jenna asked how school was going and what Mackayla's favourite subjects were this year. She wasn't surprised to hear that her niece was excelling in art and music.

All the while, Jenna watched her brother from the rearview mirror. He was listening intently, hanging on his daughter's every word. All three heavenly bodies were scrunched in the backseat of the Cherokee, Sam, Mac and Mackayla's guardian angel, making it look like a clown car.

As they pulled into the parking lot, Jenna opened the back door to grab her purse and all three piled out. Sam took his position by Jenna, Mackayla's angel and Mac took sentry positions around her.

Slinging her purse over her left shoulder, Jenna carefully checked to ensure that 911 was still at the ready on her cell phone and splayed her car keys between the fingers of her right hand. Ready for battle she walked with her niece trying not to let her anxiety show.

Once inside, Jenna asked Mackayla if she would mind Jenna waiting with her since they were a bit early. Mackayla was happy to have the company, so she readily agreed.

Mackayla was a pretty savvy kid and she knew she was taking a risk meeting someone she had only talked to online. That's why she'd picked the mall as their meeting place. It was as public as it could get. Unfortunately, what she didn't know was there was a whole world that lived behind the stores in the hallways and backrooms and it was easy to for someone to just disappear. It happened all too often.

Sitting on cushioned benches close to the entrance the girls had agreed upon, Mackayla watched for her friend while Jenna watched for everyone else. They'd only been sitting for about ten minutes when a young blonde girl hesitantly approached them.

"That's Julia," Mackayla said as she got up to meet her.

Jenna stayed put. The girl was obviously suspicious so she did her best to appear disinterested.

"Eleven o'clock, Jen!" Mac hissed as Jenna turned to look.

A man who appeared to be in his thirties was moving with purpose toward the girls. The blonde one turned to smile at him. She told Mackayla he was her father just making sure she wasn't meeting a pedophile.

Mackayla's guardian angel was whispering furiously in her ear as Mackayla turned to where she'd left her aunt. She suddenly had a very uneasy feeling and started backing away. Unfortunately, she was within arm's reach of the man who made a grab for her.

Jenna had already hit the send button to call 911, yelling their location as she sprinted across the floor, keys poised and ready to strike.

The man was dragging a screaming Mackayla toward the back rooms when Jenna caught up and launched herself on his back and hammered him with her keyed fist. During the assault, the man let go of Mackayla, who bolted for a fire alarm and pulled it, setting off the shrill sound that brought store personnel out in droves to see what the commotion was about.

The man struggled to get Jenna off his back, but she hung on as tightly as a burr on a blanket, preventing him from fleeing the scene. When security arrived, they pulled Jenna off the bloodied man and restrained him until the EPS joined them a short time after.

The blonde girl, Julia, who had been used as a lure to grab Mackayla, was slowly attempting to maneuver through the crowd, trying to be inconspicuous, when someone grabbed her by the arm and started yelling for someone to come restrain her. It was Mackayla.

When she realized her aunt was safe and the man subdued, she looked for the girl she'd thought was her friend, and saw her inching her way past oblivious people. Mackayla knew she couldn't let her get away to be used as a lure for some other lonely, unsuspecting girl.

Mackayla thought it was good luck that Julia just happened to brush past her as she moved through the crowd completely unaware that Mackayla was even there, but it was the angels working behind the scenes, whispering in ears, causing people to move subconsciously, drawing the girls together and averting Julia's eyes.

Julia struggled furiously to pull her arm out of Mackayla's grasp, but with the packed crowd and her aunt's unrelenting determination, Mackayla refused to let go until a young police officer came to her aid. The officer cuffed Julia and led both girls through the crowd to where Jenna and another EPS officer stood. As soon as they reached Jenna, Mackayla grabbed her hand and held on tightly.

Jenna gave her hand a reassuring squeeze and then put an arm around her niece's shoulders and pulled her tightly to her side.

Jenna had already filled them in on the attempted abduction. More officers arrived at the scene; some were sent into the backrooms in case there were others hiding in the wings who were working with two now in custody. When Mackayla joined her aunt, she filled in the blanks.

Julia was led to a waiting police cruiser while the man she was working for was treated for injuries to his neck. Since none of them was life threatening, he was bandaged and led out to a separate cruiser.

While the EMTs were checking out Mackayla, Jenna gave Olivia a quick call. She assured her that both she and Mackayla were fine but asked for Olivia to meet them at the West End Police Department.

Jenna was last to be cleared by the EMTs. While they were packing up their medical supplies, the officer who had initially questioned Jenna asked if she was OK to drive to the detachment. She assured them she was fine and said she would meet them there.

As Mackayla and Jenna walked to her Cherokee, Sam kept his hand firmly on her shoulder. Even though she claimed to be fine and certainly seemed to be, he could feel the waves of anxiety rolling off her and a brand new wound on her soul. With the right care, this one shouldn't leave a scar though.

Mac was fussing over his daughter, driving her guardian angel crazy with his constant need to touch her to assure himself she was unhurt. She was also left with a wound on her soul, but not nearly as huge as the one his death had left. She was young and resilient enough to heal completely.

When they reached the car, Jenna went to the passenger side to open the door for her niece and took the opportunity to give her a huge warm hug. She didn't want to let go. Mackayla returned the hug as though she were drowning and Jenna had offered her a life raft.

She got in the front seat while Jenna walked around the car, opening the passenger door on the driver's side under the pretense of putting her purse in the back but actually loading all three of the living-challenged. Then she climbed into the driver's seat and started the car. She didn't really need to let them in—apparently, they could materialize and dematerialize at will—but she didn't want to take any chances with her niece present.

When they reached the police station, Jenna put the car in park and was just about to release her seatbelt and open her door when Mackayla, who had been silent the entire trip, reached over and grabbed her arm.

"How did you know, Auntie Jen?" she asked

Confused, Jenna said, "How did I know what, sweetpea?"

"How did you know something was going to happen today?"

"I don't know what you mean, Kaylie," Jen said, breaking out Mackayla's pet name.

Olivia had just arrived and parked behind Jenna's car. She was headed toward them in a brisk, no-nonsense manner.

"So you're telling me that after months of not hearing from you, you just happened to show up today? The disbelief was clear on her face. "I don't believe you," she said as she hopped out of the car and ran into her mother's worried embrace.

Chapter 8

Therapy

They quickly gave Olivia the *Reader's Digest* version of events as they walked into the police station. Because Mackayla had been through so much, Olivia didn't allow herself the hysterical tirade she so desperately wanted to rain down on her daughter's head for having taken such a stupid risk, but she made a mental note to readdress it when Mackayla recovered from her trauma.

The police officer's questions were much the same as before, just more detailed and Jenna and Mackayla had to write it all down in an official statement. Two more people had been found in connection with the attempted kidnapping and were arrested. All four people had been on the police's radar but they could never get anything solid against them. Thanks to Mac's intel and Jenna's quick thinking, they wouldn't be luring any other girls for a very long time.

As Jenna was finishing up her statement, Mac drew her attention to Julia, sitting looking terrified at a desk where she was being grilled by a very formidable looking female officer. Mackayla was petite for her age, barely reaching Jenna's shoulder, with fine bones like a china doll, but this girl was even smaller and terribly thin, like she hadn't had a decent meal in months. Jenna nodded her head toward the officer sitting across from her and asked, "What's her story?"

"Sadly, she's probably as much a victim in this as anyone," the officer said quickly to quantify the statement. "I'm not downplaying her role in this, please don't misunderstand." He paused as the three women nodded for him to continue. "Her mom was sixteen when she got pregnant. Dad stuck around for a year or two, just long enough for the girl to get attached, then split. It seems he was pretty good at paying support for the first few years, then found a new woman and started a new family. Support payments stopped and the kid was forgotten. Mom moved a new man in. He couldn't keep his hands off the girl. Mom blamed her and kicked her out of the house at twelve years old. She made her way to the mall where she's lived for the past two years eating from the garbage or whatever she could steal and hiding behind the stores when the mall was closed. That's were she ran into those guys." He motioned to the three men in handcuffs being processed for Edmonton Remand Centre. "Apparently, they thought she would be worth more as a lure then to sell her outright. So for the price of the odd meal and protection, she learned how to manipulate other young girls into dangerous situations. Unfortunately, she doesn't stand a chance. She'll probably be in and out of the system for the rest of her life."

The officer ended the conversation abruptly, took the paperwork and stood up. He turned to Mackayla and said, "We'll need your cell phone and your laptop." His next sentence was directed at Olivia. "If you're going straight home, we will follow and pick it up."

Olivia assured him they were, then put her arm around her daughter and gave her a pointed look that said there was a further conversation to be had as she turned her toward the door. Jenna followed and they all filed out.

Once the police had come and gone, Olivia ordered takeout and they all sat around the kitchen table eating in silence. Seeing her daughter droop with exhaustion from all the adrenalin she'd been running on, Olivia made her a cup of herbal tea and sent her for a bath and bed. It was only 7 p.m., but Mackayla was too exhausted to argue, so taking her tea with her, she headed to the basement. It was finished with a theatre room, a small gym, a huge bedroom, and an ensuite. When Mackayla turned thirteen, she convinced her mom she was old enough to move down there now that she was officially a teenager. Olivia had reluctantly agreed, even though she knew she would miss having her on the same floor.

Once the door was closed behind Mackayla, Jenna, who had steeled herself for Olivia's wrath, was quite surprised when Olivia looked at her and burst into tears. "Oh my God, Jen, thank God you were there!" she sobbed. "Why would she do something so stupid, so risky? She's so much smarter than that. I've warned her and warned her about the dangers of trusting people online!"

Mac knelt beside his wife's chair, kissing her face and stroking her hair. Olivia's guardian angel assumed the guardian angel position: hand on shoulder, drawing enough pain so as not to let her drown.

Jenna got up and grabbed a box of tissues from the end table in the living room and handed it to the woman who was more than a sister-in-law. She truly was the sister neither one of them had.

Wiping her eyes and blowing her nose, Olivia continued. "I should be home when she gets home from school. She would have never taken such a chance if she had someone here after school. I told the hospital to stop putting me on evening shifts. I've been there fifteen years, that should mean something, shouldn't it!"

"It's not your fault, Olivia. Mackayla has never been the same since she lost her dad. You know that. She is lonely, but not because of anything you did or didn't do. You've lived and breathed for her for these past seven years." Jenna took a breath, "She was too young to know how to process her dad's death and you were just trying to keep body and soul together. I know what that's about. I really appreciate the appointment for the therapist, but maybe I'm not the only one who could benefit from it." Jenna said this last piece cautiously, her eyebrow raised in anticipation of Olivia's reaction.

Olivia stopped crying and looked at Jenna thoughtfully. "You know what, you're absolutely right. I don't know why I didn't think of that, especially considering the field I work in." She gave her head a self-deprecating shake. "I'll see about getting in touch with a grief counsellor in the morning."

She seemed relieved to have some course of action as she turned the conversation to Jenna.

"So, what's going on with you and Danny? Brenna gave me a brief synopsis but didn't go into a lot of details."

Jenna took a deep breath and gave Olivia the basics of some of the struggles she and Danny had been battling over the years and how they had eroded their relationship to the point that they just couldn't find common ground anymore. She explained that they were both tired of the fighting and that even though it was Danny who'd pressed the pause button on the relationship, it was something she had been considering herself.

Jenna told Olivia she actually believed Danny, as sensitive to her as he was, knew that she was getting ready to call a halt to their marriage and, in order to make it an easier break, had taken the initiative. As devastated as she'd been, she just couldn't find it in her heart to be angry with him. She knew how hard he'd worked to connect with her, but she'd only ever let him get so close. When it started to get uncomfortable, she would back away and abruptly shut down without even realizing she was doing it.

Olivia nodded her head in understanding. Mac and Jenna were very much alike. They had had to take on adult responsibilities long before they should have.

Jenna admitted to falling apart completely for the first time in her life and when Olivia asked why she hadn't reached out, Jenna simply said, "That's just not what we do. Mac and I never learned how to reach out. We learned how to hide and how to drink our problems away when they got too big to handle. Thankfully, I was able to curb that tendency when Sam died, but I just couldn't seem to get my feet back under me with Danny gone. I think I expected him to take a breather for a week or two then open up a dialogue, but he's been gone more than a month and has made no attempt to reach out."

It was Olivia's turn to reach across the table and take Jenna's hand. "I'm sorry, Jen, I had a feeling something was off but just thought you'd let me know if you needed me. I forgot how fucked up your childhood was and I have to admit, it didn't occur to me that reaching out is a learned behaviour."

Jenna patted Olivia's hand with her free one then gently extracted both. It had been a traumatic, exhausting day for all of them and suddenly all she wanted to do was crawl into her bed and pull her feather duvet over her head and sleep.

"Are you two going to be all right tonight?" she asked her sister-in-law.

Olivia assured her they would, seeing the exhaustion on Jenna's face as she got up from the chair and grabbed her purse hanging on the back of it. Olivia also got up and walked Jenna to the door. There, she gave her a warm hug and thanked her again for saving her little girl. She watched

Jenna walk to her car, throw her purse in the backseat, leaving the car door open a little longer than necessary, then get behind the steering wheel and drive away.

Both of her otherworldly friends sat in the backseat, giving her space as she drove home in silence. Mac would go back and check on his daughter later, but right now he knew Olivia would take good care of her, and he was a little worried Jenna might stop at the liquor store on her way home. He needn't have worried though, because as much as Jenna craved a drink, the events of the day combined with the conversation between her and Olivia had made Jenna that much more determined to find a new way to not just cope with stress, but live in general. She was determined to stop the cycle. She knew in order to do that she needed more than just traditional therapy, so when she got home and changed into her pajamas, she propped herself up in her bed with her laptop and a pad and pen in hand, and looked up Adult Children of Alcoholics.

After writing down the time and location of the next meeting, she shut her laptop down, put the pad and pen on her nightstand, shut off her light, and fell into a deep and dreamless sleep.

The next morning Jenna was up by 6 and out the door, sneakers pounding the pavement fifteen minutes later. She did her full five kilometres with hardly any effort at all. She was so exhilarated after her run she felt like she could take on the world. She moved through her morning routine with a renewed sense of purpose and well-being that surprised her, considering the events of the previous day.

She headed into her studio, stopping long enough to set the alarm on her phone to give her time to clean up and get to her appointment with the therapist at 2 that afternoon. Then she dialed Olivia's number to check on her and Mackayla before losing herself in the finishing touches of her painting. As she was chatting with Olivia, she looked around her studio and noted how chaotic and disorganized things had gotten. At the same time, she had what she thought was a brilliant idea, and since she had Olivia on the phone she decided bounce it off her.

"Hey, Liv, what would you think about Mackayla having an after-school job?" She heard Olivia's intake of breath, but before she could get a word out, Jenna continued. "I could use an assistant in my studio and prepping for shows and if we arranged for Mackayla to come here right after school, you wouldn't have to worry about working evenings and could pick her up on your way home." Jenna paused. Olivia was thoughtfully silent. "She would only work for me when you had to do an evening shift. What do you say? Can we run it by Mackayla?"

Olivia agreed to think about it and get back to her. Jenna was satisfied with that. After she hung up, she noticed Brenna had sent a text to check in. Jenna weighed the idea of whether to just send a quick response or call and fill Brenna in on the previous day's events. She decided on the latter. She didn't want to take a chance on Brenna hearing about it before she could tell her after everything they had just been through. So she gave her a quick call and brought her up to speed. Brenna was beside herself about what had almost happened to her little cousin and promised she would pop in to visit them and offer her support.

"Our poor daughter," Jenna said to Sam. "This will be a week she won't forget any time soon. Thank God she's so much like you, with her strength and self-assurance."

Sam shook his head and said, "Don't be so sure it's me she takes after. Look what you've accomplished with no role models to follow. If you'd been given half a chance, you would have taken over the world." His smile was filled with love.

The rest of the day went by smoothly. By lunchtime, Jenna called her painting finished and stood back take a good look at it. She'd changed the stool Brenna was sitting in to an armchair using her artistic license. The living-challenged were translucent while Brenna was opaque and there was just a hint of wings on the two angels. She shot a quick email to the hospital administrator to ask if she could deliver it in the morning, then cleaned up.

After grabbing a quick lunch, washing the paint off her hands and face, and running a brush through her crazy hair, she headed out to her first therapy appointment. She was surprised when the receptionist handed her a clipboard with several questionnaires on it and told her to "please take a seat and fill them out, ensuring to fill out both sides."

Jenna sat back in her chair, thinking: please don't let there be any essay questions. She started at the top with her name and date of birth. She must have been writing for a good half hour when a vertically challenged, grey-haired lady came into the waiting room.

"Hi, you must be Jenna. I'm Denise. Pleased to meet you," she said as she motioned for Jenna to follow her down a long hallway of offices. She stopped halfway down the hall and invited Jenna into a warm green space with the wave of her hand. "Make yourself comfortable."

A soft brown leather loveseat with two matching armchairs furnished the room and the walls were covered with simple, tasteful art that appealed to Jenna's senses. It was a room very carefully decorated to soothe and inspire calm. The furniture was positioned in such a manner that, no matter where the patient sat, Denise would be directly across from them. Jenna chose the loveseat, dropping her purse on the floor. She pulled her legs up under her, still holding the clipboard.

Denise reached out to take it from her and spent the next few minutes quietly going over Jenna's answers, making notations here and there. After a while, Jenna began to squirm, a little concerned that she had been too honest on the questionnaire. At the time she was answering questions, she felt it best to be absolutely honest. After all, she was here to get help, but she was starting to worry that she might be put in a straitjacket and sent to the psychiatric hospital. Now that would be embarrassing!

Finally, Denise looked up, smiled, and said, "All these question must seem really daunting, but it really is a good tool to determine a starting point."

Jenna indicated her understanding and asked, "So, am I certifiable?"

Denise laughed and said, "I sometimes think we're all certifiable, but the short answer to your question is no. You're definitely not certifiable. However, you've clearly been suffering. Judging by your answers, there is strong indication that you suffer from complex post-traumatic stress disorder, anxiety, and depression."

Jenna's face registered her surprise. "Wow, that's a lot of mental illness."

"Not really," Denise replied. "The diagnosis is misleading in that anxiety and depression, in cases of CPTSD, are often symptoms of the initial disorder. The good news is, with some hard work, we can teach you some solid tools to manage it."

Jenna looked at her dubiously. "Is this where you start asking me about my childhood?"

Denise laughed and said, "Well, if you find you're comfortable working with me, we will touch on that at some point. But more than anything, I'd like you to tell me what moved you to seek therapy."

Taking a deep breath, Jenna started with the events of the past month. She admitted to her binge drinking and suicide attempt, but was very careful to skirt around anything to do with Sam or Mac. She ended her narrative with her niece's failed kidnapping, while Denise listening intently and scribbled furiously.

When she finished writing, Denise looked up and asked, "What gave you the presence of mind to act so quickly? Many people would have frozen in a situation like that."

"I'm not sure. I just acted on instinct. I guess I could attribute it to my past military training."

"How long did you serve in the military?"

"About twelve years—not enough for a pension, but after Sam was killed it was just too hard to be in the army and give my kids the attention they needed. The army is a jealous wife. It doesn't leave a lot of room for any other commitments."

"So, you were married before?"

"I was."

"How was your first husband killed?"

"He was a medic in the army and died in Afghanistan while trying to administer aid to a wounded enemy soldier."

"That must have been a terribly difficult time for you."

"It was, but my kids needed me and I couldn't afford to fall apart, so I put my grief on hold just like I did when my mom died."

"How old were when your mom died?"

"I was twelve when she was killed in a car accident. My dad was driving. He completely fell apart so I had to take care of him and my little brother, Mac, and when Mac committed suicide, I helped take care of his wife and daughter."

Jenna was surprised at how much information she had just blurted out to this total stranger.

Denise was looking at her gently and asked, "So, Jenna, when do you get to grieve?"

Jenna's entire body started to shake so hard she had to grit her teeth to keep them from chattering. *What the fuck!* she thought to herself as she fought to get it under control.

Seeing Jenna's distress, Denise gently moved the topic of conversation to something safer. There would be time enough later, when Jenna had some coping strategies in place, to poke a hole in that grief and let it drain.

"Tell me about your daughter. You say she came and stayed with you for a couple of days this week. How was that?"

The trembling slowly eased at the thought of Brenna taking control of things and helping her get back on her feet.

"She's just amazing! She is so smart and strong. I honestly don't know what I'd do without her." Jenna's heart swelled as she talked.

"She sounds lovely," Denise replied. Her change of topic had succeeded in grounding Jenna again. She suggested that if Jenna was willing, they could meet twice a week for a while to set a good foundation.

Jenna agreed, so they decided on Tuesdays and Thursdays to be re-evaluated in one month's time.

Jenna left Denise's office with a handful of photocopied pages for home-work, feeling like a weight had been lifted off her shoulders. Mac and Sam, who had been witness to the entire session, high fived each other as they trailed behind.

Checking her watch, she was surprised to see how late it was. Her plan was to catch an Adult Children of Alcoholics (ACA) meeting after her therapy session but her appointment with Denise had lasted much longer then Jenna anticipated so she would have to get moving in order to make it.

Pulling into the parking lot of the church where the meeting was being held, ten minutes late, Jenna's heart started to race at the number of cars. She hated crowds at the best of times but to walk into a room full of strang-ers ten minutes late and run the risk of them all turning to look at her made her knees feel weak. She almost didn't, but Sam reached out from the passenger seat and took her hand and reminded her she was not alone.

Steeling her shoulders, she got out of the car and headed into the build-ing. As she'd feared, people turned to look when she entered the room.

They were seated at a series of tables that had been set up in a circle. A gentleman standing by the door greeted her warmly and quickly moved to grab a chair, which he added to the circle for Jenna. As quietly as she could, she sat and the meeting carried on.

Each person around the tables had an opportunity to tell their stories. It surprised Jenna to hear so many stories that paralleled her own. When the circle made its way to her, the lady beside her whispered, "It's not mandatory, you can pass if you're not ready to share."

So overwhelmed with the emotions of the day and just trying to take in all the stories she'd heard, she passed, but when she left that day, for the first time in her life, she didn't feel alone.

While Jenna was working to reinvent herself, Olivia was doing some soul searching of her own. After Jenna left the night before, she'd done her nightly routine, changed into her PJs, then gone downstairs to Mackayla's room and crawled into bed with her. She'd pulled her tightly against her like she used to when she was a tiny little girl—two spoons in a drawer. Mackayla gave a sleepy little sigh and settled into her mother.

Olivia dozed in and out of sleep, wide awake at every small sound her daughter made. It terrified her how close she'd come to losing her. Olivia was well aware that neither of them had ever recovered from the grief of Mac's death. Seven years later and it still felt fresh and new. She also understood that it was the loneliness of that grief that led her daughter to take a risk like that.

All these years, Olivia had been a walking shrine for Mac. Instead of finding her way through and helping Mackayla find hers, Olivia realized she had done the exact opposite. Her grief wouldn't let Mackayla's heal. She'd promised Jenna she would get both of them to a grief counsellor and making that appointment was the first thing on her list of things to do the next morning.

As all of that was keeping her from sleeping soundly one other thing kept niggling at her. She kept seeing the half-starved waif sitting in the police station in handcuffs. The officer's words were on repeat inside Olivia's skull. She put one more thing on her mental "to do" list for next day.

When she finally gave up on sleep her watch read 4:30 a.m. Quietly, she got up and left her daughter's room. Her eyelids felt like sandpaper on her tired eyes and she had a dull headache that came with too little sleep and too much stress.

She made herself a pot of coffee and pulled a mug out of the cupboard, poured some milk in the bottom, and leaned against the counter while it brewed. Hearing the last sputter of coffee in the carafe, she poured herself a hot cup of heaven and moved into her office and sat in front of her computer.

Because she worked in the emergency room at an inner-city hospital, they often had to call in psychiatric support for patients who came in with mental health issues. That's where she had first met Denise. Denise was a psychiatric nurse who often worked the same shifts as Olivia. Her no-nonsense manner and genuine heart for patients had earned her Olivia's respect and that had quickly developed into a friendship.

When Denise grew tired of the bureaucracy of the hospital and lack of support for the patients, she'd decided to branch out into the therapy end of things. Her hope was to give her patients the tools they needed so they didn't have mental health crises that led to the emergency room.

In Olivia's mind, Denise was the logical place to start, so she sent her an email asking whom she would recommend as a good family grief counsellor. She hoped if both she and Mackayla started the process together, her daughter would be less likely to balk at the idea.

Next, she dug Constable Sean Rafferty's card out her coat pocket. He was the officer who'd taken Jenna and Mackayla's statements. He'd handed Olivia his card as they were leaving in case Mackayla remembered anything further. She noticed an email address listed under his direct line. Carefully, she constructed an email explaining that she couldn't stop thinking about Julia and asked what the possibility was that she might be able to arrange an opportunity to talk to her.

Satisfied it said what it needed to, she hit send, then sat back in her chair and chewed on her nail in thought. She struggled to understand why she was so compelled to seek out this girl who had almost cost her her daughter. As with most people, she was unaware of the workings going on in the ether. Neither Mac nor the angels could force a human do anything they didn't want to; that went against the law of free will. But they could impress on people and if someone, like Olivia, was sensitive to their angelic impressions. They could help a seemingly impossible situation come to a happy resolution.

The angels knew too well what Julia had suffered in her short life and they also knew Olivia had the gift that would help her heal. The reason she was drawn to a profession in the health field was because she had been born with the gift of healing.

It surprised her when she received an email back from the constable almost immediately. He had been surprised too when her email popped up in his inbox, but it brought a smile to his face and in his line of work, he didn't often have cause to smile. He remembered the beautiful, tiny blonde woman in scrubs who'd come in and introduced herself as Mackayla's mother. His first thought was that she didn't look old enough to be the mother of a teenage girl but he was too professional to say such a thing out loud.

As he read the email, he felt the stirrings of a feeling he'd thought long dead: faith in humanity. Julia had been on the police radar for the past two years and he was far too familiar with her backstory, having heard it so many times. But this little girl had gotten under his skin; something kept him believing that if she could just catch a break, she could turn her life around and become a functional member of society. So when he opened Olivia's email that morning, he knew he would do whatever he could to bring the two of them together. He trusted his honed ability to be a good judge of character and somehow just knew Olivia was what this girl needed.

Olivia read his email, which told her Julia was being held in the Edmonton Young Offenders' Centre until her trial. He assured her he would see what he could do to set up a meeting between the two, but that it would most likely have to be supervised.

She sent a quick response saying she didn't have a problem with that, then got up to refill her cup. She wondered how she would explain to Mackayla that she was meeting with the girl who had almost gotten her kidnapped. She decided maybe she didn't have to tell her just yet. *Let's just see how this plays out*, she thought to herself.

Despite all the strings Constable Rafferty pulled and favours he called in, Olivia still had to jump through several hoops to get her visit with Julia. Several trees' worth of government forms had to be filled out, then an interview had be set up with both the centre's administrator and social worker in order to determine Olivia's motivation.

Olivia expected there'd be some hills to climb, but often times during the process she found herself wondering exactly what she was hoping to accomplish. Constable Rafferty—Sean, as he insisted on her calling him— was a surprising ally, and if it hadn't been for his recommendations, she would most likely have been denied access.

All in all, just a little shy of two weeks later she found herself sitting across from a hostile teenage girl. Sean and the social worker assigned to Julia's case were also in attendance, but they stayed far enough way so as not to overwhelm her while Olivia worked on opening up a dialogue.

Mac watched his gentle, loving wife with a backbone of steel work her magic with this girl who had no reason to trust Olivia—or anyone else, for that matter—with pride. But he also noticed the way Sean watched her. Mac could see a white translucent string run between Olivia, Julia, and Sean. He was sure if Mackayla was here it would connect her as well. They were meant to be a family.

Chapter 9

Danny

It took several visits to make any headway with Julia, but Olivia knew it wouldn't be easy and she could see tiny bits of progress with every visit.

In the meantime, Mackayla had been far more receptive to the idea of grief counselling then Olivia could have hoped. After the first visit, the grief counsellor recommended individual sessions in order to give Olivia and Mackayla the ability to share without worry about how one's feelings would impact the other. For the first time in more than seven years, they were finding their way through the grief.

Olivia had also told Mackayla about her Aunt Jenna's suggestion of her working for her part-time after school on the days Olivia was scheduled to work evenings. Mackayla was very excited at the idea and agreed instantly.

Jenna was still attending counselling, but only once a week now. As she was looking through the worksheets Denise had given her, she'd noticed the name of the workbook they were taken from and, being the over-achiever she was, she'd ordered it and was systematically working through it on her own at a much faster pace than Denise usually recommended. But Jenna's personality was such that she needed to drive the pace of her healing and, as long as she was still making her appointments, Denise was very encouraged to let her.

She was also still going to her ACA meetings weekly. Although she wasn't in a place yet where she was comfortable sharing with the group, the comfort of knowing there were other people who had experienced similar things gave her a huge measure of comfort. She knew there would come a time when she would need to open up if she wanted to grow, but she was learning to just be patient with herself and let things happen in their own time.

The one area of her life that still hadn't been addressed was her relationship with Danny. His pay was still being automatically deposited into their joint account and he was still withdrawing a nominal amount every month, but that was the only evidence she had that he was still alive and well. During one of her therapy sessions she talked to Denise about how much it hurt her that he hadn't called or tried to get in touch with her in all this time, but was silent when Denise asked her why he was the one who needed to initiate the conversation.

After a moment, Jenna said, "Because he was the one who left."

"OK, so . . . is that the real reason, or are you afraid of what will happen if you do?"

Jenna looked down at her hands clasped in her lap, "What happens if he doesn't want to see me?" she said in a quiet voice, tears forming. "What happens if my marriage really is over and I have to face the rest of my life without him?" Now the tears were running down her face.

"I don't know, Jenna. What happens? Isn't it better to face it than to live in limbo?

"No!" It's not!" Jenna replied, emphatically.

"Really?" Denise persisted, gently. "Here's a question for you: what if he has the same fears and feels the same way you do?"

Jenna looked up from her lap, carefully examining Denise's words.

Mac was glad to see Jenna's mind finally open enough to try seeing things through Danny's eyes. Jenna had graciously allowed him to sit in on her therapy sessions knowing full well that, with his cosmic connections, he was already privy to the intel.

With Olivia and Mackayla well on their way to healing, he had been visiting his old friend and brother-in-law more and more. He wanted to talk to Jenna so many times about how much Danny was suffering, but it seemed there was a fine line between guiding and impacting the cosmic law of free will. Every time he came close to stepping over it he found himself on the shores of Zadkiel's Lake with Zadkiel taking the opportunity to teach Mac another cosmic lesson.

Danny didn't carry the marks on his soul that Jenna did. It's what made him such a good match for her. It gave him the patience and tolerance he needed while she battled her emotional dragons. Contrary to what Olivia believed, he hadn't left because he had given up on her or their marriage. The truth was, he stopped believing he was good for her, especially when she shut him out so completely after Mac died.

There wasn't a day that went by that he didn't miss her, but he knew he was solidly committed to her. What he didn't know was if she could say the same. So he waited. Every day, he waited. He wanted to give her the time and space she needed, but more than two months had passed and he was coming to the realization that just maybe she really was done.

He worried about her, too. He had spent many nights talking her through her night terrors and holding her while her heart raced and she trembled with fear from monsters only she could see. When he saw all the automatic withdrawals from their local liquor store, his heart constricted. Her turning to alcohol wasn't something he'd seen coming. She was always so careful not to drink to excess. Sure, they would indulge in a glass of wine the odd warm evening sitting out on the patio, on special occasions when they were out at a nice restaurant or at a dinner party, even having an occasional beer at a backyard bbq but she never let it get out hand. The scars of growing up with an alcoholic father then watching her brother self-destruct had impacted her deeply. Even while serving in the army where it had been a huge part of the culture, she was very restrained. Now she was buying large amounts on a daily basis.

Even though he was terrified of her going down the same road as her dad and Mac, he knew at his core that she would have to find her way through whatever this was. She needed to be the one to reach out to him. He had always been there, wide open to receive whatever she was willing to give—but she had to be willing to give. So he just kept going to work and doing these lonely days, staying steady so he could be her rock if she wanted him for as long as he could stand it.

Because they had a joint account for household expenses, he was able to monitor the withdrawals and deposits. Jenna had always been the one to take care of the budgeting and paying bills. She said she enjoyed it and was very vigilant about ensuring everything was paid by the due dates. He suspected it was less about her enjoyment in handling the finances and more about the need to control them since she was profoundly affected by the foreclosure of her childhood home after the loss of her mother, and having to move time after time when the rent in each new place wasn't paid, or the gas and electric was disconnected for being in arrears.

When her mother was alive, their house had been the central gathering place for all the kids in the neighbourhood. Anna had always had home-made cookies or brownies waiting for them for an after-school snack and a warm hug for anyone who needed it. After she was killed, they stopped bringing anyone over unless they were sure John was gone, until the day Jenna came home to find a huge foreclosure notice tacked to their front door. Her best friend was with her to study for their mid-term exams. Jenna was so mortified she never brought anyone home with her again.

When Danny saw the bills drawing close to their due dates and then going past them, he was about to step in when he noticed Jenna had gone into their accounts and quickly put everything to rights again. As he continued to watch their accounts day after day, he also noticed the liquor store purchases had ceased. Then he noticed a large deposit from the commission Jenna was working on and he was finally able to breathe again. Until that moment, he hadn't noticed how frightened he was that she would go down the same road as Mac.

No matter what happened between them, Danny would always be grateful to Mac for bringing him and Jenna together. They'd started with the city the same day and being the two newbies, became fast friends. Even now, Danny could recall in vivid detail how he'd felt the day he first laid eyes on his beautiful wife. Mac and Olivia invited him over for a barbecue one Sunday afternoon. It was the perfect sunny summer day. Mac was grilling the steaks Danny had brought as he drank beer and bitched about work. Olivia was making salads and setting the patio table, while Mac's niece and nephew played tag in the yard with an ancient border collie named Lily. No one noticed the creaking of the old gate until a statuesque brunette in a military uniform came around the corner. The children were the first to see her and it was their shrieks that made Mac and Danny turn as the children launched themselves at her. She barely had time to brace herself when she was hit by the impact, but she exuberantly wrapped them both up in a bear hug, not letting them go till Brandon struggled to get free.

"Ewww! Mom, you stink!" He exclaimed with his six-year-old honesty, his little nose wrinkling in disgust.

She threw her head back and laughed as the tiny girl in her arms snuggled in closer and said, "I no fink Momma stinks. You stink, Brandon!" Offended on her mother's behalf.

"Well, thank you for that staunch defence, baby girl," she'd said as she sat her back down on the ground. "But I'm afraid your brother is quite right. Momma's just spent two weeks in the field in Wainwright and I should have probably stopped for a shower, but I just missed you both so much!" She ruffled her son's hair as she turned to see Mac and Danny.

She flushed a little when she realized she had an audience, but just stood up straight and tall, walked over to the two men. Sticking her hand out to Danny, she'd said, "Are you going to introduce us, brother?"

Mac laughed. "This brazen creature, Danny, is my big sister," he'd said by way of introduction.

She'd cocked an eyebrow at the use of the word "brazen" and said in a teasing tone, "Have you been reading again, brother?"

Danny had laughed instantly drawn to this charismatic and confident amazon of a woman, who really did have a pungent aroma about her.

Olivia came out of the house to see what the fuss was about. Seeing Jenna, she shouted a greeting and ran up to her with her endless, bounding energy and wrapped her in a huge hug. At 5'9", Jenna towered over her tiny 5'3" sister-in-law who was grinning from ear to ear.

"Careful, Auntie Olivia, Momma is stinky!" Brandon felt the need to warn his much-adored aunt.

Olivia released Jenna, insisting she stay for dinner and telling her to help herself to the shower. That was Olivia-speak for Brandon was absolutely right. Laughing again, Jenna had grabbed the duffle bag she'd dropped by the fence when she saw her children, and headed for the house and a much-needed, amply discussed, and much-anticipated shower.

Since Sam's death, Mac and Olivia had been the only people Jenna trusted with her children when she had to go away on military exercises.

With Jenna so self-sufficient since Sam's death, it seemed like a small thing to Mac and Olivia and they loved their niece and nephew dearly.

Twenty minutes later, Jenna exited the house again, juggling a beer, a bowl of chips, dip, and a plate of pickles balancing on top of the chip bowl. Danny was hard pressed not to stare at the difference a shower and street clothes made. Her dark hair was free from the braid it had been in when she'd arrived and it hung to her waist in glossy waves. Her blue jeans and tank top showed a woman who spent a lot of time in the gym and as a soft wind passed by him he had to admit she smelled much better also. Danny rushed over to help her with a certainty in the pit of his stomach that this woman was about to send his perfectly ordered world into a tailspin.

The sound of his cell phone brought him back from his journey down memory lane. His heart skipped a beat when he heard the telltale ring tone that signified the caller was the object of his reminiscing.

It was an unusually perfect spring day and he'd taken advantage of the weather to sit outside on the cabin porch. The dogs, who had been sleeping soundly at his feet, also jumped at the intrusive sound. With his heart beating painfully in his chest, Danny answered, not sure if this was the beginning or the end.

It had taken Jenna a couple of days to process her last session with Denise, but after she'd had an opportunity to mull it all over, she'd had to admit she needed to know where she and Danny stood. This miraculous time she'd spent being able to see Sam was amazing and she sincerely hoped it was a gift she would be able to enjoy long after she was done helping Mac set things straight. But it had also helped to cement what she had always known deep down inside: she and Sam were never meant to last a lifetime. It was Danny she wanted to wake up to when she was old and grey.

Two men couldn't have been more different. Sam was as bright and vibrant as the sun. He was a burst of light that illuminated her sky but burned out quickly, leaving a black hole. Danny was as strong and steady as the earth, ready to fill that black hole with healing and a love that could stand the test of time.

After her long deliberation, she'd picked up the phone, heart in throat, and dialed Danny's cell. Sam kept his hand on her shoulder, bolstering her courage as she heard Danny's voice on the other end.

"Hey, Jenna, what's up?" he said, casually.

"Hi, Danny. I was hoping we might be able to talk."

"OK," he said cautiously. "Talk."

"I think it should be face to face. I was wondering if you're free Friday evening?"

"I certainly can be"

"OK, would you like to meet at our old Starbucks on 199th at around 7 p.m.?"

"Sounds good, see you then." Danny had started pacing during the call and had hit a dead spot, accidentally disconnecting the call. He thought about calling her back but thought better of it. They had set a time and place to meet; he would talk to her then.

"See you then," Jenna said to an empty line. "That's not a reassuring sign," she said to herself.

Jenna had been sitting in her office for the duration of the short phone call. Getting up, she stuck her cell phone in her back pocket and headed for the kitchen. When she passed the mirror that hung on her wall, she stopped short in front of it and took inventory. Her return to the land of the living was evident. The hollows in her face had filled out and she noticed the yellow tinge to her skin had been replaced by her old rosy glow. Her eyes were clear and bright blue again, but the one thing that desperately needed attention was her hair. It was the only evidence left of her past choices. It was time, she decided. Pulling her cell from her jeans, she dialed her hairdresser and begged for an emergency hair appointment, since Friday was only a few days away. As luck would have it, there had been a cancellation the next day at 11. Jenna jumped at it.

The next day, Jenna and her heavenly entourage climbed in her Cherokee and headed to the hairdressers. Jenna's hairdresser, Courtney, greeted her warmly. "It's been a long time, even for you, Jen," she said with a smile.

Jenna laughed and teased, "I told you when we started our relationship, I wasn't looking for a commitment."

Courtney also laughed as she began brushing out Jenna's long locks. "It's gotten really long, hasn't it? What are you looking for today? Your usual dusting or do want something different?"

"Actually," Jenna said, slowly, "what would you suggest?"

Courtney stopped her brushing mid-stroke and looked at Jenna in mock amazement. As long as Courtney had been styling Jenna's hair, she had done the same thing: just trim the ends and clean up the bangs. This was uncharted territory and she wasn't sure she could trust it.

Seeing the look of disbelief on the hairdresser's face, she laughed again and said, "Seriously, it's time for a change."

While this interaction was taking place, Mac and Sam had their heads together with Courtney's guardian angel, Johiel. Jenna watched them whispering in animated conversation. After finally coming to some sort of agreement, Mac and Sam settled into the empty chairs on either side of Jenna while Johiel hovered around Courtney offering suggestions that Jenna couldn't quite catch.

Thinking she couldn't go wrong with this cosmic intervention, Jenna told her hairdresser to do what "felt right," suggesting she listen to that little voice in her head.

She had always held the premise that she would colour her hair when it started to grey. But when Courtney suggested that she felt a little colour wash would really make her hair pop, Jenna readily agreed.

Courtney was planning on putting a burgundy wash in Jenna's dark hair, but when the indigo blue kept falling off the shelf in front of her she decided to go with it. Of course it was Mac who kept knocking it off the shelf knowing how perfect the indigo colour would be for his indigo sister.

As Courtney worked, Jenna kept her eyes firmly closed. She didn't want to flinch when the hair started to fall. The only time she opened them was when her head was safely wrapped in a towel. She was so nervous, she felt nauseated.

Just over two hours later Courtney told Jenna she could open her eyes. For the second time in as many months, Jenna didn't recognize the face looking back at her. This time, however, the tears streaming down her face were of happiness. She'd never thought she would be so overjoyed at seeing her hair so much shorter. It lay just below her shoulders and instead of shortening her bangs to her usual length, just above her brows, Courtney had left them long, given Jenna a side part, and pulled them over to the left. She'd then used the blow dryer and straight iron to pull the thick tresses into a smooth, sleek style that swayed gently when she moved her head. What Jenna loved the most was how the light caught the iridescent indigo wash like the gossamer of a dragonfly's wings.

Jenna felt so much lighter. She was sure she was floating on air when she left the hair salon. She took every opportunity to look at her reflection in store windows as she passed, then in the rearview mirror of her Cherokee. She was so enthralled with her new look she almost backed into a pedestrian as she was leaving the salon. If Mac hadn't shouted a warning she might have mowed the little old lady right over.

It took a lot of effort for Jenna to focus on the task at hand, her urge to see her new hair was so strong. She really did feel like a new woman. She had once heard that a person's trauma was stored in their hair and that cutting it released the negativity of those events and caused a rebirth of sorts. Judging by the way she felt with her new cut, she almost believed it, and when Mackayla arrived after school that day stopping short at the sight of her Aunt's new "do," Jenna heard herself giggle like a schoolgirl.

"You look so hot, Auntie!"

"Thanks, sweetpea." Jenna's smile reached from ear to ear.

The painting she'd completed for the hospital had caught the attention of a small downtown gallery owner who contacted Jenna about doing a show. She decided to carry on with the theme and was working on an entire celestial series. Since she was now able to see the guardian angels of every person she came in contact with, she had no shortage of material to inspire her paintings.

The idea of having Mackayla come and work with her had turned out to be a godsend. She was a hard worker and kept the studio tidied and the supplies organized and had even started a running list of the supplies.

Mackayla also brought her aunt food and kept her water glass full so Jenna was able to work free of interruptions and could produce pieces at a much faster pace than she could alone. Jenna came to rely on her niece to such a degree she was almost lost on the days she didn't come to work.

Her niece had also become very adept at the print side of Jenna's work. Because painting was where her passions lay, the print side of things had a tendency of getting backed up a bit, so Jenna taught Mackayla how to use her equipment to make the high-quality prints. It wasn't long before her niece was handling the orders and packaging. All Jenna had to do was set up courier pick-up and order supplies.

Jenna was very vocal about the wonderful job Mackayla was doing and Mackayla blossomed under her aunt's praise. Her confidence grew as she mastered each new task.

Olivia couldn't believe the change in her daughter. She was even becoming more involved in the arts at school, auditioning for the odd small part in the theatre group, even bringing a friend or two home on occasion, just to hang out. She still attended the grief counselling and even though she was probably almost ready to lessen the sessions, Olivia kept encouraging her to go because she was concerned about how Mackayla would react to the Olivia's growing relationship with Julia. Olivia still hadn't found the right time or place to tell Mackayla about it.

Mackayla was well aware that it was a very real possibility she would have to testify in her attempted kidnapping, but she made an active choice to, as her mother often advised her, cross that bridge when she came to it. For now, she just wanted to focus on school, her new friends, and working with her aunt—and that was all right with Olivia.

Friday arrived much faster then Jenna was ready for. She woke up with butterflies in her stomach that even her run couldn't settle. She was able to do her eight-kilometre runs again and this was definitely a morning for an 8k. As hard as she tried to focus on her daily routine, her mind kept going to her "date" with Danny that night. She found it amazing that she could be both excited and terrified at the same time.

She tried to distract herself by working in her studio but, by 10 a.m., she threw up her hands and gave up, deciding to call Brenna to see if she was free for a lunch and little retail therapy. Brenna was just finishing her morning class when her mother called, and didn't have another one until 6 p.m., so was happy to meet for lunch and some mother-daughter shopping. It had been forever since they'd done that.

Jenna, who was always thirty minutes early for everything, was already settled at a table in their favourite Thai restaurant. Having never seen her mother with hair shorter than her waist, Brenna didn't recognize her. Jenna literally had to stand up and wave to get her daughter's attention and even then Brenna did a double take.

"Oh my God, Mom!" she exclaimed. "You look fantastic!"

"Thanks, darling," Jenna blushed.

Brenna couldn't stop staring at her mother. She was so stunned at how wonderful she looked. It was more than a new haircut. She was definitely back to her old self. But there was something more. Even when things were good in Jenna's life, Brenna couldn't remember ever seeing her without that haunted look behind her eyes. Brenna realized as she studied her that the haunted look was gone. She looked like someone who was finally at peace with herself, and Brenna was overjoyed. Unfortunately, she had news she was afraid would threaten her mother's newfound peace, but she decided to wait until after they ate to broach the subject.

They chatted all through lunch, Jenna updating Brenna on how things were going with Mackayla, telling her about the glowing reviews she'd received for the hospital commission and the gallery that had contacted her for a showing. She carefully avoided mentioning Danny, partly to keep Brenna from getting her hopes up and partly to keep the anxiety from overwhelming her.

Brenna told her about the classes she was taking, her frustrations with Ethan, and the women's march she'd attended. Then after a brief hesitation, she said, "Mom, there's something I have to tell you."

"OK?" The tone in Brenna's voice alerted Jenna that it was most likely not something she would want to hear. "Shoot, you're loaded."

"Brandon's in the city and staying at my apartment."

Jenna's stomach fell. For all the things she'd worked through, she still hadn't found the courage to deal with her damaged relationship with her oldest child. Because she'd pushed herself so hard to make the incredible strides she had already made, this was one area Denise didn't press during their sessions, knowing it would come up in its own time.

"I'm guessing a visit with his mother isn't on his agenda," Jenna responded, unable to hide the bitterness in her voice.

"To be honest, Mom, he hasn't mentioned you at all." Her words cut like a knife.

"Why are you telling me this, Brenna? He could have come and gone without me ever being the wiser. What's the purpose in my knowing?"

"I'm sorry, Mom, I really didn't mean to hurt you, I just wanted to give you the opportunity to reach out to him if you felt you wanted to is all."

Jenna's voice was tight with unshed tears, Sam's hand firmly on her shoulder. "Well, thank you for that, I guess. But Brenna, I'm just not strong enough for that battle yet. I'm getting there, but I'm not there yet. I hope you understand."

Brenna got up and gave her mother a hug and said, "I do, Mom, I really do."

They settled up lunch, then headed to the mall for some shopping. Jenna bought a flattering pair of jeans and a long-sleeve, shoulderless top Brenna gushed about when she tried it on. She also bought a pair of ankle boots she just couldn't resist. With the retail therapy a success, they gave each other a quick hug and parted, leaving Jenna two hours to get home, shower, dress in her new clothes, fix her hair, put on a bit of makeup, and head for Starbucks and her future, with or without Danny.

As usual, she was early. He was there at 7 p.m., on the dot. As he walked in the door, time seemed to stand still.

Oh my God, she thought to herself. *How will I ever learn to live without him if he tells me doesn't want me anymore?*

Chapter 10

The Art of Forgiveness

Danny arrived at their rendezvous point fifteen minutes early for probably the first time in his life.

He wasn't surprised to see her car already parked there. Her need to be early and his chronic lateness had been a source of contention throughout their entire marriage.

He must have set every alarm he could find in order to show that he could make concessions, but when he got there, he found it took him that extra fifteen minutes just to find the courage to get out of his truck and walk through the door.

Even though he knew they had things they needed to work through, he honestly couldn't imagine his life without her. So with that purpose in mind, he finally made the move.

She had always taken his breath away, but when he walked into the Starbucks, even with her new look, he recognized her immediately. As always, she was the most beautiful woman in the place. The indigo in her shoulder-length hair turned her gray eyes bright blue.

Doing a little stuttered step, he turned his attention to the coffee bar. Ordering his drink gave him enough time to sort himself out and get his emotions back under control.

Jenna had managed to get the cozy armchairs in a quiet corner by the fire—the perfect place to have a quiet conversation.

When Danny approached the table, she got up and met him, putting her hand on his chest and giving him a kiss on the cheek. Encouraged, he returned the kiss and they both sat down.

"You look fantastic, Jen."

"Thanks, so do you." She smiled

"How have you been?" Danny asked, not sure how to get away from the small talk and the reason they were both there. He didn't need to worry. As always, Jenna was the one to get right to the point. It was one of the many qualities he admired about her.

"To be honest, Danny, up until about a month ago, I wasn't worth a shit. How about you?"

Danny knew she didn't want a pat answer. She wanted him to tell her the truth. Had he been better without her?

"I've been about the same. But tell me, Jen, what happened a month ago?" Danny asked, heart in his throat, afraid the answer would be that she'd found someone else.

Looking him directly in the eye without wavering, Jenna said, "Well, Dan, let me tell you."

And she did.

She opened up to him for the first time about how it felt to lose her mother at such a young age and her father's descent into alcoholism. She talked about being afraid all the time and having to be constantly on guard, knowing if she made one wrong step or trusted the wrong person she would put herself and Mackenzie at risk. She felt as though she had to be perfect at all times or catastrophe would strike. And when it did, she knew deep down it was her fault because she had missed something important that she should have, somehow, known.

She talked about losing Sam and how she couldn't afford to get lost in her grief because she had to take care of Brenna and Brandon, so she put her emotions on the back burner and simply put one foot in front of the other until she was numb to the pain.

Lastly, she shared her grief and guilt over the loss of Mackenzie acknowledging and sincerely apologizing for her inability to allow Danny to share his own sorrow when he'd lost his closest friend.

She opened her heart to him in a way she never had before, even telling him about her own deep dive into the bottle when he left.

For all her honesty though, she did leave out a few details, like her suicide attempt, her new relationship with her dead brother and Sam, and her ability to see angels everywhere, including the one standing behind him with his hand on Danny's shoulder.

She was intimidating as hell before he left, but this new Jenna terrified him. She was different, more at peace. She had found her centre and Danny knew without a doubt that, no matter what happened between them, she would be OK. She didn't need him.

She smiled when he expressed this thought and said, "You're right, Danny. I don't *need* you in my life. Needing someone isn't a healthy basis for a relationship. What's more important is that I *want* you, and that's something I hope we can build on." She waited for his reply.

"Jen, I just want you to be happy," Danny replied. "It's my hope that it's with me, but if it's not, that's something I'll have to learn to live with."

Jenna nodded her understanding, saying, "It's my hope that we can be happy together, too, Danny."

It was the first time since they started dating that they were so open and honest with each other. By the time the conversation ran its course, they both agreed that Danny would stay at the cabin a little longer, but they would make a point of setting aside time once a week for a date. They didn't want to continue on from where they were. They wanted to start fresh and build a new, stronger foundation from which to grow their marriage.

When they left the coffee shop, Danny walked Jenna to her car and wrapped her in warm hug and kissed her long and tenderly.

For Jenna, being in his arms again was like coming home after being away for far too long. As she returned his kiss, the world disappeared. Mac, Sam, and Joel, Danny's guardian angel, did a happy dance a few feet away.

Jenna drove home without remembering a single thing about the drive. She pulled into her garage with a grin so big it nearly engulfed her entire face. She floated up the stairs, hopped in the shower, and crawled into her big king-sized bed and for the first time since Danny left, stretched corner to corner, and fell into a deep sleep, hugging his pillow, a smile still on her face.

Even though the next morning was Saturday and Jenna slept much later than was normal for her, she still strapped on her sneakers and went for a run. She didn't just run for the physical benefit. Jenna found running cleared her mind and got her creative juices flowing. It was almost meditative. Because of the wear and tear on her body, she forced herself to take Sundays off. She didn't pick Sunday as her day of rest for religious reasons; it was simply the busiest day on the trails and it was a pain trying to dodge unruly kids, dogs, and Sunday strollers.

As she sauntered home at the end of her run, she was surprised to see Mackayla sitting on her porch swing. Jenna looked around for Olivia's car and, failing to see it, asked her niece how she'd gotten there.

"I took the bus," she said.

"You know it's Saturday?" Jenna asked cautiously. "You don't work on Saturday, right?"

"I know, Auntie Jen, but I really needed to talk to you," Mackayla said, clearly upset and on the verge of tears.

"No problem, sweetie. Let's get in the house. I'll fix us some iced tea and you can fill me in on what's going on, OK?"

Her niece nodded, afraid to try and speak over the lump in her throat.

Once inside, Jenna filled two glasses and asked her niece if her mother knew where she was. Mackayla said no, that she'd told Olivia she was going to a friend's house.

"You know I have to let her know you're here, right?" Jenna watched Mackayla for any sign of her bolting before she could get to the bottom of what had her so upset. "Don't worry, I'll tell her I can drive you home when we've had a chance to chat. How does that sound?"

Again, Mackayla nodded.

Jenna quickly went out onto the porch and called Olivia to let her know Mackayla was safe and sound. Olivia gave Jenna a brief synopsis of what had transpired previous to Mackayla's running out of the house. Even though Mackayla had lied about where she was going, Olivia was very relieved to learn her daughter had run to her aunt.

Returning to the kitchen, Mackayla asked, "Did she tell you what she's being doing and what she wants to do?"

"She gave me the *Reader's Digest* version of events, but how about you fill me in," Jenna suggested.

"She's been visiting the girl who almost got me kidnapped!" Mackayla said indignation and betrayal obvious in her voice. "Not once or even twice, but several times! And you know what's worse?" It wasn't really a question. "She wants her to move in with us! In our house with me! My own mom! How could she do that?!" Mackayla broke down sobbing so hard she could hardly breathe.

Jenna wrapped her up in her arms and let her cry it out.

"Oh, baby, you must feel so betrayed right now." Jenna attempted to give a name to Mackayla's feelings.

She felt her niece give a little nod, then a loud sniff. Jenna pulled back, grabbed a box of tissue, setting it in front of her niece she said, "I think I know just what you need."

Mackayla looked at her with one eyebrow cocked, looking just like her dad for that split second.

"Follow me," Jenna said as she headed to her studio.

She dug around in her cabinets until she found her old easel, then grabbed a blank canvas and told Mackayla to pick her paint colours. She set everything up beside her workstation with a jar of brushes and a palette and said, "Let's paint those feelings while we talk."

Mackayla looked at her aunt like she'd lost her mind but Jenna just said, "Trust me." So she picked out her colours and sat down in front of the easel her aunt had set up for her.

"What am I supposed to paint?" she asked.

"Whatever you feel."

They sat in silence until the sound of Mackayla's stomach growling signified that it was lunchtime.

Jenna got up from her stool and looked over at the canvas her niece had been swiping angrily at. *It's definitely an abstract*, she thought, looking at the black, red, and orange slashes of colour covering the once white space.

They tidied up their painting things, Mackayla much calmer than when she'd arrived. Jenna fixed them both soup and sandwiches and they sat at the kitchen table eating in more silence.

When they'd finished their lunch and cleared the dishes away, Jenna sat her niece down in the living room and said, "OK, kiddo, now that we've gotten some of those emotions out, maybe we can try and see your mom's side of things. What do you think?"

"I just don't understand, Auntie Jen," she said, but with much less emotion. "How could she do that behind my back?"

"I don't know, honey. What reason did she give you when she told you?"

"She said Julia was just a kid who had never been given a fair shot in life. She said Julia feels awful and is willing to testify against the people she was working for so I don't have to take the stand. She said Julia wants to be a better person, she just needs someone to believe in her and show her how." Even though the heat had left Mackayla's voice, it was still that of a sullen teen.

"Could your mom be right, Makayla?" Jenna asked, gently.

"She almost got me kidnapped, Auntie Jen. How am I supposed to get over that?"

"I don't know, darling, but I know your mom loves you more than anyone else in the world and that she will help you find your way if you let her. Maybe working on the art of forgiveness is a good place to start?"

"That's what Mom said," Mackayla mumbled.

"She's a pretty smart lady, your mom. Maybe it's worth hearing her out."

"What if she's wrong? What if Julia is just trying to take my mom away from me?"

"Not possible, sweetpea," Jenna said as she ruffled her niece's hair. Then smiled and continued. "Besides, she will have me to deal with if she does."

When Mackayla smiled back, Jenna suggested she call Olivia and see if Mackayla could stay the night. Jenna thought it would give her niece a safe environment where she could digest things and give them a chance to just hang out like they used to when she was small.

Olivia was happy to agree. She needed some time to reevaluate whether or not fostering Julia was such a good idea after all. She had expected Mackayla to be upset but hadn't predicted just how betrayed her daughter would feel. They had always been so close, just the two of them against the world when Mac died. Maybe she had overestimated how much progress Mackayla had made and how well she'd been adapting.

And then there was the good constable. She found herself thinking about him more and more as they worked closely to help Julia. She knew he was attracted to her and she definitely found him interesting, but when she let herself think about him too much, she felt guilty, almost like she was cheating on Mac. She knew how ridiculous that was, but she just wasn't ready to explore another relationship yet.

Her other concern, of course, was Mackayla. With everything that had happened to her and everything that had been thrown at her, could she handle sharing her mother after all these years of having her to herself?

With all of these things on her mind, Olivia felt like she was walking in a minefield that had the potential to blow up in her face in a very big way.

Meanwhile, Mackayla seemed to have forgotten all about why she'd run to her aunt as they listened to music, played board games, then ordered take-out for dinner while watching movies on the big screen in Jenna's theatre room.

When Mackayla fell asleep on the sofa around midnight, halfway through the third movie, Jenna covered her with a heavy quilt, shut off the big screen and lights, and went up to bed. Exhausted, she fell into a deep sleep only to awaken standing in her backyard in the middle of a night terror.

She fought hard to find her way through the darkness that enveloped her mind. To remember who and where she was. She could feel a comforting hand on her shoulder and could see Mac in front of her, but she didn't know who he was and couldn't make out what he was trying to say. Seeing the back door to her house open, she ran blindly for it. She ran through the house and up the stairs to her bedroom. She wasn't consciously aware of where she was going; she was strictly moving on instinct, in blind terror.

Standing in the middle of her room with her chest heaving and her entire body quaking, Jenna let Mac's words finally penetrate. As she came out of the night terror, she sank to her knees and buried her face in her hands and cried.

Not only was she suffering the after-effects of one of the worst attacks she'd had in years, she felt all the wind leave her sails as the failure of all her hard work over the past weeks hit her like a wrecking ball, leaving her shattered on the floor. She was so sure she'd beaten these attacks, that she was healthy and strong and ready to take on the world. How could she have been so wrong?

"Don't do that, sis," Mac said quietly as he lifted her chin to look in her eyes. "This isn't a failure, it's only a setback. It has absolutely no bearing on the progress you've made or the work you've done."

Jenna refused to be comforted as she digested her defeat and what it meant. There had been periods in her past when these attacks had taken over not just her nights, but her days, as well. When that happened, she never knew how long they would last. Sometimes it was weeks, sometimes months. One period lasted more than a year. No matter how long it lasted every second felt unbearable.

Finally, Mac's words and the comforting warmth of Sam's hand got her up off her knees. Terror dwindled to anxiety, causing tiny tornados in the pit of her stomach. She reached for her emergency stash of Ativan and slipped a tablet under her tongue. Then she splashed her face with cold water, pulled on her robe, and headed downstairs to her studio to wait for the drug to take effect.

She hadn't taken a drink or used medications since her suicide attempt, but these were extenuating circumstances.

Because she didn't feel like going through the trouble of setting up her palette and brushes, she went to her drafting table, instead. She had a large piece of art paper taped to it with her graphite pencils open on the attached pull-out shelf. She sat on the stool and started to sketch. As she worked, her heart rate slowed to normal and the tornados in her stomach subsided. She knew the medication was probably taking effect, but she also became aware of how soothing the act of being creative was.

Her mind went to earlier in the day and how effective the act of painting had been in helping Mackayla clear her mind and get out the strong emotions that were blocking her ability to reason things out.

In the periphery of her mind, Jenna remembered seeing an article in one of her magazines about the incredible work being done with art therapy. Exhaustion settled over her, partially the effects of the Ativan and partially the after-effects of the previous attack. Still pondering the idea of art therapy as she got up from her table and started toward the staircase.

She stopped at her office and jotted down a note to herself to look into it further the next day.

When she crawled back into her bed, she fell asleep and stayed asleep for the rest of the night and late into the morning. For the first time in Mackayla's memory, she woke before her aunt with absolutely no idea of the battle Jenna had fought in the night.

Mackayla had decided to surprise her aunt with breakfast, and had whipped up a batch of blueberry buttermilk pancakes, turkey bacon, and a pot of fresh coffee. When Jenna awoke, it was to the wonderful breakfast smells wafting up the stairs. Grabbing her bathrobe, she made her way into the kitchen.

"You're hired!" she exclaimed. "This smells wonderful. Who taught you how to cook like this?"

Mackayla blushed at the praise. "Mom works so hard. When I get a chance, I like to surprise her with breakfast. I watch a lot of cooking shows."

Jenna sat at the breakfast nook in front of one of the two place settings and tucked into the pancakes. Mackayla poured her aunt a cup of coffee then sat down in front of the other plate.

When breakfast was finished, Jenna couldn't stop gushing. She couldn't remember the last time someone had made her breakfast and it was just so delicious!

They washed up the dishes then they they both grabbed a quick shower and Jenna took Mackayla home. When they reached the house, Mackayla asked if Jenna wanted to come in. The idea of using art as a form of therapy was still rattling around in Jenna's head and she was excited to get back to do some further research. She also decided she needed to see if she could make an emergency appointment with Denise, since her next one scheduled was more than two weeks away. So she passed, saying she would take a rain cheque.

Mackayla surprised her with a quick, impulsive hug, and said, "Thank you, Auntie Jen, for everything."

Jenna smiled and hugged her back. "That's what aunts are for," she said.

Jumping out of the Cherokee, Mackayla quickly stuck her head back in and said, "Don't think I've forgotten about how you knew so much about that whole kidnapping thing." She gave the two-finger indicator that

127

she was keeping an eye on Jenna, shut the car door, and ran up to her front door.

Jenna laughed, knowing Mackayla was never going to let it go. She knew she would eventually have to offer up an explanation.

Back at her house, she hung up her jacket and set her bag on the bench by the door. She then sat down at her desk in front of her computer. Before starting her email to Denise, she turned to Mac and Sam and thanked them for helping her find her way through the night terror and subsequent panic attack. They assured her they were just doing their jobs.

She laughed and shook her head at the bizarre chain of events that had her talking to two beings no one else could see. She still wasn't entirely convinced that she wasn't crazy but she decided she would just go with it and see where it all ended up. After all, things had definitely changed for the better with help of her celestial support system.

Once she sent off the email, with a brief description of her midnight meltdown and her interest in learning more about art therapy, Jenna started doing some research of her own. It wasn't long before Denise sent a reply, saying she had an opening at 8 the next morning and wondering if Jenna wanted her to slot her in. Jenna agreed right away, relieved to be able to get in so quickly.

The rest of her Sunday was uneventful and, for that, Jenna was grateful. She did very little, just tidied her house and caught up on the shows she'd recorded. She was tremendously grateful not to have a repeat of the night before when she finally crawled into bed at her usual 10 p.m.

The next morning she had just enough time to get in a run, hop into the shower, dress, grab a muffin and coffee, and fly out the door to make her appointment with Denise. There, she went into more detail about the attack on Saturday night and Denise offered her some grounding techniques to use when the next one came, assuring Jenna it was not a sign of any failure on her part. She explained it would take more than a few weeks to overcome a lifetime of suffering, but in time she would be able to manage them much more effectively, minimizing the impact they had on her.

This encouraged Jenna, and she was glad to have some coping strategies to put in place. But she was disappointed to learn that the city had very little to offer in the way of art therapy. Denise did say there were some very good programs available at the local universities and suggested maybe Jenna should look into becoming one herself.

When Jenna laughed and said, "Me—really?" Denise replied, "Why not? You are an accomplished artist and have several years' experience as a medical technician in the military. Surely some of your courses would transfer. It couldn't hurt to look into it, could it?"

It wasn't something Jenna would have ever considered, but suddenly she couldn't let the idea go. "You know, I just might."

"Good," Denise smiled. "Now, tell me, how did things go with Danny?"

Jenna told her about the meeting and that they had both agreed to go slowly, rebuilding on a firmer foundation.

"I think that's very encouraging, Jenna, don't you?"

"I do, I really do."

"So now that you have that relationship going in the right direction, let's talk about your son."

Jenna sighed loudly and long. "I don't even know where to start," she said.

"Well, maybe you should start the same way you did with Danny, by reaching out," Denise suggested.

"The thing is, Danny was receptive to talking to me. Brandon just will not forgive me for what he feels was the ultimate betrayal. I had him admitted into a rehab facility. He just can't let that go."

Denise challenged Jenna. "Are you positive that's what caused the estrangement? Have you ever asked him directly if that's the case?"

"Well, no, not directly," Jenna admitted.

"Maybe you should. I'm just saying." Denise replied giving Jenna a sideways look with a smile on her face.

Jenna left the counselling session with a lot to think about.

Getting into her Cherokee, she put the key in the ignition but before she turned it over, she turned to Mac in the backseat.

"You were there when Brandon started using, can you tell me at what point things went so badly?" she asked. "He's been recovered for years now, so he must have to understand that the choice I made was the right one. . . . No?

"That's a tough question, Jen," Mac replied. "I think there may have been more roads that would have reached the same destination without his feeling like you were throwing him away. But I have to agree with Denise. Brandon's the only one who knows for sure."

Jenna sat for a few more minutes pondering everything that had been said, then she turned the key and dialed her daughter on Bluetooth.

Brenna answered on the second ring. "Hey, Momma, what's up?"

"Is Brandon still at your apartment?"

"He is," Brenna said cautiously. "He'll be there for the week. Why are you asking?"

"No reason. Is Ethan home?"

"No, he's in classes until 3 p.m.," Brenna replied. "Mom, what's going on?"

"Stop worrying, Brenna. I just want to see my son. Is that OK?"

"Of course, Mom! I think it's high time you did, but you did just tell me you weren't ready for that yet and that you've been through a lot. Are you sure you're up to this?"

"I know what I said, darling, but I've had a change of heart and I think it's high time to clear the air. I love you, baby girl."

"I love you, too, Momma, just don't get too upset if things don't go the way you want them to. It could take time to break down those barriers."

"No worries, Bren, I have no illusions." That said, they ended the call.

It only took ten minutes to get to Brenna's apartment. Since both Brenna and Ethan were away, Jenna parked in their spot and headed to the door. Brenna had given her a key to the front door when they first moved in, in case of an emergency, and neither she nor Ethan could be reached. Jenna used it now, eliminating the need to be buzzed up. As she knocked on the door, she felt the rapid beat of her heart.

One of these days it's going to beat right out of my chest, she thought just as the door opened and Sam's clone stood before her with a surprised look on his face.

"Hey, Mom, what are you doing here?" he asked.

"Well, son," she replied. "It's been far too long and I think it's high time we had a heart-to-heart conversation."

Chapter 11

Letting Go

"OK," Brandon said slowly as he opened the door and let her enter, suspicion clear on his face.

She had always been a strong proponent of the premise that if you just let things lie, they eventually work their way out. Given the continued strain in her and Brandon's relationship and her own recent crash and burn, the evidence did not support a successful outcome with this particular theory, so she stood before her son, not quite sure where to start but determined to try.

"Can I grab you a coffee?" asked Brandon, the consummate host.

"Sure, that would be great."

He poured them both a cup of coffee and sat them down at Brenna and Ethan's tiny kitchen table that did double duty as a desk, covered in textbooks and various other study supplies.

Sitting across from her son she took a moment to just look at him. When he shed the last of the little boy he'd once been and became the man who sat before her, it had taken her a long time to reconcile the two. He had grown taller than his dad's six feet, two inches, and his dark hair was longer than Sam would have ever worn it and a shade lighter. But his eyes were the same—warm and deep brown—and even though his skin tone was lighter, his facial features were identical. His build was slighter but she wasn't sure if it was because Sam had been a soldier and had to be super fit so worked out regularly or if Brandon was just naturally a slimmer build.

Since Brandon worked on the rigs doing very heavy physical work evidence supported the latter.

Growing uncomfortable under her scrutiny, Brandon cleared his throat and said, "You're the one who wants to talk, Mom. The floor is yours."

"You're right," Jenna started. "Look, son, even though you've always been polite and treated me with respect, I'm well aware you do your best to avoid me and when we are together you keep me at arm's length. Even though I think I know the point in our relationship where things went wrong, I'm really only guessing." She paused, trying to read his face. "Please, son, I've come to you hoping you'll be willing to tell me exactly what thing I did that you've been unable to get over so we can, if you're willing, work on mending this rift."

Brandon looked down at the table, then up at his mother, struggling to find the words to explain what it was like living under her shadow. He had only been five when his dad died in Afghanistan. If the truth be told, he honestly didn't remember much about him. He was off on deployments most of Brandon's young life, then one day he didn't come home at all.

What he did remember with crystal clarity was how his mother reacted to the military officers at the door. She hadn't so much as flinched. Her face looked as though it were carved in stone. She said a quiet "thank you" to the officers and calmly shut the door. She stood looking at her children eating their pancakes at the kitchen table and started removing all the pictures of Sam throughout the house, packing them in a box and placing them in a closet. When Brandon asked why she was taking Daddy's pictures down, she'd simply said, "Because Daddy's not coming home anymore." Then she'd gone about her business as usual—except she wasn't really Mommy anymore. She was quieter and didn't smile or laugh or play with them anymore.

Things got better when Danny came into the picture. Brandon and Brenna met Danny before their mother did because he was often at Uncle Mac and Aunt Olivia's house when Jenna was away doing army stuff. Danny and Uncle Mac played with them a lot and when Brandon talked to him, he felt like Danny was really listening, not like his mother, who went through the motions but he could tell she didn't really hear him.

Then Uncle Mac died and his mother did a repeat performance. Packing up everything that reminded her of him and putting it away, refusing to allow anyone to mention him, refusing to allow anyone else to grieve. Brandon was beyond devastated by his uncle's death; they had been so close before he got sick. The pain was more than he knew how to bear and he had no one to share it with, since Danny was so afraid to upset Jenna. He allowed her to just erase Uncle Mac's memory.

It didn't take much for the drugs offered at school to entice Brandon. He started by smoking a joint with his buddies and when he found it offered him some peace from the pain, it wasn't long before he moved into the stronger stuff. By the time he discovered he had a problem, he was powerless over the draw of the drugs. Then his mom found out and dropped him off a rehab centre to be someone else's problem. In his young, damaged mind, she'd erased him just like she'd erased his dad and his Uncle Mac. He even imagined her boxing up all his photos and anything that reminded her of him and putting them in a closet and closing the door to him forever.

She never visited him in rehab, but Danny did. Every visitors' day Danny was there. Sometimes Brenna came with him and sometimes it was just Danny, telling him how proud he was of him and relating stories from home. But his mother, his own mother, never once came to see him in the entire three months he was there. He thought if he worked hard enough to get better, she would see he was trying and be proud of him. Maybe then she would come to visit. But she never did. Everything he did, he did to make her proud so she wouldn't forget about him. Erase him.

It wasn't his intent to relate all of this to her, but he found when he started, he just couldn't stop. Jenna suspected it had something to do with the encouragement of his guardian angel, Sam, and Mac all working diligently to open the lines of communication between mother and son.

As Jenna listened to the picture Brandon painted she was taken back to those times, and with what she'd learned over the past several weeks about herself, she could clearly see what Brandon was talking about. Because she'd been unable to deal with the traumas he described, she'd made it impossible for those around her mourn in a healthy, normal manner.

She didn't offer any excuses for her behaviours. She simply listened to her son for the first time in his memory, she really and truly listened. Tears ran down her face—not for herself but for her poor, lost boy.

He couldn't remember ever seeing his stoic mother cry; his heart softened a tiny bit.

When he finally ran out of words she only had two things to say but they were the two things he'd waited his entire life to hear.

"Son, I am so proud of the man you've become and I *am* so sorry for the pain my actions caused you."

When she left him, she hugged him tightly. He let her, even hugging her back. She knew they had made a great start but she had her work cut out for her to get him to trust her enough to let her back into his life.

When Jenna got home that day, she went into her storage closet under the stairs and pulled out box after box. Then she sat in the middle of the theatre room and went through them all, taking out the pictures of Mac and Sam, even some of her mom and dad. She slid the boxes back under the stairwell and carried the photos up to the main floor. She placed some on the mantle of her fireplace and hung the others.

When she was done she stood back and looked at her family all around her. She finally felt like she was truly and completely home. Mac and Sam beamed with pride at the progress Jenna was making.

When Brenna got home that afternoon, she found her brother still sitting at the kitchen table, deep in thought.

"So, how did it go with Mom?" she asked

Brandon smiled and said, "I think it went well." Then, looking at his sister, he said, "She's very different, isn't she?"

Brenna nodded. "Yes, buddy, she really is."

"I like the new Mom," he said. "I hope she sticks around."

Jenna spent the rest of the day researching universities with art therapy programs. The more she researched, the more excited she was at the prospect of going back to school. She had always loved learning. She'd hated high school, but she loved her military courses and then university as she worked through her art degree. The idea of giving back through a form of therapy was something she could wrap her mind around; it really appealed to her

Once she settled on a school that offered transfer credits for her military courses and art degree, she sent a request for her high school transcripts and filled out the admittance forms. She was opting for a part-time course, starting in the summer, because she still had her art commitments and didn't want to set herself up to fail.

Two weeks later, she was thrilled to find out she had been accepted as a mature student, and because she had a lot of transferrable credits, she could finish the program in a year.

She and Danny had had two more dates since she made the move to break the ice and they were enjoying one another's company like they used to when they were first dating. They had agreed on a one-month goal. There were only two weeks to go before Danny moved back into their house. She was excited but also terrified. She was terrified that she would blow it again and fall back into old habits that could risk losing him permanently.

Since Brandon was on leave because of spring breakup from his job on the oil rigs, he'd decided to spend it with Brenna and Ethan. Jenna had taken the opportunity to make a point of having all of them to the house for dinner a couple of times. They were both working hard to keep the lines of communication open. Brenna and Brandon were both pleasantly surprised to see the photos their mom had placed all around her house. But she was so careful not to do or say anything that would alienate her son again. She felt like she was walking on eggshells.

Finally, the week before Danny was scheduled to move back home and Brandon to go back to work, Jenna felt overwhelmed by anxiety. Everything that had happened over such a short period of time was threatening to pull her under, even with all the counselling and ACA meetings. So she decided a change of scenery was just what she needed to clear her head. She let Olivia know she was going away for a week so Mackayla wouldn't come to the house for her after-school job and find her gone and also, so Olivia wouldn't worry.

She told Brenna and Brandon she was taking a vacation and promised them she would text her location daily. Then she packed a bag, jumped in her Cherokee, and headed for the highway going west with Mac and Sam in the backseat jumping up and down like children chanting "Road trip! Road trip!"

She didn't have a destination in mind, she just knew she needed to hear the sound of the ocean and feel the sun on her face.

The first day she made it as far as Kamloops, BC, where she stopped for the night, too tired to see straight anymore.

The second day she made it over the border into the United States, stopping at Coos Bay, Oregon. This was where she decided to stop. She spent her first night in a hotel. The next day, she searched out a private cabin and found one on the water, perfect for soul-searching.

Once she solidified the room with a credit card, she bought a few days' worth of groceries and headed for the cabin. Renting over the internet is always risky, but Jenna was pleasantly surprised to see that it was even prettier than the pictures.

The owner of the cabin, a casually dressed lady in her sixties who introduced herself as Selma, met her when she arrived. She gave her the key and walked her through the little cabin, showing Jenna where everything was leaving her with a contact number in case Jenna had an emergency or needed anything.

Once Selma left, Jenna got down to the business of filling the fridge and putting her things away. That task done, flanked by her celestial sentries, she headed out to explore the beach. Outside, she discovered some beach chairs and a fire pit just a little bit away from the cabin. The sun was shining brightly and the waves were washing gently on the shore. Ignoring the chairs, Jenna plopped down on the damp sand, closed her eyes, and let her senses take over. *This is exactly what the doctor ordered*, she thought to herself as she breathed in the Pacific Ocean.

She spent the first day just soaking up the sun and wading at the edge of the ocean, letting the waves slap over her feet. It was nice to have the opportunity to spend time with Mac and Sam without worrying about being seen talking to thin air. Out here, there was no one for miles so she was able to express all the feelings that were churning around inside her.

She talked about how hard it was to listen to her son's description of their growing-up years. All this time she had thought she was doing the right things, staying strong and continuously moving forward. When Sam died, she was determined not to do to her children what her own father had done. He'd just quit. Quit life, leaving Jenna and Mac to fend for themselves. Being the big sister, Jenna felt like caring for Mac and her father fell on her shoulders and she did the best to set aside her own mourning in order to take care of them. That's what her twelve-year-old self believed had to be done. That was when she learned she wasn't allowed the luxury of grief, so when Sam died, she refused to let her children see her fall apart. Once more, she shut the sorrow down and did what needed to be done.

As she talked about her mother, a thought occurred to her.

"Hey, Mac, they say the people who died before you meet you when it's your turn. Did you see Mom and Dad again?" Her voice was quiet, barely daring to hope.

Mac looked at Sam before he answered, not sure what he was allowed to say and what was off limits.

Sam nodded his assent.

"Dad met me with my guardian angel but Mom had already moved into a new life," he replied.

Jenna, clearly disappointed that her mother wasn't somewhere close by keeping an eye on them all like Mac was, simply said, "Oh."

Mac smiled gently as he said, "You actually see her quite often, you know?"

"Really?"

"Um hum. Mom's new incarnation is Mackayla."

Stunned, she just stared at him for a few minutes before exclaiming, "You mean to tell me that Mom is Mackayla and Mackayla is Mom! Well how the fuck does that work?"

Both Sam and Mac burst out laughing at Jenna's outburst and the expression of total disbelief on her face.

Their laughter stopped abruptly when she suddenly burst into tears, realizing she would never see her mother again, at least not as her mother. She couldn't bear the thought.

Both of them were at her side instantly as the sobs wracked her slim frame. She struggled to get the tears under control so she could ask more questions, but she found she couldn't stem the tide. Once the flood gates opened, the tears flowed nonstop like the ocean before her, with seemingly no end in sight.

Finally, several minutes later, she was able to get herself under control enough to ask, "Does she know us?"

"No, not in the way you mean, and it's not common that someone is reincarnated into the same family, but it does happen. She doesn't know you as her daughter but you have to admit there has always been a very special bond between the two of you, a pull neither of you have even been aware of on a conscious level."

Jenna nodded. Mac was right. There had always been something special between Mackayla and herself.

Unable to process this new piece of information, Jenna got up and started walking toward the beach. This time, Mac and Sam didn't follow, knowing she needed her space. They watched her from a distance. If she needed them, they could close the gap in the beat of an angel's wing.

She walked for hours, letting her mind go back to her childhood, weighing it against what she had just learned. As she let her mind wander, she allowed herself the luxury of feeling the emotions that went with it. She raged and cried and lamented over and over until there was nothing left. She arrived back at the cabin spent from the emotions and crawled into the old iron bed with the softest mattress she had ever slept on and fell into an exhausted sleep.

As she slept, Mac could see the old raw wounds on her essence finally healing, leaving behind only the faintest scar.

Unfortunately, the wound he'd left was still open and oozing. He knew before she left this little haven they'd led her to, they would need to help her heal that one, as well.

When she woke the next morning, she was still exhausted. Deciding to forgo her run in light of the many kilometres she'd walked working through childhood trauma, she made herself a cup of coffee and warmed a croissant in an ancient microwave. She spread it with butter and jam and took her plate to the window seat that looked out at the ocean. She didn't usually eat that many carbs for breakfast, but she was on vacation so she thought, *What the hell?*

She sat there a long time just watching the waves. At one point, when she got up to take her dishes to the sink, she grabbed an old paperback she'd been wanting to read for a while and settled back down to intermittently read and wave watch. She was so exhausted from the emotional hurricane of the day before, she spent her entire day just sitting, eating, reading, and wave watching. She didn't even feel bad that she never left the cabin.

When she drifted off to sleep that night, she didn't have her usual night terror, but she woke the next morning, heart pounding and dripping in sweat all the same. She'd had a nightmare that, though it had been rec-curring for many months after Mac's death, she hadn't had in years. The setting was the city morgue and she and Olivia were standing with a police officer next to a gurney waiting for the medical examiner to uncover the body underneath.

The medical examiner only pulled the sheet to just under the occupant's neck. It was enough to illicit a moan from Olivia but when she indicated it was her husband, the police officer ushered her out. Jenna remained, demanding the medical examiner show her what he was trying so hard to hide. He advised against it but she refused to be moved.

When the medical examiner pulled the sheet down to just above her brother's waist he uncovered the careful stitches that attached Mac's head to his body. Jenna wasn't rattled by the bluish tinge to his skin or by his blue lips, but the obvious method of his death haunted her for years after. The dream had blissfully ceased a little better than a year after his death, but now it was back.

This time when she sat up in bed fresh from the horror of her dream, seeing him there wasn't a comfort. It had the exact opposite effect. When he reached for her, she backed away from him, screaming at him not to touch her. She backed right into Sam, who was there as always to help her carry the overwhelming feelings

Mac felt awful about planting the dream in her mind while she slept, but they only had one more day left here without all the background noise and distractions Jenna hid behind back home.

"I'm sorry, Jen," Mac said.

It wasn't until he apologized that Jenna realized he had been responsible for that horrible dream.

"You did that!" she screamed at him. "How could you! Do you have any idea how long it took me to get that picture out of my head? You fucking bastard!" Tears ran in streams down her sweaty face.

"Yes, sis, I do," he replied

"Then how could you do that to me!? Why, Mac? Wasn't what you did bad enough? You had to show it to me and make me relive it all over just when I'm struggling to put my life back together! I fucking hate you, Mac!"

"You're right, Jen, what I did was inexcusable and you should be angry with me."

Jenna scrambled up off the bed, waving both of them away from her as she went into the bathroom to splash her face with cold water. When she turned to grab her bathrobe, they were both standing by the door.

"Get the fuck away from me!" she screamed, "both of you! Leave me alone!"

Quickly slipping on sweatpants, socks, a sports bra, and runners, Jenna headed out the door at a rapid walk. She broke into a run as she cleared the door.

She had no idea how far or how long she ran. She just ran until the image burned in her mind faded. She had no doubt Mac and Sam kept her in their sights, but as long as she couldn't see them, she could pretend things were the way they had been before they showed up in her bedroom almost four months earlier. It had all been so surreal, she could hardly believe any of it ever actually happened.

They were sitting in the beach chairs when she got back to the cabin as if they had never left. She took off her shoes and threw them at Mac one at a time.

"Get away from me!" she screamed at him, sinking to her knees on the sand a few feet away.

Sam was behind her again. She realized she'd never even seen him move. This time instead of putting his hand on her shoulder, he knelt down and wrapped her in his arms as she broke down completely, twice in three days. When the torrential tears finally slowed, she looked at her brother, who was kneeling in front of her, while Sam comforted her.

"How could you leave me? I was there for you when Mom died, when Dad fell apart. I was there for you when you got married and when your daughter was born, I was there. Didn't that count for anything? I'm the one who took care of Dad through his disease and I'm the one who buried him. The least you could have done was stick around, don't you think?"

"You're right, Jenna. I was selfish and single minded. So caught up in my disease I couldn't think of anything or anyone and I hurt so many people in the process," Mac answered. "If I could change it, I would in a heartbeat. But I can't. Though for some reason I've been given an opportunity to try to fix some of the damage I've done and help put the lives I've derailed back on track. I didn't give you that dream to torture you, sis. I gave you that dream so you could work through it and let it go."

"You were the one loss I didn't think I would ever get over, you know," Jenna replied. "Danny and Brandon accused me of shutting down when you died, but the pain was just too big for me. I was terrified if I took the lid off it, it would consume me like a raging fire, leaving nothing but ashes. That's why I took your pictures down and did my best to erase you from my mind."

Mac handed her back her shoes. "I know, Jen."

Slowly, Jenna got up off the ground, shoes in hand. She walked in her stocking feet toward the cabin. When she got to the door, she peeled off her socks, shook all the sand out of them, and went inside. Dropping her shoes by the door, she went into the bathroom, stripped down, and stood in the shower until the hot water ran out. She went back into the bedroom after drying off and crawled back into the big, soft bed and went to sleep, completely unconcerned by the fact that it was only mid morning.

She didn't wake again until well after noon. When she got out of the bed, dressed, and went into the kitchen, Mac and Sam were seated at the tiny table. She walked over to Mac, hugged him tightly, then backed away and said, "If you ever haunt me with that dream again, I will find a way to hunt you down and kill you all over again."

Mac laughed and promised that if she had that dream again it wouldn't be him who'd put it there.

Making herself a cup of coffee, she headed back out to the beach, paperback in hand, and sat in one of the chairs. She intended to finish it but found herself deep in thought, not paying much attention to Mac and Sam building castles in the sand.

Molding the sand into turrets, Mac was watching Jenna's essence and he noticed that the wound he'd left was finally starting to heal. But what he didn't notice was a mark left by Sam. He would have thought losing her husband in such a violent way would have left some type of mark.

As unobtrusively as possible, Mac asked Sam about it. Sam told him it was because every time he left, she mourned him. She had always had a sense that one day he wouldn't come home and she'd prepared herself for that outcome as best she could. Between that knowledge and the healing Danny brought with him, those wounds were shallow and completely healed.

As Jenna loaded the car the next morning to head back home, she turned toward the ocean and closed her eyes. She visualized leaving all the emotional baggage she'd come there with behind her, symbolically letting it go. When she drove away she knew with certainty she was ready to make a brand new start with Danny.

Once again, she took her time going back, stopping overnight at the halfway point. As much as she needed the time away, she was more than happy to see her house as she turned down her street. Pulling into her garage, she unloaded her bags, kicked off her shoes, and took her luggage up to the laundry room. Once she'd started a load of laundry, she called Brenna and Brandon to let them know she was safely home.

She picked up the pile of mail lying at the front door and headed for her office. As she was going through it, Mac perched on the arm of her chair and asked, "So, when are you going to tell Brandon you were at the rehab centre with Danny every time he went to see him?"

"I'm not," Jenna said.

"Just out of curiosity, why did you wait in the car? Why didn't you go in to see him?"

"Because I wasn't strong enough to bear the hatred I was afraid I would see in the eyes of the child who taught me the true meaning of love, that's why." Her tone was final.

Chapter 12

Second Chances

Things had improved considerably between Mackayla and Olivia when Mackayla returned home from her aunt's. Olivia was tremendously relieved when Mackayla flew through the door and ran into her mother's arms after Jenna dropped her off that Sunday.

Olivia apologized for the way she'd handled things and Mackayla apologized for running out on her.

Considering everything that had happened, Olivia wasn't happy about Mackayla's lying to her, but she was incredibly relieved that Mackayla had had the good sense to run to her aunt at the very least. It didn't save Mackayla from being grounded for two weeks though.

Mackayla grumbled a little but there was no heat in it. She knew she deserved it and was grateful it was only two weeks and not two months.

Once things settled a bit, Olivia sat Mackayla down and started from the very beginning, about how she just couldn't get past the sight of Julia sitting in handcuffs, so thin, so scared, so young. She explained how Constable Rafferty believed that Julia hadn't had a lot of breaks in her young life and how he was afraid that if she ended up in the prison system, she would be lost. How she couldn't help but see something in her that Olivia believed could be rehabilitated with patience, counselling, and love.

"But, Mom! What about me! She almost had me kidnapped! How am I supposed to just overlook that? How can *you* overlook that?" Mackayla exclaimed.

"I'm not overlooking it, sweetheart," her mother answered. "I just feel that Julia was a victim in this, too." She stopped a moment. "Look, there are lot of things that have to happen before bringing her into our home is even a possibility. Constable Rafferty (Olivia was careful not to use his first name in front of Mackayla—she just wasn't ready for those questions yet) has arranged some classes for Julia to attend while awaiting her trial. Her attendance and willingness to participate will be monitored. Then there's the court case. Julia has asked to be a witness against the men who set the whole thing up. We didn't ask her to do this, she offered." Olivia put her hand up to stop Mackayla from interjecting. "Now, I know, it serves her purpose as well as ours. But it will mean you don't have to go through the trauma of taking the stand. That means a lot to me. But she needs to follow through on all of these things before I will even seriously consider it. Once you've had time to really think about it, you have to be OK with it also. But before you decide, I'd like you to come with me to visit her at least three times."

"Why three times? That's kind of random, don't you think?" Mackayla replied.

"You can't make an informed decision with just one visit. The first visit is always awkward, the second visit you're just starting to get a feel for things, the third visit means you really are willing to be receptive to her. What do you think? The ball's in your court. I won't force the issue."

"Can I take the length of my grounding to think about it?" Mackayla asked.

Olivia laughed. "Sure, why not. It will give you something to do."

The first week of Mackayla's grounding wasn't too bad because she was still allowed to work with Jenna on the days her mother had to work the evening shift. Mackayla was pretty disappointed when Auntie Jen went away the second week though, because she had to stay home alone, which gave her time to think about her mom's request. She couldn't avoid it anymore.

She was still angry at Julia. But it wasn't just because she had almost gotten her abducted. She'd pretended to be Mackayla's friend at a time when she needed one so badly. She had been so lonely and Julia had pretended to care. Mackayla had shared her innermost secrets with Julia, honestly believing they were friends and Julia was just using her to lure her into a terrible situation.

When Mackayla thought about it, the anger, the sense of betrayal, and the embarrassment of being played for the fool were so overwhelming she thought she would explode into a million tiny pieces. She knew she had to get these feelings out before they caused her do something destructive. So she went to her mother's desk, grabbed a piece of paper and a pen, and wrote a letter to Julia telling her all of the things she was feeling.

She raged on for pages, spilling her hatred onto every page. When she was done, she folded the letter and put it in an envelope for her mom to give to Julia the next time she visited her.

She was asleep when her mom got home at midnight. She saw the letter addressed to Julia with a sticky note attached asking Olivia to give it to her when she saw her again. Knowing how upset Mackayla was and how fragile Julia was, Olivia made a decision she wouldn't have normally made. She had always respected Mackayla's privacy, but she decided under the circumstances, and especially since all mail was opened by the administration before it was given to the inmates, decided that she should probably read it before delivering it.

Normally, Olivia slept a little later when she worked evenings. She was always up to see Mackayla off but she was rarely awake before her, so Mackayla was surprised to see her in the kitchen making coffee when she got up.

"Hey, Mom, what are you doing up so early?" Mackayla asked.

"I'm going to visit Julia but I wanted to talk to you about this before I do." Olivia pulled the opened letter out of her pocket.

"You opened a private letter, Mom! Seriously?" Mackayla was outraged at her mother's unusual invasion of her privacy and not a little mortified that her mother saw the poison she penned.

"I did," Olivia replied, careful to stay calm. "You do know all mail is opened before it's given to the inmates, right?"

"Actually, I didn't." Her outrage dispersed like water on flame.

"They do and I have to ask: Would you really want them to see this letter?" Olivia asked.

Mackayla, looking down at her feet, refused to answer.

"I'll tell you what, you read the letter over carefully now that you've had time to think about it and if you still want Julia to have it, I'll consider it. Deal?"

"Deal," Mackayla mumbled.

Olivia sat her down at the breakfast nook, handed her the letter, and left the room to grab a shower while Mackayla read what she'd written the night before.

When she returned, Mackayla was still seated at the nook, the letter in front of her and tears streaming down her face.

As Olivia handed her a box of tissue and put her arm around her shoulders. She asked, "So, do you still want Julia to read this letter?"

"No," Mackayla said, wiping her eyes and blowing her nose.

"Why not?"

"Because it's awful! And I don't really feel that way, I was just angry and hurt. She made me look like a complete idiot, Mom!"

"Oh, honey! Those are very reasonable feelings considering what you've been through and it's good to express them. Writing them out like this is a great idea. It gives a voice to them without hurting yourself or someone else. That is, unless you give it to that someone else."

Olivia sat on the stool beside her and turned her face to look at her. "I think it's a good idea to have this conversation with Julia. That's why I wanted you to come with me. But you're not a mean girl and I don't believe you would feel good about doing something to intentionally hurt another person in the way we both know this letter would."

Mackayla nodded, indicating her mother was right.

"Let's get rid of these awful feelings, what do you say?" Olivia pointed to the letter.

Mackayla looked at her questioningly, but nodded her consent.

Picking it up, Olivia grabbed the barbecue lighter out of the drawer and motioned for Mackayla to follow her.

Getting up off the stool, they trekked out to the patio where Olivia lifted the barbecue lid and handed the letter and lighter to her daughter. Smiling, Mackayla took it, lit the letter, and watched it turn to ash.

When they returned to the house, Olivia wrapped her daughter in a warm mom hug that Mackayla melted into.

"Mom?" she mumbled into Olivia's shoulder.

Stepping back but keeping her hands on her daughter's shoulders, Olivia asked "what, baby girl?"

"Can I come with you to see Julia today?"

"Yes, sweetheart, you sure can." Olivia smiled with pride at her beautiful daughter with hair the colour of fire, just like her dad's.

As usual, her mom was right. The first visit with Julia was awkward. It had taken a lot of time and persistence on Olivia's part to win Julia over, and even though Julia still struggled to believe Olivia could really, honestly care about someone like her, she was so desperate for someone to fill the maternal role in her life that she had been willing to pretend Olivia was sincere.

But Mackayla was a different matter. Julia had used Mackayla, pretending to be her friend, gaining her trust, then betraying that trust. So when she saw Mackayla with Olivia, she shut down instantly, putting up her protective wall without a second thought.

For Mackayla, seeing Julia for the first time since her attempted abduction was definitely not what she'd prepared herself for. Julia didn't look like the monster Mackayla had created in her mind. She was so thin, her jutting cheek bones were the most prominent feature on her face aside from her brown eyes. Those eyes that held the shadows of years of abuse. Her body was lost in oversized clothing provided by the province, and she had her dark blonde hair pulled back into a skinny ponytail so fine the elastic was barely containing it.

Where Mackayla was tiny, with her mother's fine china doll bone structure, Julia looked more like a half-starved, raw-boned pup. With the proper nutrition, she would have been an average sized fourteen-year-old girl, but years of scrounging for food had left her seriously malnourished and underweight.

Mackayla realized that she had never really *seen* Julia. On line, they only messaged one another, they had never had a face-to-face conversation. When she did finally meet her, things happened so fast, her appearance didn't register. So this was really the first time Mackayla was seeing her. She could definitely understand how her mother could be moved by

Julia's plight. Mackayla told her mother as much when they got home later that morning.

On the second visit, Julia was less guarded, so Olivia sat back with Constable Rafferty while Mackayla attempted to talk to Julia. As angry as her letter was, Mackayla couldn't summon the same level of animosity looking at the girl in front of her.

Very quietly, Mackayla said, "I thought you were my friend, Julia. Didn't you like me even a little?"

Julia looked down at the small round table the two girls were sitting at in the visitors' room. "You couldn't possibly understand," Julia replied. "You have everything. You're smart and pretty and you have a mom who loves you and a house to live in. I bet you even get to eat whenever you want to, and not food someone else has thrown away."

"I'm sorry you don't have those things, Julia, but it's not my fault that I do."

"I know. I didn't want to do it, but it was the only thing I could do, so they wouldn't beat me or let me starve. I'm not pretty like you. I wasn't worth anything to them other than to use as bait.

"How many girls did you lure to them?" Mackayla didn't want to know but for some reason the question was out of her mouth before she could stop herself. The last thing she needed was to have nightmares about girls she didn't even know.

"None, that was the problem. I kept making excuses, saying I couldn't get the girls I was talking to meet up with me. You were my last chance. If I couldn't get you to meet me they said they would kill me and throw my body in a dumpster. They said no one would even know I was gone, because no one cared enough to look for me." Julia was swiping angrily at the tears that were trying to escape.

Mackayla stayed silent, not sure how to respond. She couldn't imagine being in a situation like that and she certainly had no idea what lengths she would have gone to, to survive.

Taking her silence as rejection, Julia got up and left the table. She indicated to the staff that she wanted to go back to her room.

Mackayla was silent all the way home that day. Olivia was worried, but knew Mackayla had to process the things Julia had told her in her own way and in her own time.

She wasn't sure if Mackayla would go a third time, but she was pleasantly surprised when the following week, Mackayla was dressed and ready to go. She had to change her scheduled weekly visits to the evenings, when she wasn't working, to make allowances for Mackayla's schooling. Mackayla was almost done Grade 9 and had managed to keep her grades up despite all the events of the past few months. Olivia didn't want to jeopardize that, but she also felt the visits would be a necessary part of her healing process.

Olivia wasn't the only one surprised. Julia obviously was, as well, judging by the look on her face. Once more, Olivia took a backseat and let the girls talk.

The first thing Mackayla said was, "Look, Julia, you were right, what you said last week when I was here. I don't know what it would be like to live through the things you lived through, and I don't know what I would have done in your shoes. I do know, though, that I've had to survive some pretty bad stuff myself." She put her hand up to stop Julia from interjecting and continued. "I'm not comparing, I'm just saying everyone has stuff. But I know I've had a lot of help to work out my stuff and I think you deserve the same chance. That's all I'm saying."

It was Julia's turn to be silent, but Mackayla didn't walk away. She just sat there, leaving the ball in Julia's court. Several minutes passed while she obviously tried to work things out in her mind. Finally, she said in a tiny voice, "I'm sorry, Mackayla, I really wanted to be your friend."

The gap had been bridged. It was what Mackayla needed to hear and what Julia needed to say. Mackayla accepted her apology, letting go of the last of her animosity.

As the two girls were talking, Mackayla notice her mother and the constable chatting with their heads together. His feelings for Olivia were so obvious even a blind man could see them, but he was determined to keep things professional until the end of the trial. He didn't want anything to impact its outcome.

While they were chatting, Mackayla heard a sound come from her mother she couldn't remember having ever heard before. Turning to look at them lost in their conversation she turned back to Julia with a look of disgust on her face.

"Did she just giggle, I mean actually giggle?" she asked Julia.

Julia laughed at Mackayla's expression and said, "Yep, and she does it a lot when they're together. I think they like each other."

"Ewwwwww!" Mackayla responded, repulsed at the idea of her mom and the constable.

Julia laughed again. "Oh, he's not so bad. Trust me, I've seen worse."

Mackayla nodded in acknowledgement.

As they drove home from the youth centre that day, Mackayla told her mother that if Julia followed through on all the things they had agreed on, and if Olivia thought it would help her, Mackayla would be all right if her mother fostered her.

Olivia and Mackayla continued their weekly visits with Julia up until the trial, Constable Rafferty attending when he could.

Even though it was unlikely Mackayla would have to testify, she still had to do a deposition, just in case. Jenna would definitely have to take the stand and Julia had struck a deal with prosecution of probation and time served for her testimony.

The trial started the fifth of July and they were all in attendance. As was expected, the blonde man and his cohorts plead not guilty, so Julia was the first witness up. Even though Julia hadn't personally been able to help lure young girls, she had been witness to it as part of her training. So her firsthand testimony was the nail in their coffin.

She was so terrified her voice shook when she spoke. She kept her teeth tightly clenched when she wasn't talking, to prevent them from chattering together, but she gave a good testimony. She wasn't swayed when pelted with questions from opposition lawyers. Between her testimony and Jenna's deposition, each man received a fifteen-year sentence with no chance of parole.

It was finally over. They could all put it behind them and move on with their lives. There was a definite air of celebration. Except for one. Julia stood alone by her lawyer and her social worker while Jenna, Danny, Mackayla, and Olivia all huddled together, chattering happily over the outcome.

Constable Rafferty saw Julia standing alone and walked over to Olivia and whispered something in her ear. She turned and headed over to her.

"Hey, kiddo, good job up there. That was an incredibly brave thing you did."

"Thanks," she mumbled, head down.

"No, really," Olivia said, and lifted her chin so she could look at her face. "You were amazing and Mackayla and I would like to ask you a question, if that's all right."

"Sure, I've got nothin' to do except wait to find out what foster home I'm going to end up in."

Julia's lawyer and her social worker were deep in conversation. Then the lawyer turned and left as Mackayla made her way over. When she reached them, the social worker joined them.

"What's going on?" Julia asked, suspicion clearly evident in her voice.

""Well," Olivia started, "Mackayla and I would like know if you would be interested in coming to live at our house?"

Julia searched Mackayla's face for affirmation of her mother's question. Mackayla gave her a genuine smile. The one thing Julia had learned to do on the street was read people and she could see no dishonesty in the mother and daughter.

"Why would you do that?" She was still not quite able to wrap her mind around the offer.

"Because, Julia, everyone deserves a second chance at life, especially someone who's had the bad breaks you've had," Olivia replied. "But don't misunderstand. You'll have to follow the same rules as Mackayla and I will have the same expectations of you. It won't be a picnic, but you will have a clean bed of your own to sleep in, clean clothes that no else has worn, all the food you can eat, and a roof over your head." Olivia stopped to let her take it all in. "So, what do you say?"

Julia smiled and said, "It's the best offer I've had all day. But will they let you foster me?" She pointed at the social worker.

"Olivia has already done the paperwork and she has been carefully vetted and approved to take you, if that's what you want," the social worker replied with a smile.

Julia stuck her hand out to Olivia. "Deal."

Olivia laughed and pulled her close for one her famous mom hugs. Julia let her. Mackayla, the social worker, Mac, and three guardian angels smiled.

Mac knew it wasn't going to be easy, but he knew they were all finally firmly back on the track they were meant to be on.

Zadkiel appeared beside him and put his hand on Mac's shoulder. "Good work, Mackenzie," he said, "but it's just a start. There are more lives to realign. Don't get complacent." Then he disappeared again.

Mac sighed.

Olivia and Mackayla had already cleaned out Mackayla's old room and set up a double bed frame with matching end tables and a dresser. They still needed to get bedding, but wanted Julia to be able to pick out what she wanted. So on their way home, they stopped at the mall for a shopping spree.

Julia was hesitant at first. She had never been shopping before. Living in the mall, she'd seen people laughing together going from store to store, coming out with so many bags they could hardly carry them, but she knew it wasn't something girls like her got to do so she hadn't even let herself hope. Now here she was going from store to store, picking out bedding, clothes, and shoes just like a normal teenager. It felt surreal.

Olivia kept a close eye on Julia, trying not to overwhelm her. When she started to show signs of a meltdown, Olivia paid for what they had picked and ushered both girls out the door to the car.

There was just one more stop to make before they were able to get home and let Julia set up her room and put away her new clothes: the grocery store. If Julia was overwhelmed with the clothes and bedding, she almost burst into tears when Olivia asked what she, surrounded by more food choices than she'd ever seen, would like to eat.

Olivia put her arm around her and said, "Just tell me what you don't like to eat and I will pick this time, how does that sound?"

Julia nodded, too close to tears to speak. Olivia would point at a grocery item and Julia would shake her head yes or no. It turned out there was very little Julia didn't like, so it was a rather painless process for Olivia.

Finally, they arrived at home. Olivia put Julia's new things through the wash, and started a pot roast for dinner. While Olivia was doing that,

Mackayla showed Julia around the house. Then the girls flopped on the sofa in the family room and turned on the TV.

While Mackayla looked for a show they might both like, Julia fell into an exhausted sleep. Mackayla covered her with the sofa throw and went to join her mother in the kitchen. As she was working alongside her, helping swap out laundry and make dinner, she turned to her mother and asked, "So, Mom, what's the story with you and Constable Rafferty?"

Her mother turned to look at her with on eyebrow raised. "What are you talking about?"

"Don't give me that. I've seen the way he looks at you."

"You're imagining things, young lady. We're just good friends."

"Yeah, OK," Mackayla said with a smirk.

"Stop smirking, it's the truth." Olivia swatted at her with the tea towel from her shoulder.

"Methinks the lady doth protest too much," Mackayla teased as she ducked out of reach.

"You're a brat," her mother said, turning back to dinner.

Mackayla also turned back to the task at hand. Looking at her mother out of the corner of her eye, she said, "You know, Mom, you could do worse."

Chapter 13

Trucker Joe

Jenna and Danny had been living back in the same house for almost as long as they had been separated by the time the trial came up. Jenna filled Danny in on the events of that day but the trial brought it to life for him in a very real way. He was terribly upset at the danger his wife and niece had been exposed to. The outcome was tremendous relief to both of them as justice was served. Everyone involved could move on.

They were both a little surprised to hear that Olivia had decided to open her home to Julia. But seeing the frightened girl on the stand, refusing to be cowed, gave them a vision of the person she could be with the right influences and opportunities. If any could offer her those things it was Olivia.

Jenna was so proud of the progress Mackayla made in not only finally coming to agree with her mother's decision but her capacity for forgiveness. She knew adults who held grudges to their deathbeds because they couldn't let go of slights much less significant than Mackayla and Julia's.

With the trial over it could all be put behind them. Jenna and Danny settled back into their newly established normal. At first it was challenging for Jenna to get used to Danny and the dogs being back in the house. She had recreated her routine, which wasn't easy after three months of having only herself to think about. Danny had to find his place in her world again. But at night when they curled around one another in their king-sized bed, they both agreed it was worth the struggle.

Now that Danny was back where he belonged, Mac spent more time searching out others whose lives were negatively impacted by his choices.

Sam just made himself scarce. He knew Jenna and Danny needed time to reconnect. If Jenna was aware of his presence, she would be uncomfortable and distracted. That was the last thing she or Danny needed. So when they were together, he disappeared, but was well within helping distance if she needed him.

When she was alone in the house, he would reappear, letting her know he hadn't left her. Mac also popped back in from time to time.

Danny was thrilled when she told him she was going back to school and he thought her choice of study was perfect. She was still very busy with her art but now she had her studies to concentrate on and that's what she was doing when Mac suddenly popped in beside her, scaring her half to death.

"Jesus, Mac!" she exclaimed, her hand clutching her heart. "Give a girl a heart attack, why don't you?"

"Sorry, Jen, but I really need your help and I don't have a lot of time." Mac was obviously worked up about something.

"What's going on, Mac?"

"Well, remember the truck driver I hit when I died?"

"Not specifically. I don't remember if I met him, did I?" she asked, confused.

"Maybe not, but he was at my funeral." Impatiently, he waved away any further explanation as to how she may have met him. "Anyway, he hasn't been doing so well since the accident and he's decided to follow in my footsteps, if you know what I mean."

"He's planning to hit a truck?"

"No! He's planning on committing suicide by jumping off the High Level Bridge. I need your help to stop him," Mac exclaimed.

"My help? Don't you have"—she waved her hand in the air—"other more qualified 'people' to help with that?"

"No, I don't! It's your help I need to help with this. Please, Jen!" He was frantic now. "I just need you to get there before he jumps and talk him down. I can tell you exactly where he's going to be but that's all I have the power to do. I told you the night you almost died that I would need your help, that's why they lifted the veil so you could see me."

"OK," she conceded with a heavy sigh. "Let's go. You can give me the directions on the way."

She rushed out the door, grabbing her bag and keys en route. They all piled into the red Cherokee. Jenna drove as fast as she safely could, following Mac's directions until they reached the spot on the High Level Bridge where Mac's truck driver was supposed to execute his suicide attempt.

Since there was no place to park, Jenna pulled over as far as she could, put her four-way flashers on, jumped out of the Cherokee, and lifted the hood, feigning car troubles. It was the least conspicuous way she could be there without attracting suspicion. She knew other than an angry horn or two, odds were no one would bother with her.

Once her hood was up, she climbed back into her car to keep watch. It wasn't long before Mac pointed to a lone person walking along the bridge's pedway, overlooking the water.

Searching for an access point, Jenna finally found an opening at a crosswalk at the entrance of the bridge. She would have to pass him to get to it then double back. She was concerned he would see her and be suspicious.

She needn't have worried. He was so engrossed with his own thoughts that even when she passed him with only the iron railing between them, he didn't look up. She ran for the opening and slowed as she came up behind him, careful to keep a good distance between them so she wouldn't spook him, no matter how unlikely that was.

When he stopped at the mid-point of the bridge, she could she his angel whispering furiously in his ear. He swiped at him like he would a bothersome fly, not able to see and too distraught to hear.

Jenna stayed a good distance back and dialled 911 into her phone for the second time in fewer than a six months, thinking if she kept having to call them they would eventually end up investigating her. Once more, she didn't hit dial—at this point she had no real reason to. He was just a pedestrian watching the water.

Then he made his move. As he slung one leg over the iron railing, Jenna forgot all about her phone and screamed "Stop!"

She ran to where he was standing, one leg still on the sidewalk and one over the edge and with a startled look on his face.

When she got within arm's reach of him, she stopped, out of breath from the anxiety and her record sprint. Now that she was close enough, she could smell the alcohol wafting off him in waves.

Fuck! she thought to herself. It was hard enough to reason with a distraught sober person, but trying to talk sense to someone who was three sheets to the wind was going to be much, much harder.

"It's going to be OK, Jen." Mac was beside her. "You've got this. Just tell him what I tell you to, OK?'

"Well, you'd better talk fast, I'm losing his attention," she said as the man turned back to the bridge.

"Hey!" she said, trying to draw his attention back to her. "What's your name?

Mac nodded his approval at her question as the man turned back to her.

"What difference does it make to you, huh?" he slurred.

"It makes a lot of difference. If I have to watch a man die, I want to know his name."

"Ish Joe—Joe Burns. Now leave me alone."

"I can't do that, Joe, not before you tell me why you're on a bridge getting ready to jump."

"Ish none of your buishnesh lady, jush go away."

Mac told Jenna to ask about his daughter, the little girl who used to ride with her dad in his truck every summer. He called her "Daddy's girl." She was in university now, struggling with the stress of her full course load and trying to take care of her dad, after his wife finally gave up and left.

"Hey, Joe, what's your daughter going to think, if you leave her like this?" Jenna said. "After all, she was the one who stayed with you. This is an awful way to repay that, don't you think?"

Joe turned his blurry eyes to her in confusion.

"How you know all that?" he asked

Jenna shook her head. "That's not important, I just know. Now, why don't you take your leg off the ledge? You don't look very comfortable like that. Then you and I can talk. What do you say?"

"Look, lady, jush, go away" was his reply as he looked back over the water.

"Jen! Ask him about his sons. One was a baby back then so he would be around seven or eight years old. The other one would be around thirteen.

"What about your sons, Joe? Thirteen is terrible age to lose a father. Who's going to teach him how to be a man? Who's going help him with his first broken heart? Help him buy his first car?"

Joe spun around, so fast that if his leg wasn't still over the ledge he would have fallen flat on his face. Who was this strange woman throwing information at him that she shouldn't know?

"Are you a friend of my wife's?" he asked, clearly unsettled.

"No. My name is Jenna Walker and my brother is the one who committed suicide by driving his car into your truck seven years ago. He sent me to help you."

Mac glared at her for going off script. Sam sighed.

Jenna could hear sirens in the distance. She didn't know just how anxious she was until the relief washed over her, making her knees give a little.

Her words were like a bucket of cold water, as his befuddled brain cleared for a moment.

"How is that even possible?" he yelled at her. "The fucker's dead. I know 'cause I've seen his head laying on the pavement every fucking night for the past seven fucking years." He was almost screaming. "That bastard destroyed my life!"

"No," Jenna said. "He hasn't destroyed your life, but he will if you choose to jump." She paused for effect. "And how many lives will you destroy if you do the same thing?"

A police officer had arrived and was slowly walking up to them. Jenna reached out her hand. Joe pulled back so quickly he lost his balance and would have toppled right over into the water below if Jenna hadn't grabbed him. But she wasn't strong enough to keep him from going over. She was able to slow him enough that the officer arrived just in time to get a hold of him and help drag him back over the railing onto solid ground.

When the officer was sure Joe was safe, he let him go. Joe collapsed to the ground in defeated sobs and Jenna's knees finally gave way as she, too, slid to the ground. She was leaning against the bridge trusses when the paramedics arrived. They waited until the scene was secure before they rushed in to assess the situation.

They would have stopped to treat Jenna first but she waved them away, indicating Joe was the one who needed their attention.

Jenna's head popped up like a jack-in-the-box when she heard a familiar voice.

"Hey, Jenna, seriously, this is becoming a pattern. You mind telling me how you came to be here at the same time as a potential jumper?"

Jenna laughed. "Hey, Raff, just lucky I guess." Constable Rafferty reached out a hand to help her get back on her feet. They had gotten to be friends throughout the kidnapping investigation and then subsequent trial. Even better friends when Olivia finally agreed to go out with him.

"Did you draw the short straw?" she asked.

"Nope, some concerned citizen called in your plate number as a potential suicide attempt. I thought I'd better find out what was up."

"Didn't my 911 call go through?"

"Not to my knowledge."

Pulling out her phone she realized that in all the kerfuffle, she'd failed to dial the call.

"Oh, well, I really am glad to see you."

While they were talking, the paramedics loaded a dazed and sobbing Joe onto a gurney and started toward the ambulance parked behind Sean's police cruiser, which was parked behind Jenna's Cherokee. Jenna and Sean followed.

"What's going to happen to him?" Jenna asked.

"They'll take him to the psych ward of the University Hospital and do an assessment," Sean replied.

"Do you think I would be allowed to visit him?"

"Not for probably the first week; he'll be in lockdown for at least twenty-four hours because of his suicide attempt. But once he's been stabilized, you should be able to. But if you don't mind me asking, Jen, who is this guy to you?"

"He's the truck driver my brother used to end his life," Jenna replied.

Sean looked at her with one eyebrow raised. "And you just happened along. My Spidey senses are tingling, Jen." With that, they had arrived at her car. He held open the door as she crawled in behind the steering wheel.

"Are you sure you're OK to drive?" he asked.

She assured him she was. He closed her door and she started her engine, signaled, waited for traffic to clear, and merged back onto the main road to home.

It was two weeks before Jenna was finally allowed to visit Joe. She had made arrangements to meet him at the hospital cafeteria and, of course, she was thirty minutes early since her classes with the University of Alberta and the hospital were within walking distance.

She grabbed a coffee and settled close to the entrance so she would be easy to see and dug out one of her textbooks, taking every opportunity to do some extra reading.

She was so engrossed in her book that she didn't even notice Joe until he sat down across from her.

"Hi, I'm guessing you're Jenna," he said.

"I am," Jenna replied.

"I don't really remember much about the day we met. I was a little inebriated. But I understand I have you to thank for the fact that I'm sitting here today."

"No, I just happened to be at the right place at the right time," Jenna said.

"Something tells me that's not entirely true, but I am grateful anyway," Joe replied.

Jenna waved away his gratitude and said, "I've been thinking about you a lot since that day. How are you?"

"I'm pretty heavily medicated, but otherwise, I feel better than I have in a long time."

"I'm so glad to hear that," Jenna replied, genuinely relieved.

"I have a really strange question about something I'm not sure is a memory or if it really happened," Joe said with caution. "When you were talking to me on that bridge that day, did you say you were Mackenzie Doyle's sister?"

"I did and I am," she replied.

"That's quite a coincidence, don't you think?" Suspicion was clear in his voice. "How did you know who I was and how did you happen to be there that day?"

Jenna sighed. She'd been hoping he wouldn't remember that but now that he did, he deserved an explanation, an explanation she wasn't sure how to give.

"I'm going to be honest with you, Joe," she started. "If I told you how I really knew you were going to be there, you probably wouldn't believe me. Just know it wasn't your time. Mac set your life on a path that wasn't your destiny and I'm here to help you get back on the right one."

Joe just shook his head. "Well, I don't really care how you knew, I'm just glad you did."

They talked until Jenna had to go to her class but she asked if he would mind if she stopped by again. He said that would nice and asked what she was studying. When she told him art therapy, he said that that made sense and they parted with a handshake.

He was there for another week, then he started his outpatient program with a psychiatrist and because Jenna had classes three evenings a week, they made a point of having coffee on those days at a nearby Second Cup.

He wanted to know as much about Mac as she was willing to tell him and for the first time in her life she talked about her brother freely. She talked about the boy he'd been before their mother died and the man he'd had to become when their dad spiraled into alcoholism. She talked about how protective of her he'd been and how devoted he was to his wife and young daughter. She told Joe how Mac and Olivia helped her with her children when Sam died and she told him how she'd met the love her life, Mac's best friend, at a barbecue at their house.

She also told Joe how when the pressure to succeed overwhelmed Mac, he had no tools to combat it, having no example to follow, with their dad as their only role model.

While she tried to give Joe some ideas as to why he would do what he did, she was careful not to excuse it. She was very open about the path of destruction Mac had left.

Mac, who was listening to these commentaries, cringed at her honesty, but he stayed to hear the conversations between his sister and the man he'd dubbed Trucker Joe. Truth be told, he couldn't have left if he wanted to—he was compelled to listen.

Jenna was also very open about her own suicide attempt. She talked about how, after it, she'd realized that she, too, needed to learn a new way of handling the trauma's past, present, and future if she wanted to have the life she believed everyone deserved.

Joe, in turn, talked about the day Mac used him to end his life. He was very careful at first, not wanting to hurt this beautiful lady who, literally, had saved his life. But when she assured him she needed to know in order to continue her own healing, he told her everything.

There was one thing about the telling of the events of that day that disturbed Jenna, a lot. That was the description of the reaction of the police officers and the two young paramedics that attended the scene.

But not just them. Joe also described the two men and a woman who were called to the scene to pull the car from the truck. The tow truck drivers.

Mac's body couldn't be recovered until the car was removed from the undercarriage of the truck. Even though Mac's head had been covered with a sheet, they were well aware of its presence. Joe said they worked in solemn silence as they pulled the car away from the truck and sat on the side of the road while the body was removed from the wreckage.

Joe was sitting in the back of one the ambulances watching their faces, so stoic and haunted. He was pretty sure this wasn't the first scene they had to clean up but what caused him the most heartache was when he overheard one of the officers say to other, "Do you think we need to get the recovery workers in touch with a trauma worker?" Then the other officer said, "Why would they need a trauma worker? They're just tow truck drivers."

Jenna's breath caught at what Joe had overheard. Mac nodded confirming that Joe had heard right. She couldn't wrap her mind around that kind of ignorance and said as much.

As she sat and listened to Joe, an idea started to worm its way into her mind. She made a mental note to run it by Danny when she got home that night.

Every night after her visits with Joe, she'd gotten into the habit of talking things through with Danny. It took some time to get used to being this new, open Jenna, but now she looked forward to sharing things with him. Not only did it bring them closer together, he had fresh ways of looking at things that gave her a different viewpoint.

Jenna and Joe chatted for a bit longer that night. Jenna asked him how things were with his family. His daughter was, understandably, distraught at his attempt to jump off the bridge but she was joining him, on occasion, at his therapy sessions. Just the fact that he was taking his medication as prescribed and was finally getting the help he needed took a huge weight of her shoulders.

His wife, on the other hand, was a hard sell. He knew she may never want to take him back, but he hoped they could at least find some peace and a place where he could begin to rebuild his relationships with his sons. It was a work in progress and Jenna knew it wouldn't be without its pitfalls. But according to Mac, he was well on his way to getting back on his path.

That night after class, she was deep in thought on her drive home. She couldn't get the police officer's mindset toward the recovery workers out of her head. She really wanted a chance to talk to Raff and see if this was just a couple of ignorant officers or if it was the general consensus amongst the officers.

Choco met her at the door before Danny could get to her. He jumped up and licked her face, did his happy dance all over the place with Cara close behind. Danny finally fought his way to the front and helped take her things so she could remove her shoes and get into the house.

My God, I missed this when they were gone, she thought to herself as she took the time to kiss Danny, giving him a proper hello. He had a cup of herbal tea at the ready and followed up the stairs behind her as they she made her way, tripping over the excited pups on every second step.

Danny put the cup of tea on her bedside table and turned back the bed for her while she washed her face, brushed her teeth, and changed into her pajamas. She crawled into bed, propped herself up with pillows, and took a sip of her tea.

As she was getting settled, Danny asked her how her night had been. She told him about the conversation she'd had with Joe and how much it had disturbed her.

"How does one group of people think they have the market cornered on trauma?" she asked Danny. "I mean, I get that police officers see some of the most horrendous things and deal with the worst of humanity, but it's outrageous to me that they would have the audacity to suggest other people don't experience trauma. It's asinine!

"I think I'm going to do my thesis on PTSD. I'd like to research all the occupations and events where people have shown symptoms. What do you think?"

"I think it's a great idea, and if anyone can do it justice, you can," Danny told her as he kissed her cheek, then her shoulder, then worked his way down her arm.

She put her teacup down on her nightstand and slid down in the bed, wrapping herself around him as she kissed him deeply.

Lips still connected, Danny ran his hands down her body. She smiled as she said, "Does this mean this conversation is over?"

"Nope," he murmured, as he rolled her on top of him. "Just postponed."

Chapter 14

Karma's a Bitch

The next morning after Danny left for work, Jenna called out to Sam and Mac. She'd never tried to reach them before; she usually just waited until they showed up, which they always did. Most mornings, Sam appeared after Danny left and Mac showed up willy nilly throughout the day. But today she was anxious to get some celestial feedback.

As expected, Sam popped up beside her. She suspected he never really left, just made himself scarce as the situation dictated.

"You summoned," he said in a deep, creepy voice.

"Stop that!" She swatted at him, laughing. "Yes, I did. I need to talk to you guys about what Joe told me yesterday. I just can't seem to let it go."

As she was talking to Sam, Mac showed up and motioned for her to continue.

"It always surprises me when I hear such a lack of compassion coming from someone who, I guess, I expect to be above it." She was pacing as she talked. "I mean, look at Raff, he's a perfect example of what a police officer should be." She spun to look at Sam and Mac who just stood and waited until there was a break in her thought flow.

"Well, actually, there are a lot of officers who think Raff is the opposite of what a police officer should be." Mac was the first to cut in. "Some of his co-workers think he's too 'liberal,' too soft for the job."

"You're kidding me!" Jenna sputtered. "Being compassionate isn't the same as being soft. I would think it's necessary when you're dealing with society's most vulnerable, no?"

"Unfortunately, the police don't just deal with society's most vulnerable, they also deal with some of the worst atrocities one human can do to another, day in and day out. It doesn't take long for a human to become very jaded," Sam replied. "And you're absolutely right, Jen, about Sean Rafferty being an exemplary police officer. You could even say it's his calling. He has the capacity to be tough when he needs to be, but his instincts are very well honed and he is able to see when compassion is the right call. He really is as honourable and honest as he appears to be. That's because, even though he doesn't know it on a conscious level, he has always been deeply connected to the source of life.

Jenna did a double take. "Pardon?"

"Have you ever met someone who had an extremely well-developed intuition?" Mac cut in. "Someone who always 'follows their gut instincts' and never seems to take a misstep?"

"You mean like mother's intuition?" Jenna asked.

"Sort of. Mother's intuition is a bit different, but it comes from the same general place. But take a look through history. Even now, there are people that seem to function on a much different level then everyone else. You have three-year-old prodigies who can play music that literally makes the angels weep. You have scientists who just know things long before they find the scientific law to define it."

"Are you talking about God?" When Jenna's mother was alive they went to the little community Baptist church on the corner of their block. Even so, Jenna's parents were never as strict or rigid as some of her friends. When her mother died though, John gave up all pretenses and turned his back on religion and everything it stood for and the only time he brought up God was during his rages with his fists raised to the sky.

"Well," Sam began, "most people's idea of God is that of an ancient being with white hair and a long white beard prone to fits of anger. We've given "God" human qualities because that's what people understand and can relate to. I'm sure you've heard the Bible verse Genesis 1:27 'So God created man in his own image?'" When Jenna nodded that she had Sam comtinued. " This is true…ish. Except it's not our physical bodies that are the likeness of 'God' but our spirits or energy. The source of all life is not an entity it is where all life begins and ends.

"What do you mean? is humanity way off base? because *that* I would believe," Jenna said.

"Well, I wouldn't say entirely. Some people have a pretty good grasp of things, while others are so caught up in their fear of the unexplained they just cannot move past what they have always been taught to look at the possibilities. But the truth is this, all of life, is just a fragment of a larger life source.

Jenna put up her hand. "OK, just stop. Is this another Mackayla-is-mom type talk, because if it is, I'm just not there yet."

Sam laughed. "Let me come at if from a different perspective. Think about a light bulb. That bulb is just an empty vessel until it's plugged into a socket. Once it is though, if there is nothing interfering with the current, it shines brightly illuminating the room. If there is interference or a break in the connection it flickers and eventually withers away.

Plants, animals, oceans, sky all exist in perfect synchronicity with the life source. When a human becomes disconnected from the source their spirits flicker and eventually die. These people will eventually lose all ability to connect and will wonder through life spiritually blind. But there are those like Raff who are connected with no interference and they see things very differently. They understand that we are all a fragment of that one source of life. We are ALL one."

"The reason you're so bothered by the insensitivity and cruelty of people like that police officer is because you, too, are very connected to the source. That's where you get the ability to produce such beautiful art and empathize with people the way you do."

"OK, that's all fine, but where does that leave me with this burning need to make this better somehow?" Jenna asked in exasperation. She felt overwhelmed and completely out of her element. She knew she was at a pivotal point but wasn't sure which direction was true north.

"Honestly, Jen." It was Mac's turn again. "You just have to wait to see where it all leads and be open to the possibilities."

"Oh, what kind of cryptic bullshit is that, Mac?! Jesus fuck! That's of no use to me at all!" Jenna exploded, running her hand through her hair in utter frustration.

Mac laughed. "I hear you, sis, but that's how it works. You'll know when you know and not one minute before. Sorry." He lifted his hands in apology.

Sam nodded his agreement.

"Well, that was informative!" Sarcasm dripping from her voice, Jenna stomped off to her studio and the painting she was working on. The hospital had loved the first one so much they'd asked her to do another for the maternity ward.

As she painted, she tried to make sense of everything Sam and Mac had told her. It honestly made her head spin. She just couldn't wrap her mind around it all and she was never good at just waiting for some cosmic sign. She could see the three recovery workers sitting by the ditch, their heads in their hands, in her mind's eye as clear as though she'd been there herself.

With a deep sigh and shake of her head, Jenna made a note to call Raff later in the afternoon. Then she let her painting take her away from the images and information that were making her brain hurt.

She was making good headway by the time she broke for lunch. She found her new ability to see angels everywhere gave her a ton of inspiration, and people seemed very receptive to her new paintings. People were drawn to the idea even if they didn't always believe the premise.

She had noticed that every day she seemed to be able to see more and more angels—not just guardian angels, but her world seemed to be getting quite crowded with beings. Mac and Sam explained that there were a few people who were legitimately able to see through what they referred to as "the veil," but they were very few and were often diagnosed with some mental illness to explain it away.

This was partially the reason Jenna had never brought it up in any of her therapy sessions. Jenna herself still hadn't quite figured out if she was imagining these beings because she needed to or if they were really there, but she did know they were helping her to get stronger and be better and she just needed the idea even if it was a fairy tale.

So she kept it her sacred secret and just laughed when people looked at her strangely if she walked around someone they couldn't see. For the most part, she couldn't always tell the difference between living, breathing people and what she believed to be angels. She knew Sam had wings, but she'd only ever seen them twice, once was with Brenna, the second time was at the cabin on the beach; they were otherwise invisible.

So that's what she painted. Today, she was working on a labour room scene. The mother had just given birth and was lying in her hospital bed looking exhausted but overjoyed as the doctor who'd delivered her precious bundle was presenting it to her surrounded by nurses. The people in the painting were opaque like the scene around them, but for every person, there was an angel. In her painting, the angels were more translucent than the people and the scene and she was able to illuminate them so they appeared as though they were standing in rays of sunlight. The effect should have been cliché but somehow it worked.

After cleaning up her painting mess, Jenna fixed herself a chicken salad, made a cup of tea, and took it all into her office. She had a class that night so she needed to leave a list of jobs for Mackayla who was still coming over a couple times a week to work. Jenna got the feeling it gave Mackayla a break from Julia.

Things seemed to be settling since Julia had moved in with Olivia and Mackayla, but Julia had suffered a lot in her young life and there was a definite adjustment period. Julia needed a lot of time, attention, and reassurance from Olivia and it only stood to reason that Mackayla would get less of her mother. To Olivia's credit, she worked very hard to ensure that the time she managed to set aside with Mackayla was individual and uninterrupted.

For Mackayla, though, Julia was always present. They lived in the same house, went to school together, and because Julia was having a hard time fitting in, Mackayla was her only friend. Her niece never complained, but Jenna got the distinct impression that the time she spent at Jenna's house had become a reprieve for Mackayla and since Danny was always home in the evenings, she got to spend some time with her favourite uncle, who in her fathers' absence filled that void as much as possible, too.

Once Jenna finished her job list she picked up her cell phone and called Sean. He answered on the first ring.

"Hey, Jen, what's up?

"Not much, Raff. I was just wondering if I might be able to schedule some time to pick your brain?"

He laughed at that. "That's some slim pickin'," he said. "I work tonight, but if you wanted to, you could bring me a Papa Burger and a root beer and we could chat over my lunch break."

"It's a date. How does five o'clock sound? I have a class at seven and that should give me plenty of time."

"Sounds good. If I get a call I'll shoot you a text; otherwise, I'll see you at five, food in hand."

"Deal." Laughing, Jenna said her goodbyes and they disconnected.

List completed, phone call made, and lunch eaten, Jenna put her dishes in the dishwasher. As she was closing it, Choco and Cara came up behind , whining to go out.

"I have one better for you, guys. How about we go for a walk instead?"

At the word "walk," the dogs almost lost their puppy minds. They spun in circles and ran to the door, tripping over one another as they scrambled to get to their leashes hanging in the entrance.

"Silly beasties," she said as she snapped each leash on its respective dog and gave their excited heads a pat. Slipping into a pair of sneakers, she grabbed a heavy sweater and headed out the door. They were so excited they almost pulled her off her feet. She didn't usually let them pull, but it had been so long since she'd taken them out she didn't have the heart to reprimand or be too firm. They settled down after a couple of minutes, as they joyfully took in all the wonderful smells of the boulevard.

There was a bite to the air as they walked along—not uncommon for fall in Alberta. Even though it was only September, Jenna knew they could get snow anytime. It likely wouldn't stay, but it had happened and when it did it made for a very long winter.

Spring and fall were the two seasons she loved the most. Spring with its promise of rebirth and new life and fall with all the amazing colours. The oranges, reds, and yellows against an Alberta sky always made her feel so at peace. The summers felt so short here. Albertans crammed as much as they could into them with cleaning, camping, gardening. And because winter roads were often so treacherous, people tended to try and keep their travelling down to necessity, but summer road trips were definitely a thing.

Jenna had always felt a distinct mood change with the fall, almost like an overfilled balloon that was finally able to release some of its air. She always wondered if this season was the human form of hibernating. Preparing for days indoors, running to cold vehicles, scraping ice off windows.

They walked for a good hour, scoping out the neighbourhood. The dogs sniffed every blade of grass along the way. When they got home, Jenna wiped their feet and gave them each a treat, then took off their outside clothes. Checking her watch, she decided she had time to put on a pot roast for Danny and Mackayla. Then she would shower and head for the police station.

Turning the oven on low, she peeled carrots, potatoes, and parsnips and laid them beside the browned beef roast in a large roasting pan. She sliced an onion over the other vegetables, mixed up what would be a rich gravy out of the beef drippings, and poured it over the roast and all. She put a lid on top and popped it in the oven. Then she whipped up a quick salad and sent Danny a text so he wouldn't stop at McDonald's on the way home, which was his usual MO when she wasn't going to be home.

Upstairs, she stripped out of her sweaty, paint-stained clothes and got into a nice, hot shower. She wasn't in a rush so she took her time, letting the steam work out all the tension and aches and pains of the day. Slowly, she lathered shampoo into her hair, then conditioner. Then she scrubbed her body in her favourite soap. Breathing in the smells and the steam, she wondered how a simple shower could feel like the lap of luxury.

She rinsed the soap off with her eyes closed, then opened the shower door and was preparing to step out and grab her towel when she felt fur under her foot. Opening one eye, she saw Choco lying right in front of the shower.

"Buddy, you have to move. You almost tripped me, you silly beast," she said to the dog, who was looking up at her with one ear cocked.

Stepping around him, she grabbed her towel and dried herself. The dogs always suspected something was up whenever Jenna or Danny showered and they wanted to get in on the action. They hated being left behind, but she knew they would only be alone for a little while and when Danny got home they would be ecstatic.

Dried, dressed, and out the door, she was on the road with more than enough time to grab the burgers and meet up with Raff. She loved A & W, especially the onion rings, but she rarely let herself indulge so she really had no problem when Raff requested it. She salivated all the way to the police station.

She sent a text to him to meet her at the door. When he did, he took the bags out of her arms and she followed him to the breakroom. There were a few cocked eyebrows and she was sure he would be met by the Spanish Inquisition once she left, but Raff didn't seem worried so neither was she.

She waved away the twenty he offered and said, "Let's call it the cost of doing business."

He laughed. "That sounds ominous."

Swallowing a sip of root beer, she shook her head. As they ate, she related the story Joe had told her and asked how common this belief was within the police community. As an ex-soldier, she knew military personnel avoided the subject of PTSD like the plague because to have it associated with you at all was career suicide. She also knew it was soldiers coming back from war zones who were generally considered in relation to post traumatic stress.

Raff told Jenna there were those in the department with the same mindset as the officer at the accident scene, but that the department was really trying to get away from that way of thinking. If the powers that be got wind of a situation like the one Jenna described to him, the officer in question could be sent for further education on the subject.

"Do you mind if I look into this a little bit?" Raff asked

"Not at all. But just out of curiosity, would you be able to share the outcome with me? I would be careful to keep names confidential, but I would like to add it to my research."

"I trust you will, Jenna. I'll keep you posted," he assured her. "Alas, though, my lunch break is over and I must get back to the criminal element." He stood and walked her to the door.

Two days later, Jenna received a text message from Sean saying he had some information that might interest her. They arranged to meet for coffee at a local Tim Hortons halfway between Jenna and the station before his shift that day.

Since it was just after the lunch rush, there were very few people when Jenna arrived. For once, she wasn't the first one there. Sean had gotten there first and he sat in a corner far enough away from the three other occupied tables in an effort to keep their conversation from being over-heard. Mac and Sam tagged along behind her as she ordered a coffee and sat across from Sean.

"Hey, Raff, how's it going?"

"Pretty good so far, but I expect its subject to change once I get to work and have to interact with the underbelly of our society," he said, his bright smile and light tone taking the edge off the words.

Jenna knew how much he loved his job and that this was just his attempt at levity.

"So . . . whatcha got for me?" She couldn't bear the suspense any longer.

"Well, you're probably going to want to get your pad and pen. I suspect you'll want to take down some information."

"OK." She drew the word out, intrigued. Reaching for her backpack, she did as he suggested and, once settled again, said, "Let's have it."

"Well, it seems the officers who attended the scene of your brother's accident were Constable Candace Jacobson and Constable Peter Buchanan. Jacobson is a good officer and very compassionate. She was the one who suggested recommending trauma support for the three recovery workers." He paused as Jenna jotted the information down on her note pad.

"Now, please be clear, I only know Buchanan by reputation. I've never actually had the privilege of working with him, but according to the grape-vine, he's not our most shining example of law enforcement and this isn't the first time he's made a poor judgment call or been overheard saying something offensive. Consequently, he is now on desk duty until he can be placed on mandatory sensitivity training."

Jenna looked up from her writing. "What does that entail?"

"I thought you might want to know that," Sean grinned. "Just so happens he's required to go to an intensive weekend PTSD conference to learn about what constitutes PTSD." He held up his hand as she was pre-paring to interject. "Uh, uh, uh, hold on, I have more." He took a piece of paper from his pocket and passed it over to her.

"All the information about the conference is here. It's being held at the Fairmont Hotel in Lake Louise and there are still spots open. It's a little expensive, but if you were interested you could attend and, not only get to meet our illustrious officer but probably get some amazing information for your thesis."

"No way!" Jenna exclaimed. "You're the best, Raff!"

Sean puffed out his chest. "I know, I know, but I never get tired of hearing it."

Jenna just laughed and shook her head.

As they finished their coffee, she asked how things were going on the Olivia front. He blushed a little but said he was making headway. Jenna knew that meant he was at Olivia's house more than he was home.

She and her sister-in-law had a standing lunch date again and she kept Jenna filled in on the relationship front. Jenna just liked tormenting Sean because he was so easy to rattle when it came to Olivia.

When they parted ways, Jenna quickly ran a few errands. She was anxious to get home and look into the conference. When she looked it up on line, she saw that Sean was right. There were still plenty of spots left open. He was also right about the cost. It was very expensive. It was a three-day event running Friday to Sunday, but she would need to drive up on Thursday to check into the hotel and get the itinerary.

As excited as she was to register, she knew she needed to talk to Danny about it first. The funds would have to come out of their vacation account and she couldn't just arbitrarily make a decision like that without his OK. So when he came home from work that night, she could barely wait until he had his shoes and coat off before launching into her meeting with Sean, ending with what he thought about her going to the conference.

Danny laughed at her exuberance and said, "I think you'd better hurry up and book it before it's too late." He pulled her into a hug. She kissed him warmly, then bolted for the computer that was already on the webpage and finished her registration.

The conference was still three weeks away and Jenna didn't think it would ever come. Finally, just after lunch on her travel day, she loaded up her car and headed for the mountains. It was about a four-and-a-half-hour drive, so she would be there just before dinner and the information session wouldn't be until 7p.m. She would have lots of time to check in, freshen up, and grab a bite before heading for the conference centre.

The trip itself was a blast, with Sam and Mac as her travel buddies, singing to the radio stations until they cut out, then fighting over who got to pick the next one. Other than their angelic antics, the trip was uneventful and went by quickly passing the incredible mountain scenery that, no matter how many times she'd seen it, took Jenna's breath away.

There was a valet waiting as soon as she drove up to the hotel. Her bags were whisked away and she was directed to the check-in desk with quick, friendly efficiency. Once her bags arrived, she was able to have a quick shower and change out of her travel clothes. Then she headed back downstairs for a light dinner at the hotel restaurant/bar. As she ate, she watched other patrons check in and tried to guess which, if any, were Buchanan. She tried to get Mac or Sam to tell her but they refused, saying she would know soon enough.

By 6:45p.m., she was settled in the conference room as the staff buzzed around her making final preparations. She knew it was a husband-and-wife team who were holding the conference and that this was the third one they'd put on, the first two conferences having received very high reviews. She was excited not only to get a bead on this Peter Buchanan person, but to learn more about PTSD itself.

The facilitators arrived just as the other attendees started to funnel in. As people took their seats, Jenna once again looked for anyone who might look like the picture of Buchanan she had created in her mind. By 7:05, every seat was taken but one. As they checked the names on the sign-in sheets with their list, the facilitators agreed to wait until 7:15 p.m. If the last person still hadn't arrived, they would start assuming they were a no-show.

At 7:10, a man in his late thirties strolled into the conference room. Jenna nodded to herself, thinking this had to be Buchanan, especially as she noted the hostile look on his face as he made his way to the last seat left, which just happened to be dead centre, front row.

Jenna was seated one row behind him and off to the left, the perfect position to study him without being obvious. She tried to pay attention to all the dynamics, but Mac was driving her crazy as he stood behind her, laughing uproariously. Placing her arm on the back of her chair in a feigned relaxed position, she gave her elbow a little nudge, catching Mac in the midsection. He stopped his laughing but was still grinning like the Cheshire Cat when the facilitators took to the podium and introduced themselves.

"Good evening, and welcome to our third PTSD conference here in beautiful Lake Louise. My name is Pamela Simmons and this is my husband, Rick. We're not going to take up too much of your evening as many of you have travelled a long way and are, most likely, exhausted. But we will ask you all to fill out your name cards and, if we could, to introduce yourself and tell us where you're from. Let's start with you." Of course she pointed at Peter Buchanan whose facial expression had changed from solemn to shocked during Pamela's introduction.

Jenna whispered quietly to Sam and Mac, "What's going on?"

"It would appear that your facilitators for this weekend are none other than two of the recovery workers who worked the scene of my accident, and Officer Buchanan has been ordered to spend the entire weekend being schooled by them. Karma really is a bitch."

Chapter 15

True Story

Jenna's mouth was still agape when it came her turn to introduce herself. She recovered quickly and responded automatically, her mind still befuddled with this new information. People were starting to rise and amble out of the room by the time she got her wits about her. While some of the others stopped in the bar for a nightcap, she headed straight to her room to grill Mac and Sam about this turn of events. She started asking questions before the door was shut behind her.

"What the fuck, guys? I know you knew about this. One of you is an angel and the other," she glared pointedly at Mac, "is a ghost. So why didn't either of you give me a heads up?"

Sam was the first to speak up.

"We're not allowed to tell you everything all the time, Jen. You have to trust that when the time is right you'll know everything you need to if you keep your mind open to the universe around you."

"Well, fuck you, too," she vehemently replied, frustrated at being caught so completely unaware.

Sam laughed at her colourful response.

"Wait till tomorrow. You'll get the entire story and it's a good one." This was Mac's contribution and no amount of cajoling or coercing could get either one of them to budge.

"Fine," she hurrumphed, and preceded to get ready for bed. It was already after 10 p.m., and breakfast was served at 6 a.m. with yoga at 7:30.

After all the hours sitting in a vehicle, Jenna definitely wanted to catch the yoga class.

While she snored softly, Mac and Sam hung out with the other Fairmont ghosts. It was almost a reunion of sorts, even though they hadn't known one another in life. The Fairmont ghosts were always happy to entertain. Since the hotel was busy most of the time, the ghosts were used to the angels that accompanied all the guests and staff members, but ghosts weren't as common. Mac being, well, Mac, was the life of the party.

Sam wouldn't stray far from Jenna, but Mac let them show him around the hotel and regale him with stories of the pranks they'd pulled on the staff. They didn't bother the guests too much but sometimes a sensitive soul would check-in and they just couldn't resist having some fun; after all, unlike Mac, who could travel the world, they were trapped at the hotel. When Mac asked why they were trapped, he learned that some of them had been so obsessed with the hotel in life and loved it more than life itself. They were sentenced to stay there until they learned what was of real importance. Mac noted there were some slow learners amongst them, judging by the age of their clothes.

Others were victims of terrible tragedies, from horrific accidents to murder. These ghosts had their own karma to work out, each one with a different lesson to be learned as to how they got to the place that ultimately led to their dismissal from life.

Mac joined in on a few of their pranks, but made it very clear his sister was off limits.

"We would never. We're not allowed to bother humans like your sister," the charge ghost assured Mac.

"What do mean 'like my sister'?" Mac asked.

"She's marked. She's special and one day she will help ghosts like us find our way to our next stage, just like she's doing with you."

"Marked? What! Where?"

"When you look at her all you see are her scars and wounds. You're too close to it. If you look past that, you'll see it."

"Now I know how Jenna feels," Mac replied.

Jenna woke at 5:30 the next morning feeling refreshed and eager to get the day started. She was very curious to see how things would play out in the conference. She knew none of it was random; it had all been carefully orchestrated and the players carefully maneuvered, herself included.

After a quick shower, she dressed in her yoga gear and headed down for breakfast. Breakfast was light—a coffee, some yogurt, and fruit—then it was off to the yoga class. Out of her eighteen classmates only six showed up for the yoga. She couldn't say she was disappointed by that. She hated trying to move into the poses bumping into people, struggling to work around them. The small intimate group was definitely welcome. The instructor was knowledgeable and the routine was simple but effective. By the time the class was over, Jenna felt very zen.

The class was only an hour long, so Jenna had an hour to run to her room and change for the conference. As she was changing into her jeans and a long-sleeved T-shirt, she noticed Mac kept studying her like she was some sort of science experiment. Finally fed up with feeling like a bug under glass, she turned to him and said, "Jesus, Mac, what's up with you today? Why are you staring at me?"

He was so intent, looking for this special mark that was supposed to be on his sister, he jumped when she busted him. He'd asked Sam about it when he got back from his romp with the other living challenged, but all Sam would say was that all he had to do was look.

Mac shot him a glare then went to examine his sister.

Giving Sam a belligerent look, he said, "Apparently, you have some special mark that other ghosts can see but it seems I can't."

She gave him the raised eyebrow look and said, "Really?"

"Um hum."

"And just what does this mark signify?" she asked.

"That you're some sort of ghost helper," Mac replied.

"Well, knock it off already!" she barked, disconcerted by it all.

Giving herself a shake, she finished dressing and made her way to the conference hall. They'd left their name placards in the spot where they'd sat the night before; she made her way to it and set her things on the floor under her chair and watched the others as they slowly filled their seats.

Peter Buchanan wasn't the last one in the room this time and the hostility from the night before had been replaced with a wariness.

While the participants were getting settled, Pamela and Rick were placing booklets and a questionnaire at each seat. Once everyone was seated, they moved up to the front of the room, this time minus the dais. It was Rick who spoke first this time while Pamela stood back getting a feel for the room.

"Good morning, people. This morning, we're going to start by getting each of you to fill out the questionnaire in front of you. It is only for our conference and will not be kept or used for any other purpose, so please be completely honest. You're not required to put your name on in it as it will be kept completely confidential. Once you're finished, put it on the table face down." He motioned to a long table filled with brochures, pens, pins, and pamphlets of all sizes on PTSD.

People had already started filling out the papers before Rick finished talking. There were 100 multiple-choice questions, so it took a while to finish. When the last person did and placed their paper on the table, Rick started talking about how he and Pamela ended up becoming psychologists who specialized in post-traumatic stress.

"As Pamela mentioned last night, this is our third conference on trauma and its long-term effects," he started. "Previous to this, our lives were very different. Pamela started off as a physical education teacher and I worked on a large mixed farming operation with my parents. We built a house not far from my parents and, for fifteen years, we eaked out a living."

Pamela stepped up. "It didn't take long to become disillusioned with our education system. My first struggle was with the jocks who didn't think a female teacher could give them the direction they needed to excel in the competitions, then there were the kids who found phys ed more of a gauntlet and just wanted to put their time in and get their credits for graduation. These were the kids I wanted to reach. I wanted them to learn to love fitness and sports. Alas, it was an uphill battle and any new thing I attempted to implement was met with disapproval from the school board. They didn't like change. I pushed that boulder uphill for fifteen years and, finally, sick, exhausted, and burned out, Rick and I agreed that the only choice was for me to quit and work the farm with him. Every summer I helped drive our harvest to sell so I was fully licensed to operate our 18 wheeler. It just made sense."

"I loved working the farm," Rick said. "I fully expected to inherit it and carry on. But what I didn't know was my parents had never recovered from the collapse of the cattle industry in the '90s. They were over-extended and could no longer keep the farm running. Our only viable option was to sell. We were devastated.

So, to keep a long story short, we sold the farm, my parents moved into a small house in Colinton, and we moved to the city where we were able to get work in heavy equipment recovery. It was crazy hard work but I think I can safely say we both loved it. Unfortunately, we often had terrible accidents to recover and after a while, it started to take its toll."

Pamela stepped up. "We simply weren't mentally prepared to deal with the things we were encountering. Then seven years ago, one accident in particular changed the direction of our lives—and here we are now."

Jenna could see that Buchanan's relief was almost palpable when Pamela stopped her story. But it didn't last long when one of the others piped up and asked them to share what happened.

Pamela went on to say, "The accident was horrific by any standards, and the trauma to myself, Rick, and a fellow co-worker was undeniable. But the most important event of that day was overhearing one police officer telling his partner that, and I quote, 'They are just tow truck drivers—why would they need trauma assistance?'"

Buchanan quickly looked down at the desk as his face glowed vibrant red.

Someone gasped at the audacity of the remark and total lack of empathy. Jenna held her breath.

Pamela carried on. "Rick and I looked at one another and knew this was another moment in time when our lives would take a sharp turn. We just didn't quite know how. We both really struggled with the idea that there was so much ignorance around the idea of who could suffer trauma and what trauma meant. So we did the only thing that made sense. We quit our jobs, enrolled in university with our area of interest being PTSD, and the rest, as they say, is history."

After the introduction, the Simmons went into detail about the many different types of PTSD and the wide variety of symptoms that went with them. They explained that anyone could suffer any one of the forms of

PSTD. It was no longer a soldier's disease. Under the right circumstances, anyone could be affected by trauma. Of course, it was very common amongst soldiers, police officers, nurses, doctors, paramedics, and, yes, even recovery workers.

When the day ended, Jenna was overwhelmed with the information. She'd done her best to take detailed notes while keeping an eye on Peter. She'd stopped thinking of him by his last name as she watched him systematically unravel. It was probably not noticeable to anyone else at the conference, but because she was studying him so closely, she could see the strain around his eyes and mouth as the Simmons described the symptoms of PTSD and the slow descent if it wasn't acknowledged and treated.

There just might be hope for this guy yet, she thought to herself.

As she was leaving the conference room, a couple of the others asked her to join them for dinner. She'd chatted with them a bit during the breaks and they seemed really interesting, so she agreed. It turned out they worked together as trauma nurses and were also, very apparently, really good friends. Jenna had a blast listening to their colourful stories and quips. She couldn't remember when she'd last laughed so much.

It was well past 10 p.m., when she finally excused herself and headed up to her room. Stripping down, she got in the shower and stood under the hot spray for a good thirty minutes, letting the events of the day wash down the drain. After drying herself off, she didn't even change into pajamas, she just wrapped herself in a fluffy hotel towel and crawled under the clean sheets. She was asleep before her head hit the pillow.

The next morning was much the same: breakfast, yoga, change, conference room. This time though, the tables had been removed and the chairs placed in a circle. She stopped as she entered the room, unsure where to sit.

Pamela laughed and said, "Just sit where you feel comfortable."

Jenna chose the very back seat so she could watch everyone as they came in. She snickered to herself as they all had the same reaction she did.

This time, Rick and Pamela sat in the circle with everyone else. Pamela started things off.

"So as you've noticed, we're changing the format today. Yesterday, we filled your head with our story and information about PTSD. Today, we are going to learn about each other."

Everyone groaned. No one liked being vulnerable or put on the spot so this was always uncomfortable.

Rick reached under his chair to grab the envelope of papers he'd brought in with him.

"Let's start by going over the questionnaires you did yesterday. How many people out of this group do you think tested with possible symptoms of PTSD?" He waited for someone to respond.

"Fifty percent." A guess from one of the trauma nurses.

"Nope, anyone else?"

No one responded.

"It might surprise you—or not—but 100 percent of the questionnaires showed signs of possible trauma. Of course a diagnosis requires more than a questionnaire, but every single one of you could, potentially, suffer from PTSD."

Jenna balked at this. As much as she trusted and respected Denise, she simply didn't agree with her diagnosis of complex post-traumatic stress disorder. She knew she'd had some challenges, but while she was in the military, she'd worked with people who had a legitimate reason to suffer PTSD. She didn't believe she'd suffered anything that would warrant a similar diagnosis.

When Rick came out with this information, she became very guarded as, she noted, did the others seated in the circle as they all started to exclaim and deny.

Rick held up his hand and said, "Hold on, hold on. Let's not get our hackles up. This is a very common reaction, but let's just keep an open mind."

Everyone quieted down.

"Now, if you'll notice," Pamela said, "I've written a list of PTSD symptoms on the flip chart. We're going to go around the room and each of us is going to share a little bit about why we came. Then I want you to go up to the flip chart and check off the symptoms that relate to you, if any."

Another groan from the room.

"Let's start with you, Shakira." Pamela pointed to a very pretty woman in her thirties who had been very quiet throughout the conference and kept to herself.

With a sigh, she started her story. She had been a Syrian refugee. She told her story of fleeing her war-torn homeland only to be met with racism and hatred in her new adopted country. She talked about her children being targeted and how she feared every time her young son left the house he would not come home. She talked about having nowhere else to turn; she couldn't go back to Syria and her new country hated her.

Tears streamed down her face as she told her story and when she got up to put her check marks on the list, Jenna noticed she checked every single symptom. Jenna thought no one else could possibly top that, but it turned out she was wrong.

She heard stories that day of abuses against children she couldn't even try to comprehend; of brutal rapes, murders, and horrific accidents. Then Jenna realized there were only two more stories to be heard, Peter's and hers. Peter went first.

He cleared his throat. "The first thing I feel I have to confess is that I was the officer at the accident scene you and your husband attended. I'm the one who made that ignorant, uneducated comment."

He looked at Pamela, then Rick. "You're right about me and, actually, that's why I'm here. I didn't come of my own accord. I was suspended for that lack and ordered to attend this conference and, boy, was I pissed! I came here because I had to get back to work but thanks to two people I refused to offer assistance seven years ago, I'm leaving here with a whole new perspective."

Then it was like a dam burst, and he talked about how he grew up in an average, middle-class home with a loving mother and an attentive father and how one career day at school a police officer came in to talk about his job. Peter knew right then and there that this was what he wanted to do with his life. His parents were very encouraging, and supported him as he worked toward his goal.

He'd worked hard and made it to top candidate then got his first assignment with the Edmonton City Police Service. It wasn't long though before the shine wore off the badge and he was exposed to things for which his happy, middle-class life could have never prepared him. It also didn't take long for him to learn that you didn't show weakness to anyone and that no one was your friend. You had co-workers and partners, but you didn't have friends. He'd seen other, seasoned officers come apart from the things they had to see and do and he'd seen how quickly their so-called friends scattered like rats on a sinking ship. He'd seen too many of them self-destruct. It had made him bitter and cynical and so fucking angry! He'd completely lost all sight of the reason he'd become a police officer in the first place.

"Then I got called out to an accident where some self-centred, self-entitled piece of shit decided to take the coward's way out and become another fucking mess to clean up. I prayed when I got out of my car that day. I asked, please God, don't let this be another nightmare I can't unsee. He didn't listen."

Jenna saw red at Peter's description of Mac's accident and she wasn't the only one. Rick and Pamela also took exception and Pamela said as much.

"Look, Peter, we really appreciate your honesty and opening yourself up to the process, but I would challenge you to ask yourself what brought the victim of that accident to that particular end. And please remember: you're talking about another human being. Someone who had people that loved him."

Peter mumbled something under his breath then got up and put his checkmarks on the flip chart.

Now it was Jenna's turn. She was still trying to get her temper under control so it took a minute to form a sentence. Sam's hand was firm on her shoulder and Mac just smiled at her in encouragement.

"Well, I have to admit when I signed up for this conference I was in for more than one surprise. You see, I'm a successful artist who had a complete breakdown. Even though I was diagnosed with complex PTSD, I didn't buy into that diagnosis because I didn't feel like I had ever suffered anything bad enough to earn it." She paused. "You see, I was a soldier, but I'd never seen combat, although I lost my first husband in Afghanistan. Why would I have PTSD? Could it be that seven years ago I had to bury my baby brother after he drove his car under a semi?" As she said it, she looked pointedly at Peter. "He would be the 'piece of shit' you referred to."

When the whole room gasped, she looked around the circle and said, "True story!"

Once again the psychologists struggled to gain control over the room.

"OK, OK, we understand this turn of events has everyone in a bit of a tailspin, ourselves included, but let's remember why we're here." Rick's calm voice of authority broke through the buzz.

Turning to Peter, he said, "Peter, we are very sorry. We had no idea you were the officer in our story. If we had, we would have met with you ahead of time and given you a heads up."

Then he turned to Jenna. "Jenna, I am so sorry for your tragic loss. Again, we would never have risked retraumatizing you." He looked at both of them. Jenna was still bristling with fury and seemed ready to launch herself at Peter. "I think this is a good place to take a lunch break," he said. "But I would ask Jenna and Peter to stay back. Everyone else, be back in ninety minutes, starting now."

Most people were good about vacating the scene but there were a few stragglers who couldn't resist trying to listen in. Pamela ushered them out, then shut and locked the door. Moving four chairs across from each other, Pamela sat beside Jenna and motioned for Peter to sit across from her, beside Rick. Both were watching Jenna closely for any sudden movements, but they needn't have worried; Sam had his hand firmly on her shoulder.

"Jenna, tell us about your brother," Pamela started the conversation.

"Make me look good, Jen," Mac teased, encouraging her to speak.

Jenna looked Peter in the eye and said, "He was my best friend, my partner in crime, my defender. If he loved you he never, ever let you down; that is, until he did."

Jenna talked about the boy, the adolescent, and the man. Bringing him to life in such a real way, she had all three members of her audience enraptured, tears streaming down their faces. When she was done, they all sat in silence, taking in the picture of the man they'd only been able to see as a tragic accident.

As Jenna was telling her story, she refused to look at Peter. Now a loud hiccup brought her attention back to him. She was shocked to see his body wracked in sobs, his shoulders shaking violently. His guardian angel wrapped him in his wings and Rick had an arm around him, passing tissues to him, one by one.

Pamela started talking in a quiet, soothing voice. "When we're met with these terrible events day after day, it's a defence mechanism to depersonalize, but at some point we have to allow ourselves to see the humanity in it or we become very damaged and jaded, even dead inside. I know for me, cleaning up accident scene after accident scene felt like I was carrying a huge burlap sack over my shoulder and every scene was another rock of sadness dropped into that sac until I couldn't carry it anymore."

While Pamela was speaking, Peter managed to get himself under control. Turning to Jenna, he said, "I am so sorry for what I said. I didn't mean those things. I was just so angry and, honestly, I couldn't even tell you what I was angry about. I don't expect you to accept my apology—I don't think I would if I was in your shoes—but there it is."

Jenna looked at him for a long moment, then said, "I appreciate your apology and I accept it with the sincerity intended. Having said that, I have to point out that you are in a very unique position to truly help people. Get the help you need, Peter because, trust me when I say, life on the other side of trauma is worth it."

With only thirty minutes left until the others returned, they got up and replaced the chairs. As they were headed to grab a quick sandwich, Jenna stopped Peter out of earshot of the Simmons and said, "By the way, if I ever hear you call my brother a piece of shit again, I will fuck you up and you can take that to the bank!"

Chapter 16

Can't Win Them All

The rest of the conference was much less eventful, but very informative. The information Jenna took back with her was invaluable and when she mentioned to Pamela and Rick that she was studying to be an art therapist, they asked if she might be interested in working with them. They were very excited about the idea of adding art therapy to their program. Jenna was too and they agreed to get in touch with them when she completed her schooling.

What was most fascinating to Jenna though, was watching Peter Buchanan's slow transformation. Gone was the angry, surly man who'd started this process and in his place was a man open to change, eager for understanding. Jenna just hoped he was able to maintain the growth he made once he was back in the trenches again.

Mac was relieved to see Peter was headed in the right direction and was even feeling a little cocky when Zadkiel showed up for his next check-in.

"You're doing well, Mackenzie," he said. "But just remember: you haven't done it on your own. There have been a lot of angels working beside you, not to mention Jenna's efforts.

This brought Mac back down to earth, so to speak.

"I'm sorry, Zadkiel, it just feels good to see the people whose lives I've interrupted get back on track, is all. Your right, I've gotten a little ahead of myself."

Zadkiel nodded his agreement.

"So, what's my next assignment?" Mac asked.

"Well, there were two paramedics at the scene. It's time for you to check in on them, don't you think?"

It was Mac's turn to nod.

Mac remembered the two paramedics who'd attended his accident scene. They were the only ones he hadn't checked in on since his return to earth. At the scene, he watched them working calmly and efficiently, tending to Joe's injuries, careful to keep their attention from the rest of the scene around them.

The woman who exited the driver's seat of the ambulance first was obviously the one in charge. Her name was Rita and she was in her early forties and quietly dispensing orders to a younger man in his early twenties. Mac could feel the deep sadness and frustration that emanated from the woman as she quickly took in the scene. Her essence was one of the most unusual Mac had come across. Everyone has a colour or a chakra that dominates and Mac had seen people whose essences were predominantly green, like his sister's. These people lead with their hearts. He'd seen people who were led by their sacral chakras vibrating orange. On the very rare occasion, he'd seen people whose chakras were perfectly balanced. They resembled an iridescent rainbow, shimmering with all the colours perfectly balanced and aligned. These people were usually very old and had spent a lifetime cultivating love and connection with the world around them.

Rita was a true indigo, but her essence was covered with a dark grey that made it look dirty to Mac's eyes. He could see the cracks and fissures that decorated her soul, some very old, some fresh. He watched her hold herself with quiet confidence, carefully moving past the carnage around her to the only accident victim she could help. Even though her outward appearance showed a very capable person operating like a well-oiled machine, her essence showed the weight pressing down on her soul, the weight of having seen too many horrific things had her spirit bent almost in half.

The young man chirped quietly beside her as they worked, making inappropriate comments about Mac's remains until Rita fixed a steely, unwavering glare his way that spoke volumes more than mere words could. Because Mac could see past the facade to the young man's core, he understood his comments as gallows humour that hid the fear that consumed him; he felt no malice toward this boy trying so hard to be a man.

The man/child was barely twenty and his essence was already battered and bruised from the hand life had unfairly dealt him. As a matter of fact, despite the contempt in which Rita held him, Mac could see he had done an admirable job of pulling himself out of the ghetto and rising above the world's expectations. If he could learn better and healthier ways to cope, he would do amazing things.

But Rita was tired, tired of these millennials who expected everything for nothing and appeared to have no regard for human life and suffering. She was one of the oldest paramedics in the city. It was a young man's gig and the job expectancy was ten years. She'd been doing it for almost twenty. She had been just sixteen when she her father died of a heart attack in front of her. As she did everything she knew to do, she was devastated when it wasn't enough and swore she would never be in that position again. If she had just taken first aid when the school offered it, he might still be alive, but she had been more interested in cheerleading and the first aid class interfered with practices. She initially thought she would become a doctor or a nurse but knew from experience it was paramedics who could make the difference between life and death, so that was where she turned her energies.

She graduated high school at eighteen and by the time she was twenty was a fully trained paramedic. Things were different back then, more professional. Paramedics took their jobs very seriously and took their enormous responsibilities to heart. Not like the kids coming up today. She found they had very little respect for those who had earned their stripes and had not only better training, but experience only time on the job could provide. As result, she had become very bitter and her outlook for the future was grim. She was fearful of the day the old guard had to stand down and let these shallow, lazy, self-centred children step up and take over.

The kid fell silent, as they worked together to assess their patient for life-threatening injuries. He had been warned when he read the rotation and realized he was partnered up Rita. She was notorious for being hard and humourless except with her patients. With them, she was kind, gentle, and compassionate to the nth degree. She was the best, but didn't suffer fools lightly. She had no time for her co-workers and kept to herself whenever possible. To his knowledge, she wasn't married and never had been.

She kept her own counsel and God help the fool who tried to get beyond the barriers she kept firmly in place.

Rita was well aware of how the people around her saw her and it suited her just fine. She had a comfortable cabin on an acreage forty-five minutes out of the city where she lived with her two dogs, five horses, and several wild cats. She learned early on in life that trusting people was a fool's errand, that the only thing you could count on is that they would eventually let you down, one way or another, and you would ultimately be left alone. The scene around her only served to reconfirm her beliefs, as Rita was certain the actions of the driver of the car had let an awful lot of people down as she listened to her patient recount the events to the police officer questioning him. As she worked, another chink in her armour clicked firmly into place. She made a decision at that moment that this was the last waste of a life she would witness. She was done. She had nothing left to give. The next morning she handed in her resignation.

Mac was saddened as he thought back to the scene. Rita had just turned fifty and wasn't doing well. Over the years, she had completely isolated herself. She never found another job after she left the ambulance service— she had no need, having invested wisely. Her dad left her the cabin she lived in and, with solar panels, well water, and a wood stove she didn't pay a lot for utilities. She had a few chickens and grew her own vegetables in the summer, preserving them in the winter, so other than the twenty dollars a month for taxes, a few groceries, and gas for her old pickup, she lived well within her means.

She didn't go into the city at all anymore and only ventured into Stony Plain, a small town ten minutes away, once a week to stock up on supplies. Her interactions with the store clerks were her only human contact and she kept that to a minimum. Although she'd managed to convince herself through the years that she was very content with her life, Mac could see past the facade. Under the tough, unapproachable shell was a frail and delicate soul. The hard, concrete exterior hid a soft and gentle interior that could be damaged much more easily than most. Her shell was a necessity for the world she was forced to live in, but the loneliness from years of having no intimate human contact had taken their toll. Rita had stopped growing; her life's purpose was not being fulfilled. She was in danger of having to repeat the lessons of this life over and over until she learned what she needed to in order to move on.

Mac stood beside her guardian angel watching as she moved in sync with the world she had so carefully created. First, she washed out the dog dishes. Next, she filled them with food and water. As she sat them on the floor, she hugged both dogs before heading out the door to feed and water the horses and wild cats. Mac was mesmerized as he listened to her soft, hypnotic voice crooning to the big black gelding who was the first to greet her. She wrapped her arms around his neck and Mac watched the horse lay his head on her shoulder. The connection between the two was beautiful to behold. It was a love so pure, so simple. It was the foundation of life.

Rita allowed herself to briefly enjoy the warmth of her equine friend before turning toward the granary where she filled two buckets with oats. Leaving them outside the fence, she crawled through, pulling the buckets through behind her. All the horses were jousting for position now, trying to get their noses in the buckets. She clicked at them and they backed away a bit so she could make a small pile for each horse. Because there was a clear hierarchy amongst them, she always kept a ration in a bucket for the one at the bottom of the pecking order, a pretty little roan mare. The little mare was very timid so it always took a bit for her to approach Rita. Every morning Rita would wait quietly and patiently while the little mare found her way to her. Rita wouldn't move a muscle as the little mare ate her ration. Rita never forced her attentions on her; respecting her timid nature, she only took what the horse was able to give.

She was a rescue pony. She was found half-starved on an acreage a few miles from Rita's. The family bought her for a spoiled child who had pitched a fit, demanding a horse for her eighth birthday, but after the novelty wore off, the pony was all but forgotten, left to forage for food and water more often than not. The child was cruel to her, hitting her with rocks and sticks if she paid attention to her at all. When she was finally rescued, it was one of Rita's co-workers who asked if Rita would take the little mare, knowing she already had horses, so was set up to care for them. Rita didn't hesitate. She gave the little mare a home and never asked anything of her, just let her live out her life in peace. She was always thrilled when the mare nuzzled her hand when the oat pail was empty.

Once they were given their oats, Rita forked fresh piles of hay over the fence for them, then pumped buckets of fresh water, filling the trough. Her ten acres had a dugout that always had water in it, but Rita still kept fresh water in the trough by the cabin since the dugout could get mucky and the horses didn't always like going down into the mud to drink.

Horses cared for, Rita made her way to the chicken coop where four hens clucked about. She scattered some grain for them, filled their water, then collected their eggs. She usually got two or three so she always had fresh eggs for her breakfast. The cats were the last to get fed and watered. She kept their dishes by the garden gate because they were too wild to come up to the cabin. Only when the animals were cared for would she have her own breakfast. She always believed in making sure they were fed before she allowed herself to eat.

Mac could see the energy of the universe connecting Rita to her animals and the nature around her. It was a beautiful thing to watch and it confused him. Rarely had he seen such a connection. It was common to see it between humans, parents and children, siblings, close friends, and lovers, but it was less common to see it between a human and their environment. When Zadkiel appeared when Mac called out to him, he questioned him about it.

"She's so connected to her world—why does she need more than this?" Mac asked.

"Because she's only connected to this safe world she created for herself. She cannot learn the lessons she needs to, to move to her next level of spiritual growth, without reaching out to the world around her and making human connections," Zadkiel replied. "There's a whole world she has closed herself off to. It's easy to find peace in a peaceful environment, but those who are truly connected can find peace in chaos. That's where we need to be in order to be fully human."

Mac nodded his understanding but couldn't help but envy this woman who had found the peace that eluded him in life. He understood what Zadkiel was saying, but he had longed his whole life for the peace this woman had created for herself. He watched her set her eggs in the old porcelain sink then turn her radio to CFCW, her father's favourite station and hers by default. He saw her stop as she heard an old song. She closed her eyes and let the music fill her soul and take her back to a happier time when she was little girl dancing on her daddy's feet in her childhood kitchen to this very song. She was an only child and definitely a daddy's girl. She'd spent every minute she could with him. Her mother often lamented when Rita would come in the house after being in the garage with her father, in the pretty little dresses she always put her in. Her dress would be covered in grease stains and her blonde pigtails would be full of dust and dirt. No matter how hard her mother tried, Rita looked less like a well-cared-for little girl and more like a street urchin.

Rita's mother was still alive, somewhere. She remarried within a year of her husband's death, which was an injury Rita could never forgive her. Rita left home as soon as she was able and never spoke to her mother again. Her mother's heart was broken, but after years of trying and two children with her new husband, she finally gave up and moved on. But there was always a hole in heart where Rita belonged. How could she explain to her daughter how much she loved her father? How terrified she was to be alone. How she didn't love the man she married, but she liked him and he was steady and kind. But she didn't have to worry about being destroyed if she lost him the way she was, when her soulmate left her so suddenly and completely.

Rita was aware of all of this on some level. She lived with the fear of losing her mother, too, when her father died. For months, her mother wouldn't get out of bed and ate only enough to sustain life. Her hands shook constantly. She roamed the house at nights, holding her husband's T-shirt to her face so she could smell him again. She was devastated when the shirt lost his scent.

Her father's best friend had always been half in love with Rita's mother. It broke his heart to see her so distraught. He started coming by every day, then several times a day. His quiet and constant presence eventually broke through her mother's grief. When he proposed, it was more like a business arrangement than an actual proposal. He gave her all the reasons it just made sense. Her mother had never been alone, she needed him. In Rita's own grief, she could only see it as the ultimate betrayal of her father. A betrayal she could never forgive.

Rita moved throughout her day. She weeded her little garden, walked through the woods, collected wild mushrooms, communed with nature.

Her two faithful dogs were her only companions. She sat on the pier of her dugout and let the sun shine on her face, basking in the warmth, soaking in the sun's energy.

She ate a simple lunch of greens from her garden topped with fresh tomatoes and buffalo mozzarella cheese. Once she'd cleaned up her lunch dishes, she headed back outside where she kept herself busy with the upkeep of her cabin, fence, and outbuildings. Tomorrow, if the weather held, she would take her old black gelding around the perimeter and check the electric fence that surrounded her acreage. It wasn't to keep the horses in but to keep everyone else out. It was the one thing she was willing to splurge on for peace of mind.

She kept a running list on the magnetized white board she kept on her fridge of all the supplies she would need when she went back to town.

After her evening meal, she sat on her porch with an old dog on either side of her, a book, and her dad's guitar. She read for a while, then picked up the guitar and started to lightly strum. Before long, the guitar was joined by the lullaby of the crickets and frogs all around her like nature's surround sound. She closed her eyes and let herself get so lost in the music she was genuinely surprised when she opened them to a dark night. Putting her guitar down, she leaned back in her chair and gazed out at the night sky.

The stars were bright, unrefined by the lights of town out here in her paradise, and it wasn't long before the starlight was joined by vibrant greens and yellows. It didn't matter how many times she witnessed the dance of the northern lights—each time took her breath away. She remembered her father waking her up and taking her out to sit on the porch as a little girl. When she'd ask what they were, he would tell her they were angels dancing.

Mac could feel the peace and contentment that emanated from her soul. He still didn't really understand why she needed to experience anything more than this, but he also knew there was so much more to heaven and earth than he could comprehend. As he stood with Rita's guardian angel, he pondered how to go about convincing her that she needed to open herself up to the world around her. He was so deep in thought he didn't notice her turn and look directly at him until she spoke.

"Who are you and why are you haunting me, spirit?" she asked.

Mac was startled to realize that she could see him and he said as much.

"Yes, I can see you," she responded. "You and many others. But what I want to know is why you've been following me around all day."

Mac suddenly understood her indigo essence. She was a seer. Someone who could see past the veil between the living and the non-living.

"Can you see the angels, too, or just those of us who haven't moved on?" he asked.

"I can see the angels, too, but you haven't answered my question. Why are you haunting me?

"I'm sorry if you feel haunted—that wasn't my intent," Mac answered. "You attended my accident scene several years ago."

"I attended a lot of accident scenes. You'll have to be more specific," she said.

"I was the man who committed suicide by driving my car into a semi. You attended the truck driver. My actions were the catalyst that caused you to leave your job and isolate yourself out here. I can't move on until I make it right."

"Oh?" She raised an eyebrow in question. "And just how do you plan to do that?"

"I'm hoping to convince you to open yourself up to the world around you."

Rita snorted.

"Good luck with that, spirit! Look around you, why would I give this up to go back to a world of selfish, cruel, self-centred people? Why?"

"Because we are communally created. We need to connect to one another to grow and expand spiritually. If you shut yourself off, you can't learn this life's lessons. You'll have to live this experience over again and again until you can."

Rita got up from her chair on the porch and moved to the door of her cabin. She opened it and paused until the dogs that had been watching the exchange between her and Mac got up and moved into the cabin.

"Ignoring me won't make me go away, Rita," Mac said as he followed her into the cabin.

"Why not? I've been ignoring spirits my whole life," she said, then turned to look at him, washcloth in hand. "Look, I've spent most of my life trying to help people in crisis and what I've learned is that most people create those crises. I've seen what humans are capable of doing to one another and themselves. Look at you, for instance. In one thoughtless and selfish act, how many lives did you destroy? I mean, besides your own?" Rita's face was flushed with emotion as she continued. "Let me tell you what I've learned in this lifetime, spirit. I've learned that every action is like a stone being thrown in a pond. You may not see the impact but that stone causes a ripple effect because water is one body. Out there in the world, people are moving through their lives with a singular focus, themselves.

Do you know how many heart attack victims I've attended in my life-time? They have no idea how their actions impact the world around them. They get up in the morning and fill their bodies with garbage that will send them to an early grave only thinking about their gratification, not about the people they are selfishly leaving behind. And if that's not bad enough they feed their children the same garbage, sabotaging their health and perpetuating the cycle.

"Now let me tell you about the drug addicts who stick poison in their arms or smoke it or sniff it. They are so out of their minds they don't even realize they're assaulting the people who are trying to save their lives. That's not to mention the victims of violent crimes, many perpetrated by the people closest to them, like spouses or parents. Then there are the horrific accident scenes. I've seen the worst humanity has to offer and, let me tell you, if I choose to live out the rest of my life alone in this little piece of paradise I've managed to carve for myself, keeping my impact to a minimum, who could blame me? I've done my time, spirit, and if that means I have to come back again and relearn lessons not learned, then so be it." She turned back to the sink and finished washing up.

Mac could see the grey tinge on her essence turn black and he knew she would not be moved. As he turned away, leaving her standing in front of the mirror, Zadkiel appeared beside him again.

"What am I supposed to do, Zadkiel? She won't be moved," Mac asked, deeply saddened by his failure.

Zadkiel put his arm around Mac's shoulder and said, "Unfortunately, Mac, that's her choice to make. That's what free will is about."

As they moved back through the ether, Mac asked, "How do I make amends if she won't let me?"

"All you can do is your best, Mac. You have helped many of the lives you knocked off course, but you just can't win them all."

Chapter 17

The Kid

Mac didn't want to give up on Rita, but Zadkiel explained when the hue on her essence turns black it indicates an unmoving soul. There was nothing more that could be done. With a resigned sigh, Mac moved on. There was still the other paramedic to check in on.

His name was Adam and even though they were both paramedics that was where the similarities between Adam and Rita ended. He was twenty-seven years old now and any evidence of the man/child he'd been at the accident scene was gone. He had matured exponentially, even beyond his years. For all his immaturity in the beginning, he turned out to be a quick study and very competent in his field. Now he was the senior paramedic, shaking his head at the young girl he'd been partnered with.

His partner was a twenty-two-year-old blonde. When he first saw her, he thought it wasn't her intellect that had gotten her through school, but more likely her cute smile or double Ds. *Oh, well*, he thought to himself with a sigh. *Might as well make the most of it.* If she didn't have a boyfriend maybe they could hook up. Never once did it occur to him that she might not be attracted to him. He'd never met a girl who didn't like him, with his wolfish smile and sparkling blue eyes. He was six feet tall and the time he spent in the gym was more than apparent. His face would be described as chiseled, giving him a very masculine appearance but the dimple to the right of his mouth softened it just enough. He had short, thick dirty blonde hair that grew faster than he had time to keep trimmed so as often as not it was falling in his eyes, driving him crazy.

Getting their first call of the day, Adam held the door of the ambulance open as she pulled herself up into passenger seat. He wasn't being chivalrous, just making sure she was clear he would be the one in the driver's seat. He was careful not to let her see him checking her out—the last thing he needed was a harassment complaint. He knew it took just one complaint, justified or not, to end a guy's career. He'd seen it happen too many times to count. He might be attracted to her but he prided himself on being a professional and worked very hard not to let a pretty face jeopardize that. Until he got the lay of the land with her he would keep things at arm's distance.

Mac was surprised to see the difference between the boy Adam had been and the man he was now. If Rita's indigo essence surprised Mac, Adam's violet hues were just as surprising. Violet was the colour indicative of a deep spiritual connection. Spiritual was something Mac wouldn't have accused Adam of being on first blush. He bore the scars of his existence on earth but there was a purity that belied the hard, professional exterior. Mac's curiosity was definitely piqued. He was very interested to learn more about this young man.

They drove to their first emergency scene in silence, Adam navigating the vehicle through heavy traffic with smooth assurance, knowing driving at a breakneck speed wasn't necessarily the quickest way to get from point A to point B. They were notified that it was a crime scene and that the fire department had already dispatched a truck, common practice in these situations. Even though Adam was aware the new girl had been on several ride-alongs and would have been taught the proper protocol for a crime scene, he still went over what was expected. She nodded in acknowledgement.

A police officer was watching for them as they arrived on the scene and motioned them forward. Parking the ambulance beside the firetruck, they quickly grabbed a gurney and emergency kit from the back of the ambulance and moved to the victim, who was lying on the ground. The fire rescue had covered a small, battered body with a blanket and were administering oxygen when they got to her. In seconds, Adam was able to take in a multitude of details as he shot orders at his partner, rapid-fire.

The girl Adam had written off as a bit of fluff responded to his orders with an efficiency that caused him to admit he just might have misjudged her.

They worked in perfect synchronicity to assess the victim, start an intravenous, and get the patient secured on the gurney. The body was so beaten up it was impossible to tell much about it. If dispatch hadn't told them it was a sixteen-year-old girl, raped and beaten, they might have mistaken her for a young boy. At least until they were able to uncover her and do a quick examination of her injuries.

Anyone looking at Adam would never guess how deeply this patient impacted him. Outwardly, he was the calm, cool professional; inwardly, he was horrified and sick. It didn't matter how many years he did this job or how many horrific things he witnessed on a day-to-day basis, he never became immune to them. He would care for this little girl to the very best of his abilities, along with whoever else crossed his path during his shift. Then he would go home and change out of his blood-soaked and (only God knew what) -encrusted uniform. He would take a hot, twenty-minute, shower scrubbing every inch of his body. When he was finished, he still wouldn't feel clean. Then he would dress in a pair of jeans and a T-shirt and head out to his favourite watering hole. Once there, he would drink too much, pick up one of his many girlfriends with benefits—if he was lucky, take her home, and do his level best to erase everything he'd seen that day. The next morning, no matter how hung over, he would get up at six and work out for two hours before breakfast, head for work, and repeat it all over again. The only time his routine changed was on his days off. He always made a point of heading out of the city on his down time and losing himself in the thrill of skydiving, rock climbing, para-sailing, racing his speed bike on the local race track—anything to get his blood pumping enough to silence the images in his mind. Friends had accused him of being an adrenaline junkie. That was an understatement.

Mac could see this young man was a train wreck. For all his outward calm, there was a powerful undertow of fear that motivated his actions. Paramedics worked very hard to keep their minds from going to the place that reminded them that any change of fortune throughout the day could put them exactly where many of the victims they tended were: on some stranger's gurney dependent on them to do what was needed to save their lives.

Adam was an only child raised by a single mother who did her best, but didn't have the skills to teach him how to process these feelings and work through them. So he found his own way and that was running from them. Mac knew at some point very soon that his house of cards was going to come crashing down if he didn't change the trajectory of his life. Mac also knew that his actions were the pivotal point in Adam's life and it was up to him to figure out a way to reach him. Unfortunately, Adam wasn't like Rita or Jenna and couldn't see him, but Mac had a feeling he could sense him on some level.

Mac watched the way Adam reacted when his guardian angel whispered in his ear and, judging by Adam's actions, he seemed to be able to hear him, in much the same way a dog can hear a whistle the human ear can't hear. It was Adam's ability to tune into his angels' whisperings that made him such an outstanding paramedic. He seemed to always know just what the patient needed even before assessing them. Mac thought he would stick around and give it try before he reached out to Jenna for help.

Adam and the new girl, whose name was Amy, had barely dropped off their patient when another call came in. They were sent to a residence in nice middle-class neighbourhood to a forty-eight-year-old woman in distress. Apparently, her neighbours had heard her screaming and called the police. When they arrived, they found her sitting on her kitchen floor in a pool of blood. It seemed she had stabbed herself in the face. As before, the police secured the site, and fire rescue was attempting to dress her self-inflicted wound. But every time they touched her face she would back away, kicking and screaming like a wounded animal. She was backed up against her cabinets now, sobbing with her hands in a defensive position to keep the fire rescue team back.

Adam knelt down in front of her and took her hands. His guardian angel was whispering furiously in his ear and Adam was listening intently.

"Ma'am, can you tell me why you stabbed yourself?" he asked in a quiet, soothing voice.

Her face contorted as she struggled to speak. "Trigeminal Neuralgia."

Shit! Shit! Shit! He thought to himself. Adam knew exactly what he was dealing with and would rather have dealt with anything else. This was a brutal disease that left health-care workers feeling helpless and incompetent because there was just no cure and the pain had been known to drive sufferers to extremes, even suicide. It's why it had been known throughout the medical community as the "suicide disease."

"Have you taken anything for the pain, ma'am?" he asked, still holding her hand.

Even the action of shaking her head "no" caused her face to contort as pain like a lightning strike shot through her face again at the slight motion.

"OK, we're going to give you some morphine just to give you some relief. Then we will take a look at that cut on your face. How does that sound?"

She just blinked her eyes. Adam took this as consent as Amy started an IV. The woman didn't even seem to notice the needle being threaded through the vein in her hand. It didn't even rate on her pain scale.

Adam kept an eye on the deep gash just in front of her right ear. It was bleeding profusely, but he knew if he didn't get her sedated the pain of treating the cut would cause her to lash out. He didn't blame her—he'd seen this evil disease before and really didn't want to add to what she'd most likely already been through.

The morphine took effect quickly and, as her eyes drooped, Adam began working on the gash. As he worked to get the bleeding stopped and dress the wound she cried and moaned in pain, but didn't fight him. The cut was definitely deep enough to need stitches and would most certainly scar, but it wasn't deep enough to do the nerve damage she was trying for. Even though he knew this was ultimately a good thing, he was pretty sure she wouldn't see it that way.

As they lifted the patient into the ambulance, Adam was once more impressed with his new protegé. She definitely lifted her share of the weight. His level of admiration and respect rose sharply as she crawled into the back of the ambulance, gently checking vitals and talking to the patient in a calm manner that communicated kindness and empathy. He reevaluated his initial snap judgment, admitting to himself that she had the foundation to be an outstanding paramedic.

They had a few more, much less dramatic calls: an asthma attack that was managed quickly with Ventolin, a minor heart attack, and a pregnant woman in a fender bender—both baby and momma were going to be fine.

All in all, nothing even remotely in the neighourhood of the first two calls that he kept going over and over in his mind all day.

Shift over, he headed to his apartment on Whyte Avenue, where he quickly got out of his nasty uniform and jumped into the shower. Changing into jeans and a T-shirt, he headed back out and down the avenue to his favourite pub, where he ordered a beer and the evening special. This had been one of those days that he really needed to process. He didn't want to do it alone in his apartment. He needed to be around people, but he didn't want to have to engage. So this was the perfect solution. He could have a couple beers, some food, and just sit and try to make sense of it all, before going home to his empty, deafeningly quiet 600-square-foot box.

As he ate, he thought about the first call. The sixteen-year-old girl, so small she was like lifting a feather. Beaten so badly, she was unrecognizable, and that was just the injuries they could see. He knew she had been raped by multiple men, but that was all the information they'd been given. She'd managed to crawl to a house and cry out for help, but the occupants of the house were so afraid they'd refused to open the door. Thankfully, they'd called the police or the girl's outcome would have been dire. As it was, Adam knew she wasn't out of the woods yet. She had a long road ahead of her. The outward injuries would very probably heal, but the psychological ones would not. He knew that only too well, having been raised by a mother who suffered her whole life from the abuses inflicted on her as a child.

He remembered getting up for school and finding her sitting at the kitchen table staring blankly into space, a cigarette dangling from her fingers, inch-long ash ready to fall onto the Formica tabletop. He learned to be very careful not to startle her. If he did, she would scream and jump a mile. Then it would take forever to calm her down. So he would quietly call out. It usually took several times but his voice would eventually reach her. She would shake her head, pulling herself back from where she was lost in her mind, and come back to the present.

She would smile at him like everything was perfect and say, "Good morning, baby." Then she would stub out her cigarette, open her arms, and pull him into a huge hug that smelled like coffee, cigarette smoke, old perfume, and a hint of sweat. She'd get up, dig out the cereal, milk, a bowl and a spoon.

"You want some toast with your cereal today?" she'd ask. He always said no. She just looked so tired, he never wanted to add to her burden. She would pour herself another coffee, light another cigarette, and commence staring into space. Her hands always had a slight tremor.

He knew she wanted to do and be better. She had every self-help book in print and she'd read them cover-to-cover, highlighting the parts that spoke to her and flagging pages she would go over again and again. She never told him about the things that kept her up at night, the trauma she'd suffered, but he got good at listening to conversations whenever her family was around. They would forget he was there and talk about things that he knew she probably didn't really want him to hear. It gave him some insight and, as the years passed and he entered his troubled teens, it allowed him to forgive her her many failings as a parent.

For all those failings, he watched her work and fight to pull them out of poverty and make a comfortable home for them. He was fourteen when they were finally able to move out of the tiny, run-down condo they lived in to a house in a nicer neighbourhood, much like the one where the lady who had cut her face lived. As a matter of fact, that lady reminded him of his mother. They were both in their late forties and with tall, slim builds. Where his patient had shoulder-length dark hair, his mother was blonde, with a short cut she kept looking neat. She also never wore makeup, whereas the other lady's mascara made her look like a raccoon from the tears that caused white trails through her foundation.

Adam knew he should visit his mother more often, but he found it really difficult to be around her. He couldn't explain why, he just felt the weight of being the only person in her life. She'd never married and most of her family had left or died, so she was alone in the huge house she'd bought for the two of them. He loved his mom and knew he would be devastated if he lost her, but he just wasn't comfortable with her and that made him feel tremendous guilt.

With a sigh, Adam finished his second beer, paid his bill, and walked back to his apartment where he had a few rum and cokes while losing himself in his new video game. He would play and drink until he reached that sweet spot where he could fall asleep easily without being hung over the next day.

That night he had an old reccurring dream of one of his first accident scenes. He had been paired up with Rita. It was her last call out. She quit the next day. In his dream, the severed head was talking to him, telling him not to knock it until he tried it. Adam woke with a start. He sat up bathed in a cold sweat, his heart pounding as he tried to catch his breath. It had been years since he'd had this dream. *Why now?* He wondered, struggling to get his panic under control. His guardian angel was talking to him, soothing him until he was finally able to lie back down and return to sleep.

While Adam slept, Mac had an idea. He noticed a stack of old *Edmonton Journals* sitting by in Adam's recycling bin waiting for the next collection day. He was pretty sure there was an article in one of them could have an impact on Adam if he just looked at it closely enough. Quietly, he went through each paper until he found what he was looking for halfway through the stack. Putting the rest of the papers back in a pile, he opened this one to the page he wanted Adam to see and set it beside the coffee machine.

Adam kept his apartment immaculate, so Mac hoped the paper sitting open and out of place would impress him to take a closer look. He got up the next morning, dressed in his workout gear, and headed out of his apartment for a 10-kilometre run. Forty-five minutes later, he was back to finish his workout with some pushups, sit-ups, and pull-ups. He would go to the gym in the basement of his building the next day and do two hours of weight training. His routine alternated, with a day of weight training and a day of cardio three times a week, giving him one day off.

After his workout, he grabbed a glass of water then went to his bathroom for a hot shower. He put his sweaty workout clothes directly in the washing machine stacked in the corner of his bathroom, with his clothes from the day before, and filled the dispenser with laundry detergent. He waited to start it until he was out of the shower.

As he padded naked back to the shower and got under the spray of steaming hot water, Mac had to admit he was an impressive-looking human. He was sure the statues of the Greek gods would be jealous. In his current state, he found he saw the beauty of the human body in a much different way than when he was alive. When he was living, a man like Adam would have intimidated him. He would have been just one more person Mac would never be able to measure up to. As a spirit, Mac saw each living person as their own style of beautiful art work. Adam was a perfect example of realism. Some people were abstracts, some whimsy, some impressionism—but all were beautiful.

Once Adam was showered, shaved, and dressed, he finally made his way to his coffee machine. It was preprogrammed to brew a cup at the same time every morning. Adam made sure his mug was clean and sitting under the filter so all he had to do was grab it and add a little cream. This morning, he stopped mid-grab.

"What the . . ." he exclaimed as he picked up the newspaper. "How did you get here?" His face mirrored the confusion he felt. He was sure he never left it there but for the life of him couldn't figure out how it had gotten there. He noticed it was the arts and entertainment section and knew for sure he hadn't left it there. He never read that section. Usually, he pulled out the sections of the paper that were of interest to him and put the rest in the recycling bin right away.

Without thinking, he picked up his coffee and set in on the table. As he was adding cream he inadvertently spilled it all over the table when he read headline: "Local artist gains acclaim from tragedy." As he looked at the picture that took up a third of the page his heart started racing. The article was about a local artist who did a painting for the West End Health Centre that was getting a lot of attention. The painting was of a young woman sitting in an armchair with an angel on one side of her and another man sitting on the other. The face of the other man was what Adam kept staring at, knowing there was something familiar in it.

The article said that the angel represented the artist's deceased husband and the other man was her brother who had committed suicide several years before. A chill went through his body as he realized the severed head that haunted his dreams was the man in this painting. Now he was convinced he hadn't left the paper by the coffeemaker. This was too bizarre to be a coincidence. Adam was sure someone was messing with him—he just couldn't figure out how or why.

With a sense of purpose, he headed to his computer and clicked on the security feed. He'd had a camera installed just weeks before when a rash of break-ins were plaguing his apartment building. Rewinding to just after he went to bed, he played back the entire night. When he came to a section of feed when Mac was going through the papers, he stopped. Rewound it. Played it again. Stopped. Rewound it. Played it again. The camera recorded the movement of the newspapers and the chosen newspaper moving through Adam's kitchen to sit by his coffeemaker, but there was nothing else in the feed. The papers had moved of their own accord.

Adam sat for a long time staring into space, not believing his eyes, trying to figure out how this could be real. Then he took a deep breath and continued reading the article because it was obviously meant for him to see. The end of the article spoke of how the artist was now studying art therapy, specializing in trauma in first responders.

Back at his computer, Adam looked her up and sent her an email saying, "I'm one of the paramedics who attended your brother's accident scene. I think you and I are supposed to talk."

Mac smiled.

Chapter 18

Jenna and the Paramedic

That day Jenna got up later than usual. She'd worked late into the night on her thesis, since she had to have it turned in it at her evening class. Her problem wasn't trying to figure out what to write. She had so much information, if she used it all it wouldn't be a thesis it would be a saga. She struggled with what was imperative and what could be left out because, to her, it all felt imperative.

She stretched with a groan then rolled out of bed. Knowing how late she'd worked, Danny had gotten up with the dogs to let her sleep, then shut the bedroom door so they wouldn't come back upstairs and wake her. But after Danny left for work, they laid at the door outside the bedroom listening for the slightest movement. Hearing her rustle, Choco scratched lightly on the door and Cara whimpered. Jenna laughed as she opened the door and braced herself for an onslaught of exuberant puppy loving. True to form, they jumped on the bed, pounced on her, and gave her a very thorough puppy bath. When they finally settled, she headed down the stairs with both dogs hot on her heels threatening to trip her in their excitement. It was as though they hadn't seen her in years instead of a couple of hours.

It was late morning before she got to her emails. She was alone this morning, neither of her celestial sentries in attendance, so when she opened a strange email sent by someone she'd never heard of and read the contents she called out to Mac.

"Hey, brother! How about filling me in on your shenanigans?"

Sam showed himself instantly, reading over her shoulder, but Mac took a couple of seconds to appear. With a sheepish look on his face, he relayed the events of the evening and admitted that he hadn't noticed the security camera as he rifled through Adam's recycled papers. Jenna sighed and turned back to her computer to reply to the email.

She responded that she was free most of the day, but would be in classes after 6:00 p.m. Then she moved on to her other emails. She was a little surprised when Adam responded almost instantly. He wrote he was off shift at 2:30 p.m., and wondered if they could meet for 3 p.m. With a sigh, Jenna shot Mac a look, then replied that she could make that work, adding her cell number so he could text her the location.

Between her classes and her paintings garnering so much attention, she found spare time at a premium. Since she didn't have any paintings on the go and her thesis was finished, she had been looking forward to a few quiet hours today. This meeting with Adam would eat into that.

Oh, well, she thought to herself. *I guess I'd better make the most of the time I have.* Shutting down her computer, Jenna sent Danny a text saying she was turning the ringer off on her phone for a few hours, then she grabbed a novel she'd been dying to read and headed to her lounge chair on the back patio.

It was a beautiful day with the sun shining brightly. Settling into the chair, she opened her book and began reading, the dogs lying in the shade a few feet away. It wasn't long before the song of the birds and the warmth of the sun caused her eyes to droop and she was napping peacefully, like a contented cat, book forgotten.

She woke a couple of hours later, slightly sunburned but feeling more rested than she remembered feeling in a long time. Stretching and yawning, she looked at her watch to find it was just past noon. Thankfully, the sun had moved at some point during her nap, leaving her in the shade so she wasn't as burned as she could have been. As it was, the angry red would most likely turn into a nice tan in a day or so.

Picking up her book, she moved back into the house and made herself some lunch. Once she'd eaten, she took dogs for a long walk. The location Adam sent to meet up with her was a Tim Hortons only about twenty minutes away, so she had time to shower and change before heading out.

She slipped on a light summer dress, put a bit of bronzer on her face in an effort to tone down the red, grabbed her bag and a sweater, patted each pup on the head with a promise to be back soon, and headed out the door.

It was plenty early enough to miss the chaos of the city schools being let out, so traffic was reasonably light. Jenna arrived fifteen minutes early but instead of going in and getting a table, she sat in her car in an effort to centre herself. The past days of painting, school, and cleaning up Mac's messes were taking their toll. Now with the reaction she was receiving from her Angel series of paintings, everyone suddenly wanted an interview. She was struggling to maintain her routine, but often felt like she was on an endless amusement park ride. There were many evenings she still just wanted to lose herself in a bottle of wine, but she was more than a year sober now and couldn't let her hard work be for nothing.

Mac could see the emotional toll helping him was taking on his sister but he also knew it wasn't just his mess she was cleaning up. In seeing the devastation he'd left behind, the universe was giving her a glimpse of what could have happened if she'd chosen the same course. Mac prayed it was enough to keep her from sliding back into that black hole of hopelessness.

Closing her eyes, Jenna took a deep breath and pictured the end result toward which she was working so hard. As she allowed herself to stay in this space, Mac could see a beam of white light emanating from the crown of her head and connecting with the universe around her. In that light, he could see her vision taking form, preparing to become reality. A soft sigh escaped her lips as she came back to the present. She had a small smile of contentment on her face as she got out of her car and prepared herself to have an awkward conversation with a stranger.

The Tim Hortons Adam chose was within walking distance from his work, so he was early. Grabbing a coffee, he found a table in a corner far enough from the other customers so as not to be overheard. He recognized her from the newspaper article as she came through the door. He stood and waved. She smiled and walked over, holding out her hand.

"Adam?" she asked, just to be sure.

"In the flesh," he replied, then realized how that sounded considering why they were meeting. He gave an embarrassed laugh and apologized for the potential faux pas.

"No worries," Jenna laughed. "I'll just grab a tea then we can sit and you can tell me what impressed you to reach out to me."

Ears pink, Adam nodded and sat back down as Jenna placed her order, then rejoined him. While she was ordering, Mac sat at the table across from Adam. He was leaning on his arms studying him, as though searching for some flaw. As Jenna pulled the chair out, she pushed him over and he fell out of the chair. Mac shot her an indignant look as she struggled not to laugh out loud, and he repositioned himself in the chair beside her. Sam took his usual stance behind her with his hands on her shoulders in a manner mirroring Adam's guardian angel.

"So, you were one of the paramedics on the scene of my brother's suicide?" Jenna jumped right into the conversation, seeing no need to waste time. "That must have been very difficult for you."

Inwardly, Adam cringed as he remembered how flip he'd been back then, trying so hard not let how deeply affected he was show.

"I was." He paused. "I had recurrent nightmares for a long time after. I still have them from time to time," he admitted.

"I'm not surprised. That's a pretty normal response to a situation like that. But tell me: why now?"

"Pardon?" Adam's face reflected his confusion. "Why now what?"

"It's been years. Why contact me now?"

Adam hesitated, not sure how to even begin explaining the events of the night before.

"That's pretty hard to explain. Let me show you instead." He pulled his cell phone out of his pocket. The recording of his security camera was already cued as he handed it to her and indicated the play button.

Jenna watched the video of the newspapers moving by themselves as though someone was searching through them. She gave Mac a glare from the corner of her eye and he pretended not to notice. She saw a section being pulled from one of the papers, then it being carefully folded and placed by Adam's coffee maker where it rested until Adam picked it up the next morning.

As Jenna was watching the video, Adam pulled the paper out of the large side pocket on his pant leg and unfolded it to the article it was opened to, when he found it. Jenna saw the interview she'd done a few days previously.

"I see," she said.

Adam looked at her with a frown on his face, then said, "You don't look particularly surprised by all this. I'll be honest, it's not the reaction I was expecting." He was starting to feel like some game was being played at his expense and he didn't like it one bit. "Care to explain what the fuck's going on here?"

Jenna could only guess how he must be feeling considering what he'd witnessed. She could certainly see how he would be suspicious. She weighed it all very carefully before speaking, not sure how to approach it. After a moment, she decided he deserved the truth, even knowing he probably wouldn't believe it. She took a deep breath and started at the beginning. She told Adam about her mother's death, her father's descent into alcoholism, and the battle with mental illness that had ultimately led to Mac's death.

She watched Mac's face carefully as she described her own fight with depression and subsequent suicide attempt and how Mac had saved her life. Mac just shrugged as she proceeded to tell Adam that since that moment she could see and talk to Mac. There was no cosmic rule that said she couldn't tell people about him or Sam for that matter. The only risk was people seeing her as unstable. If she was willing to take that risk, who was he to interfere.

Jenna admitted that it was Mac who'd placed the paper for Adam to see in order to bring them together, so she could help Adam find his way through the traumatic event that still haunted him.

As she told her story she watched all the emotions play out on Adam's face. Anger, disbelief, suspicion, back to anger. When she finished, they sat in silence as he absorbed everything she said.

After a few minutes, his face emotionless, he got up from the table and said, "I don't know what I expected when I contacted you but I can honestly say this bullshit story was not it." With that, he turned and walked out of the coffee shop.

Jenna looked at Mac. Mac shrugged again. Sam squeezed Jenna's shoulders as she said quietly, "Well, that certainly didn't go the way I'd hoped." Then she too left the coffee shop.

Getting into her car, she noticed the time and realized on top of the fact that this young paramedic thought she was some sort of psycho con artist, she was also going to be late for her second-last class of the year. As it turned out late for her was actually right on time for everyone else. Digging her thesis out of her bag, she placed it on the professor's desk as she made her way to her seat.

It was a good thing this class was just a review for the final exam, because Jenna didn't hear a thing. She kept replaying the conversation with Adam over and over in her mind. She'd shared things with him that she hadn't even shared with her psychologist and he'd dismissed her as an unstable nut. Even though she couldn't really blame him considering all things, she was still upset and deeply embarrassed by it all.

Adam was also upset, but anger wasn't the emotion overwhelming him. He was livid when he left the restaurant, but couldn't figure out at whom. Was he angry with Jenna for trying to feed him her bullshit story? Or was he angry with himself for taking the bait? He also understood at some level that the force of emotion he was feeling was more inflated than the situation warranted, but he felt powerless against it.

He knew part of the anger stemmed from the feeling of being violated. Someone was in his home when he was at his most vulnerable, asleep in his bed. Not only did they break in, but had somehow managed to prevent their image from being recorded. And this woman was in on it somehow. They were trying to set him up for some sort of scam. They were trying to play him. Well, he would show them. Instead of heading home, Adam stopped at the Whyte Avenue police detachment.

As he walked in the door he was met by a pleasant-looking officer who was, as his dad would describe him, built like a brick shithouse. He introduced himself and told the officer his story, including everything Jenna had told him. When Adam was done, he showed the officer the security video. The officer's face showed his disbelief as he watched it. When the video was over, he told Adam it was definitely suspicious. He gave Adam the police email address for Adam to forward the recording for further investigation and asked that Adam make a written complaint so they could investigate it further. Adam was happy to oblige, finally feeling some relief as the possibility of retribution began to come to light. The officer assured him they would get back to him when they had more information.

If Adam hadn't been so angry he would have heard his little voice furiously trying to reach him, begging him to keep driving past the station. But Adam was so immersed in his own outrage, he closed his ears completely and, like so many, refused to hear. His guardian angel looked at Mac and shrugged. They would have to let the chips fall and do their best to protect Jenna from the fallout.

The police officer Adam had spoken to was very concerned and frustrated. Law enforcement always seemed to be one step behind the criminal element. They would just get ahead of one scam when they'd be faced with another—and those were just the ones they heard about. Technology was moving faster than they could. The scammers were far better versed on it than the police. He had to admit, though—this one was pretty impressive. Luckily, Adam was smart enough to shut it down before the scammers reached their end result, which he knew was ultimately a big payday.

But why this lady? She seemed to be successful, didn't look like she needed the money. Even though this confused him, he knew criminals came in every shape and size and that it sometimes wasn't about needing money as much as the thrill of the scam. Maybe there was a revenge element to it. After all, Adam was the paramedic who'd attended the scene of her brother's accident. Whatever the story was, he knew there definitely was one. And he planned to get to the bottom of it.

Sitting in front of his computer, his first course of action was to send the recording to the IT department for analysis. Then he began a search of Jenna's name to see if she had a criminal history or any other reason to be under the eye of the law. The more information he found on her, the more things didn't add up.

Not only did she have no run-ins with the law, he found she was a military veteran with an exemplary service record. He also learned that her first husband was a decorated soldier who was killed in Afghanistan, leaving her alone with two small children. Once again, he knew this didn't mean anything, but one never knew the circumstances that could lead to criminal activity and, judging by the story she'd shared with Adam, she had hit some pretty rough patches.

He'd gotten so caught up in his search he didn't realize his shift was up until the next shift tapped him on the shoulder.

"What are you working on so intently, Glen?"

Surprised at the interruption, he looked up at the woman sitting on the corner of his desk.

"Hey, Shelley, a guy came in here about an hour ago with a complaint and it's a doozy." He proceeded to pass on the details and what he'd found so far, then shut down his computer and prepared to head home.

Shelley assured him she would take a look if things were quiet and they said their goodbyes. Glen grabbed his kit and left the building.

Mac knew that if this investigation proceeded it had the potential to derail Jenna's future and that it would be his fault. He knew somehow he had to contain the number of officers who were privy to this complaint and somehow get Sean Rafferty involved. As he was trying to figure out the best way to intercede, he was approached by two nonliving residents of the detachment, who asked what his business was there. They were sure to let Mac know the building was full enough and he would need to find another place to haunt.

Mac laughed and explained his situation. As he shared his need to keep Jenna's information contained and somehow sent to Constable Rafferty, the oldest ghost nodded his understanding and said it could be fixed easily enough. With that, he went over the circuit box and placed his hand on it, shorting out the entire police detachment.

Shelley and a cleaner were the only staff in the building when the power went out. She called the power company and they assured her they would be there right away. Two people showed up ten minutes later and, within twenty minutes, one of them approached her to say the news wasn't good. Somehow the entire circuit box had been fried, almost like it had been struck by lightning, and there was no telling how long it would take to fix it. Shelley contacted her superior and was told they would have to find another detachment to work from. She was instructed to sit tight until they solidified which one had the room to house an extra office for a few days.

She told the cleaner to finish up what he could then to head home. Then she tucked her cell into her uniform pocket, secured the front door, and walked to a nearby Tim Hortons to grab a coffee while she waited for her call back. She sat in a booth in the back and sent the other officers on staff that evening text messages to give them a heads up. As it turned out, the closest detachment with the room to house them was the West End detachment.

Mac asked his co-conspirator, who had just reappeared after a lengthy absence, how that happened. He gave Mac a mischievous grin and shrugged his shoulders. Mac just laughed and shook his head.

Shelley forwarded a group text to all members of the Whyte Avenue office, notifying them of the situation, so when Glen woke the next morning for his shift he had to scramble to get to work with an extra fifteen minutes added to his commute. He rushed through the doors of the West End location, his first task to seek Shelley out and ask if she had had time to work on the case he'd left. With the power outage and everything else, she admitted it had completely slipped her mind. But the mention of Jenna's name caught someone else's attention.

Sean Rafferty's desk was close enough to overhear the other two officers' conversation. When he asked them what they were looking into Jenna for, Glen couldn't see any reason not to bring Sean up to speed, especially because Jenna was technically in Sean's jurisdiction. He gave him the *Reader's Digest* version of events. As the two men talked, Shelley, exhausted from a long problem-filled shift, left them to it. In the spirit of full disclosure, Sean told Glen he may be able to help fill in some of the blanks, but that he would prefer to do it in a more secure environment.

Glen laughed, understanding that even though they were in what should be the most secure environment, it wasn't. Conversations overheard often made it to the outside world and came back to bite people in the ass. He agreed to go grab a coffee with Sean after he signed himself in and got comfortable in his new digs. He signed into his account and checked his email. He'd gotten a response from the IT department but it provided no answers, only more questions. There was positively no evidence of tampering on the security recording and there was no possible way someone could erase themselves without leaving some indication of it, nor was there technology available that could prevent a human from being captured on the security camera. He printed the email and met up with Sean, feeling more confused than ever. There was something really strange going on, he could just feel it.

As the two men settled in a booth, Sean said, "Before we start, I have to be completely honest with you. I know Jenna Walker and her family—very well, as a matter of fact, as I'm dating her brother's widow. I just wanted to put that out there before we start."

Glen was a little taken aback by that information, and wondered, in light of it, how much he should disclose. Deciding to be equally honest, Glen chose to give him all the details and let the chips fall where they may.

Glen was impressed at Sean's ability to keep an emotionless face, as he told him about Adam's complaint, including the meeting with Jenna and the tale she wove. When he finished, he handed Sean the email from the IT department. When he finished reading it, Sean set it face down on the table and leaned back in his chair, looking blindly over Glen's shoulder, deep in thought, his fingers steepled.

In their line of work, waiting out a suspect was a skill they had to learn, so Glen had no problem sitting silently until Sean had a chance to process all the information he'd heard. When he finally returned his focus to Glen, he said, "I don't know what this is all about, but I do know Jenna, and I would be very surprised if there was any sort of scam involved. I would ask though that, as a professional courtesy, you give me some time to talk to Jenna and see what she has to say before you go any further in the investigation."

Glen agreed under the condition that Sean keep him in the loop. Sean readily agreed to those terms and shook Glen's hand and thanked him.

When Glen got back to the detachment, his first action was to call Adam and give him the information he'd received from IT. He told him the situation was still being looked into but they had no proof, as yet, that anything criminal had taken place.

Adam was deeply frustrated that a clear and simple answer hadn't been found, but he still refused to give any credence to the story Jenna told him. This was creating a barrier between him and his guardian angel and Adam was getting less able to hear the angel's guidance every day, until finally the voice went silent. This was the voice that kept him from taking that one step too far, the voice that fed his intuition on the job, giving him the exact information he needed at the right time. Adam's work was suffering as a result.

He found more and more that he froze when he reached an emergency scene, unable to assess or make a decision, and it was costing precious time that was threatening lives. He'd even received his first reprimand in years, since Rita spoke to him about professional behaviour with the crack about Mac losing his head.

Desperate to get his mojo back, he decided to take some banked vacation time and head to his parents' cabin just outside of Canmore. He hoped the mountain air would sort him out.

Jenna was more than a little surprised when Sean showed up on her doorstep in full uniform with a serious expression on his face.

"Hey, Raff, how's it going?" she greeted him as she opened the door and invited him in.

She handed him a pair of boot covers from when she was in the army. It was a pain to unlace the combat-style boots officers and military wore; the boot covers saved her time and trouble, not to mention her floors.

Slipping on the fleece-lined covers, Sean followed her into the kitchen, where she started a pot of coffee. She turned back to him as he sat on a tall stool at the breakfast nook.

"So? What's the nature of your visit, officer?" she said in a teasing voice. A small jolt of alarm shot through her when he didn't respond in kind.

"Seriously Raff, what's going on? Is everything all right with Olivia and the girls? What's going on?" She was starting to panic.

He held up his hand before speaking. "No, Olivia and the girls are fine. I'm here on official police business, actually. There was a complaint filed against you and I need you to answer some questions."

"Fuck! Let me guess, the complaint came from a paramedic by the name of Adam. Am I warm?"

Sean nodded yes then went on to fill her in on the details.

"A scam! Really, this guy contacted me. I didn't know him from, well, Adam, until he emailed me. Maybe he's the one trying to pull a scam. As I see it, I'm the one with the most to lose if this cockamamie story gets out." Her voice dripped scorn.

"True. But, Jenna, did you really tell this guy it was your dead brother was messing with his papers and that you see dead people?"

Jenna didn't answer. Instead, she said, "That's his word against mine."

"Not an answer, Jen!"

She refused to look at him.

Realizing she wasn't going to answer, he took a different tact. "Look, Jen, I'm not the only one who's noticed the weird shit that happens around you. You seem to have an inside track, knowing things that you shouldn't. Now I do believe in instincts and intuition—every cop worth his salt works as much on those things as they do on the tangible—but there are an awful lot of coincidences around you and I'd just like a straight answer. Did you try to commit suicide when you and Danny were separated?"

"Yes."

"Do you see and talk to your dead brother?"

"Yes."

"Prove it."

Looking at Mac who was sitting on the tall stool beside Sean, she asked, "Mac what can I say that will make him believe me?"

Mac shrugged and said, "Maybe ask him when he plans to propose to Olivia with that ring he bought on the internet. Tell him she'll love it. It's very tasteful, but he better do it soon before the baby starts to show."

"Say what! What baby?" she yelled in surprise. Covering her mouth, she turned to Sean. "Seems like you have some 'splaining to do, Lucy," she said, mimicking Ricky Ricardo on the old I Love Lucy show. "Oh, and Mac says propose already. She'll love the ring you bought her."

Sean stared at Jenna in disbelief. How could she know that? Olivia could have told her about the baby but no one knew about the ring. He'd been alone in his apartment when he ordered it and had just received it in the mail yesterday.

Chapter 19

Secrets Revealed

As much as the logical part of Sean's brain told him he was a fool and there had to be a reasonable explanation, deep down he believed her. As unlikely an explanation as it was, it certainly made everything make sense, from knowing Mackayla was in trouble to just happening by Joe Burns when he was preparing to jump off that bridge. These and so many other things Jenna just seemed to know that she shouldn't.

He looked her directly in the eye and studied her for any sign of deceit. He found none. Even if he was having trouble believing everything she was saying, he'd always believed in his own ability to assess people and his instincts told him Jenna was everything she claimed.

With a heavy sigh, he shook his head and said, "Oh, Jenna, Jenna, Jenna! What are we going to do about all this?" Getting up off the stool, he gave her a big hug and headed to the door. She took his hand after he'd peeled off the boot covers and gave it a little squeeze. "I will just have to be whole lot more cautious about who I impart that information to," she said, smiling. "No worries, Raff. It will all work out. Just do what you have to and the powers that be will take care of the rest." It sounded more convincing than she felt. She knew if this was not contained, her ability to work in the mental health field would be in jeopardy. As much as she wanted to believe it would all work out the way it was supposed to, she still had a lump in the pit of her stomach.

When Sean got back to the station he found everyone in a tailspin. It seemed there had been some sort of massive computer glitch and information had been lost. Mysteriously, none of the files of legitimate offenders had been damaged, but the complaint against Jenna and Glen's emails regarding it had disappeared.

Glen was assigned to a new investigation and, within a short time, he forgot all about it.

As soon as Sean was able to find a quiet corner where he wouldn't be overheard, he called Jenna, happy to pass the information on, hoping the knowledge would give her some peace. It did.

Almost a month later, Jenna opened the door to a hollow-eyed, dishevelled stranger. As she studied his face for some recognition it hit her that she was looking at Adam. This time, she was very cautious in her approach to him, stepping out on the front porch instead of allowing him in her house.

"Hi, Adam. What brings you here?"

He was very formal in his response. "Can we talk, ma'am?"

She snorted, "Don't call me ma'am. I work for a living."

He gave her a blank look. She just shook her head and said, "Inside joke, don't worry about it."

Gesturing to a chair on the porch, she motioned for him to sit. Taking the other seat she waited for him to start the conversation. She appreciated that the first thing he did was apologize for the way he had treated her before.

Jenna learned at a very young age that trust was a luxury she could not afford. It was rare for her to offer it up. In the past she would have never offered someone a second chance to betray it in the way she felt Adam had.

She could understand his disbelief, but going to the police with the intention of having her charged with a crime stung. A lot. Giving him an audience was a strong indicator of how much she'd learned and grown over the past several months. But she still treated him with same distance and caution she would a wild animal.

"Apology accepted," she said, keeping her voice cool. "So, what brought about this change of heart, if you don't mind my asking?"

Adam knew he was taking a chance coming to see her. Frankly, he was surprised she hadn't given him the bum's rush right out of the gate. Her willingness to listen, however grudgingly, gave him hope.

Clearing his throat, he began to explain. "Look, I am truly sorry for the way I reacted to the situation. I realize now that it was totally and completely over the top. But you have to admit the things you told me were a little out there. I mean, I know some people believe in ghosts and that certain people can communicate with them, but it's not mainstream thinking."

"That's true," Jenna interjected when he paused. "However, your reaction could have had a very detrimental effect on my career before I've even finished my degree. It felt mean and retaliatory when I was being open and honest with you in order to help you. That hurt."

His face flushed as he looked down at his feet. "I know, and if I'm being honest, my actions were mean and retaliatory. The anger behind them tainted every aspect of my life. I was like a rabid dog, alienating my friends, making mistakes in my job that could have been critical if it hadn't been for my partner. The same partner I initially thought was a piece of fluff who made it through life on her looks pulled my ass out of the fire over and over again. That is until my mistakes became too big to hide and my supervisor suspended me. When that happened, I decided it was time for a trip to the mountains." He paused again.

During this confession, he looked up from his feet and let his gaze rest on a point over Jenna's shoulder, still unable to look her in the eye. Then he continued to explain. "You see, I was raised by a single mother. I never knew my dad so it was just her and me against the world. Her dad left her a little cabin just outside Canmore and whenever life threatened to overwhelm her she would pack me up and we would head there. She used to say when you couldn't hear God's voice for the noise and commotion of the city it was time to head to the mountains. She always used to tell me to listen to that still, quiet voice, because it would never steer you wrong. And if you couldn't hear it, you needed to get somewhere quiet until you could. I knew exactly what she meant because all my life I could hear that voice she talked about—until the situation with you." Another pause as he shifted to get more comfortable in his seat.

"My mom and I stopped talking a couple years ago. She just annoyed me with all her spiritual crap and, if I cared to admit it, I was a bit embarrassed by her. She never really did a lot with her life, always seemed to fail at everything she tried. Actually, that's not completely accurate. She

227

didn't fail, she would just quit and go a different direction, never finishing anything. I wanted her to be someone I could be proud of but that never happened. So I stopped visiting and answering her phone calls. Imagine my surprise when I got to the cabin and she was there."

When he shifted again, Jenna got up and invited him inside where it was more comfortable. She motioned to the sofa and offered him something to drink. He accepted a glass of water then carried on with his story.

"When I saw her sitting on the porch, I was beyond livid. I needed to be at this cabin and here she was in my space, preventing me from finding the solitude I needed to find my inner voice again. I screamed at her, asking her why she always had to be there. I watched the absolute joy on her face at seeing me turn to pain with just a few horrible words.

"As the tears streamed down her face, she said, 'Look, son, I don't know what I've done to you to make you hate me so much, but let's make one thing perfectly clear: this cabin is mine. When I'm dead, it will be yours. Then you can be alone out here. But until *then*, IT IS MINE! I will come and go as I please and you should be bloody grateful I didn't change the locks with the way you've treated me over the past few years.'

"In that moment I felt like a deflated balloon. The fury of the previous weeks just disappeared and left me empty. I looked at my mom, who I hadn't seen in two years. I saw the grey in her hair, the lines around her eyes and mouth. She'd aged ten years in those two and I knew it was due to grief from the rift in our relationship that she just couldn't understand. I stayed at the cabin with her for two weeks. I left my prejudices and anger at the door and opened my eyes to see the woman who'd raised me and loved me most of her life. No matter what I did, she loved me. Yes, she made mistakes, but it's our mistakes that make us human." He stopped and took a sip of water.

As he told his story, Jenna felt herself warming up to him in spite of herself.

He continued. "Not only did I get the opportunity to see my mom as a person, when I got rid of the background noise, I found I could hear that small, quiet voice again, and it challenged me to open my mind to the possibility that, just maybe, what you said was true and even if it wasn't, I had to believe that you believed what you said. And if I really searched my heart I would have to admit that there was no malice in you, nothing to be gained. So I guess what I'm trying to say is, I don't know if you can really see your dead brother, but I'm willing to keep an open mind."

Jenna looked at him for a long time weighing his words. If Mac was still alive, he would be holding his breath for her response. Sam just stood behind her with his hands firmly on her shoulders. She looked over Adam's shoulder at his angel in the same position behind him. He smiled at her and nodded.

"Adam, I'm going to take another chance here and trust you again, even though it's not normally in my nature. If you betray that trust you better never darken my door again—do you understand what I'm saying?"

"Yes, ma'am."

"Stop calling me ma'am."

"Yes ma—. Sorry, yes, Jenna."

"You have your own abilities. Everybody does. Unfortunately we still live in a world where people only believe what's right in front of their noses, despite the advances we've made in science that tell us there are so many things that can't be seen by the human eye. So we ignore our senses and connection with the spiritual realm and eventually lose it. You're a rare human who never lost your ability to hear that still, small voice, the voice of your guardian angel, who is currently sitting behind you with her hands on your shoulders."

Adam held up his hand, stopping her. "Wait, wait, wait. You can see angels, too?" His voice struggled not to show disbelief that would risk getting him kicked out of her house.

Getting up off the sofa, Jenna said, "Follow me."

Hesitantly, Adam did, thinking she was going to show him out the back door. Instead, she led him into an art studio filled with paintings of people doing everyday things and the angels that watched over them. One painting in particular caught his eye. It was him, sitting in the cafe with his angel behind him. He recognized her, knew her the minute his eyes met the canvas. Tears streamed down his face as he sank down hard on the stool Jenna scrambled to place behind him when she saw his knees starting to buckle.

When he was able to get himself under control again, he said, "The angel you painted standing behind me was my only friend when I was a little boy. I knew she was real but my mom kept telling me she was imaginary because she couldn't see her. After a while, I believed my mom and my friend gradually disappeared. And now after all these years, I've finally found someone else who can see her, too, and you're telling me it's her voice I've been hearing my entire life."

"It would seem so, Adam." Jenna's voice was much gentler now as she watched him struggle to take in everything that had happened to him over the past few weeks. She knew what a stretch it was to believe something so fantastic, something so far from mainstream thinking.

He rose slowly from the stool and walked over to the painting. Then he turned to Jenna and asked, "How much?"

"I'm sorry? How much what?"

"How much for the painting? I'll pay whatever you're asking. I'd really like to buy it."

She walked over to where he was standing, picked up the painting, and handed it to him.

"I couldn't charge you for it. It was meant to be yours."

Taking it from her, his eyes welled with tears again as he attempted to express his gratitude.

"Don't mention it," she said. "You were the inspiration behind it anyway."

He gave her a quick little hug and headed to the door, painting in hand. As Jenna followed, she said, "I don't mean to be presumptuous, but there's a group led by some really cool people you might find helpful with all the stuff you've been carrying around."

He stopped at her front door and turned to her. "Really?"

"Yes. They were the two truck drivers that worked with you the night of Mac's accident. Shortly after that, they changed their career courses and are trauma counsellors now. They help front-line workers make sense of all the stuff they see on a regular basis. Would you be interested?"

As he listened to her explanation, his angel was urging him to say yes. He gave Jenna a little smile and said, "Someone thinks it's a good idea so I guess I better say yes."

She laughed and stopped at her office while Adam waited at the door. After rummaging around in her desk for a minute, she pulled out a stack of business cards and handed him one. Jenna stayed in touch after the conference and even volunteered to work with them when she had a bit of free time, which wasn't as often as she would have liked. They'd invited her to work with them for the practicum portion of her studies next year and she was thrilled to agree. She saw the difference they made. The people who had been able to get their lives back on track with their support and guidance.

Handing Adam the card, she said, "I hope we can get together again sometime, Adam. Thank you for suspending your beliefs long enough to give me a chance."

Adam gave her that little smile again and said, "It's you who deserves my gratitude. You don't even know how much your taking a chance on me helped."

Jenna smiled back and gave him another hug before he turned and headed out the door.

She headed back into her kitchen and noticed it was past lunchtime. She fixed herself a quick lunch and, as she ate it, made a prioritized to-do list. Her classes were done now for the summer and wouldn't be starting back up until early fall. That was a huge chunk of time she could use for her much-neglected art.

Mackayla was still working for her a few afternoons a week and was scheduled to come by that day. They had talked about her working with her aunt on a more full-time basis once her classes finished, but still hadn't solidified anything, so Jenna made a note to discuss that with her when she got there.

Olivia still hadn't mentioned the baby or an engagement to Jenna and Jenna hadn't asked. Their friendship was built on respecting one another's boundaries, so Jenna wouldn't press until Olivia was ready to share. Which meant she didn't question Mac about her sister-in-law's business and he didn't share unless it pertained to something he needed Jenna's help with. So Jenna knew when Mac popped in on her that the afternoon wasn't going to go the way she planned.

With a sigh, she asked, "What now, Mac?"

"What do you mean?" he said, feigning hurt feelings. "Can't a brother just pop in and see his beautiful sister?"

"Not if the brother is you," she retorted.

"Ouch! That hurt." But the smile on his face belied the statement.

"I do have a life, Mac, and as it turns out it's a very full life. So can we stop the theatrics and get on with what you need from me?"

The smile left Mac's face as he told her why he was there. "Mackayla is having a tough time of it again," he said. "Olivia told her about the baby and Sean's marriage proposal and Mackayla didn't handle it well. That's why no announcements have been made. Not even Julia knows yet, but she certainly knows something's up and she's blaming herself. Julia thinks Mackalya is upset because of her."

"Shit!"

"Right."

"Sean doesn't understand. He thinks if Olivia really loved him she would go ahead with the wedding plans. He feels like Mackayla will eventually come around. He's ready to call the whole thing off. It's a pretty huge mess right now."

Holding up her hand to stop his verbal vomiting, she said, "Stop, I get it. I'll see if I can get Mackayla to confide in me then we'll go from there. OK? Now just leave me alone for a couple of hours so I can sort out my own life." She shot him a pointed look.

With his sister's assurance, Mac smiled, kissed her on the cheek, and disappeared again. Jenna sighed and rubbed her hands over her face. She got up and started clearing away her lunch mess, then headed for her studio to work on another commission. She had slowed down on her commissions and gallery showings while she was taking classes, but had scheduled a few for the summer break. This one was a piece for a private residence and she was almost done. A couple of productive hours would see it complete.

Even though Mac had taken off to do his Mac things, Sam loved watching her work and was her biggest fan. She loved talking to him as she worked and often got his advice on a painting. He would guide her in knowing what would be perfect and where, even challenging her to expand her experimentation with her colour combinations. And he always told her just when to stop. That was the hardest part of working on a piece, finding that sweet spot when the painting was perfectly finished, not stopping too soon or going too far.

She also had a habit of talking her problems through with Sam as she worked and today was no different. It broke her heart to think things were going so sideways for Olivia and Mackayla. They deserved some happiness for a change.

When Mackayla came in that afternoon, Jenna was so intent on finishing the painting and talking to Sam about the situation with her niece and sister-in-law she never heard her come in. When Mackayla first started working with her, Jenna had given her the code to her door so she didn't have to stop her work to let her in.

Normally, Mackayla would have stopped in the office to check on emails and supply orders, but when she heard her aunt talking to someone in her studio, she headed back to investigate. Stopping at the door, she couldn't see anyone other than Jenna. Listening a little more intently for a second voice, she heard Jenna talking about her, her mother, the baby, and Sean's proposal. No one was supposed to know about those things. Who did she know and who was she talking to about something so personal and private to Mackayla.

She was furious when she burst into the room where Jenna sat on a stool, putting the finishing touches on her work. Sam's quick warning came an instant too late as Jenna's brush jerked, startled by the interruption ruining the painting she been working on for weeks.

"What the hell, Mackayla!" Jenna barked, grabbing for a damp cloth to try and minimize the damage. "Why would you come into my studio like that?"

Normally, Mackayla would have been devastated that her aunt was barking at her but this time she was too upset to even notice.

"Who were you talking to about me and my family and what right do you have to talk about things that you shouldn't even know about!?" Mackayla yelled back.

Stunned, Jenna stopped what she was doing and stared at her niece, trying to figure out to what she was referring.

"What are you talking about, Mackayla?" Her voice was firm but no longer held the previous anger.

"I heard you. You were talking to someone about stuff Mom said she never told you yet. Mom promised she wouldn't tell anyone about the baby and Sean until I was ready. Did she lie to me? Did she tell you?" Mackayla's face was red and angry tears were forming.

Understanding dawned on Jenna as she realized that Mackayla must have overheard her talking to Sam. Mac must have sensed the upheaval. Popping back into Jenna's view, she jumped and shrieked, unable to hide her startle response. "What the fuck, Mac!" she yelled without realizing.

Mackayla went deathly quiet as she stared at her aunt who was glaring at an empty space. "Auntie Jen, what's going on? Who are you talking to?" Her voice was much quieter now, sounding like the frightened little girl she was.

Realizing her faux pas far too late to repair the damage, Jenna said, "I was talking to your dad, Mackayla." Having gone this far, Jenna thought she may as well go the distance. She continued. "Look, your mom didn't tell me anything. When you came in I was talking to my first husband, Sam. It turns out he's my guardian angel. The reason I know the things I know is because I can see and talk to angels. And your dad, as it turns out. I know that sounds hokey, but it's the truth. No one betrayed your trust."

Jenna didn't know what she expected, but what she didn't expect was for Mackayla to let out a shriek of laughter and launch herself into Jenna's arms, jumping and dancing like a kid who had gotten their first pony.

"I knew it! I knew it! I knew I wasn't crazy!" Jenna just looked at her with one eyebrow cocked. "He leaves me things and plays our favourite song, doesn't he? I always felt like he was with me. He was, wasn't he?"

Jenna looked at Mac. He nodded his affirmation.

"Yes, baby girl, that was your dad and he really wants you to give Sean a chance. He wants me to tell you the baby won't replace you. No one could. Your mom is so amazing, her love is as big as the universe and she will never stop loving you."

Mackayla looked at Jenna with uncertainty in her eyes and said, in a subdued voice, "Can you ask my dad if he'll stay with me forever?"

"He says, he's pretty sure he can promise that." Jenna stroked her niece's hair.

"Can you ask him if he can show me a sign from time to time, just so I know?"

"Sure. He says how about an angel's feather?"

Mackayla smiled widely. "That would be awesome!"

Jenna laughed. "He says consider it done. When you see a white feather, it's from an angel's wing, and he sent it." That said, Mac plucked a feather from one of Sam's wings and let it fall at Mackayla's feet.

"Hey!" Sam exclaimed.

Mac winked at him and Mackayla squealed in sheer joy.

Chapter 20

Baby Makes Five

Jenna's summer passed in the blink of an eye, as time does when you're not paying attention. It was a whirlwind of painting, gallery showings, and, surprisingly enough, working with Sean. It turned out Jenna's unique ability to communicate with angels and her dead brother came in quite handy at times in Sean's line of work. He tried not to abuse their relationship but when things just didn't add up he couldn't resist, and Mac was having a blast referring to himself as "a cosmic private eye."

Because Sean firmly believed in paying attention to his strong and well developed intuition, he was a very good police officer. Unfortunately knowing someone was guilty wasn't the same as proving it and Mac had become invaluable at helping him find the evidence to prove it. Consequently, Sean was being noticed by his superiors and it wasn't long before a promotion was being bandied about. The timing couldn't be better for him either, because soon he would have a family to support.

Out of the blue, Mackayla, who had been fiercely resistant to her mother marrying Sean, had had a change of heart. One day she bounced into the house, hugged her mother, and said she was thrilled at the idea of having a baby sibling and would be happy if her mom said yes to Sean's proposal. Just like that. No rhyme, no reason. Mackayla gave no explanation whatsoever.

So Sean and Olivia set they're wedding date for June the following year. It would be a small backyard wedding with only family and close friends. Sean was already in the process of selling his condo and moving in with

Olivia. He felt a bit odd about living in the house Olivia and Mac shared, but it was a sacrifice he was willing to make for Mackayla's sake. It was lot to ask for her to adapt to all the changes that had already taken place, without asking her to leave the only home she'd ever known, and there was Julia to consider also. She was finally showing signs of recovering from her traumatic start in life and seemed to be settling in. They didn't want to uproot her either.

They talked about getting married before the baby was born but decided the stress of planning a wedding wouldn't be good for Olivia who, being over forty, was already considered a high-risk pregnancy. So baby would be six months old when they said their vows. Neither Olivia nor Sean were traditionalists so although the marriage itself was an outward show of their commitment to one another, the rest was just semantics.

Still, Sean couldn't wait until the day he could call this beautiful woman who had turned his life on its axis, his wife. She was everything he didn't know he wanted and everything he needed in a life partner. They were definitely partners in every aspect. She stood shoulder to shoulder with him, sharing the good and the bad. He didn't know that all these years he'd been existing as half a person until he met Olivia. As corny as it sounded to him, the only way he could explain it was to say she was his other half.

Jenna had to admit they were the perfect couple. Mac and Olivia had been on fire but Sean and Olivia were the slow burn that had the potential to last a lifetime. She was touched beyond words when Olivia asked her to be her maid of honour. When Jenna got emotional, Olivia just laughed and said not to be too thrilled, that she'd only asked her because she knew she'd do all the work. Jenna laughed and hugged her sister-in-law.

Life had also gotten a lot easier for Jenna with Mackayla and Sean in on her secret. She didn't feel so alone anymore and the fact that they didn't treat her like she was completely insane allowed her to relax and just go with the flow. Without classes to juggle and Mac's demands on her diminishing, she was able to focus on her paintings and learning what she could about the spiritual realm from Mac and Sam. They told her as much as they could explain. She was like a sponge absorbing it all.

She was also pleased when, one day out of the blue, Adam reached out to her. She hadn't heard from him since the day he'd showed up on her doorstep. She thought about him periodically and wondered how he was doing. She had Mac keep tabs on him and knew he would let her know when or if he needed her help again. She was surprised at how happy she was to see him looking happy and healthy. He'd just gotten back from the same conference she'd attended, and he was excited to share his new insights with someone who would understand.

She felt bad that she was still keeping this huge secret from the person closest to her, Danny. He was her rock and the separation that felt like a lifetime ago had revealed just how much she loved him. As frustrated as she still got with him at times, she honestly couldn't picture getting older without him by her side. They'd worked hard over the past year and a half, learning how to talk to one another without getting defensive and figuring out how to actually resolve issues as opposed to just not talking about them and letting them fester.

As much as they had settled into a much healthier and happier routine, every so often she caught him looking at her with a strange look on his face. With all the things going on around her all the time, she knew Danny must have a million questions. She also knew he would never ask her. He would wait until she was ready to tell him. She worried that his infinite patience would come to an end before she could figure out how to share all that had happened to her and the things she could see. Every so often, when he looked at her like that, a fist of panic would grip her stomach and leave her breathless.

Even if she could tell him, would he leave because she was batshit crazy? Or would he be pissed because three other people knew before he did? He'd walked in on her many times in the middle of conversations with Mac and Sam. When he asked who she was talking to she would just laugh and say she was talking to herself. When he could see no one else in the room, she assumed he believed her. He would just shake his head and walk away. She noticed lately though that he was getting quieter. She felt like she had to do something to get them back on track. She couldn't risk letting a rift grow between them that could cost her her marriage. He had three weeks' vacation booked in August, so she kept her calendar clear for that time and they planned a trip to their cabin forty minutes outside the city. It would just be her, Danny, and the two silly poodles. She hoped it would give them an opportunity to reconnect before her classes restarted and life got crazy again.

Jenna was busy the day they were leaving, making lists and packing the old truck that would take them down bumpy country roads to their little piece of heaven. .When Danny got home from work she was standing by the truck checking items off her list so intently she didn't even hear him walk up behind her until he wrapped his arms around her waist and laid soft kisses on her neck.

Leaning into him, she murmured, "Hey, baby, how was your day?" She turned to let him wrap her in his arms and took in the musky smell of him. She breathed deeply, loving his scent: a mixture of outdoors, Irish Spring, and sweat.

"Much better now," he responded as he tilted his head and leaned in for a deep, knee-weakening kiss. Packing forgotten, she returned his kiss, taking his lower lip between her teeth. She heard him groan. He pulled back, looking down at her half-closed eyes and kiss-swollen lips, then took her hand and led her into the house and upstairs to their bedroom. Forty minutes later, Jenna stretched her liquid limbs, and rolled over to kiss her sexy husband to find him looking at her with sleepy, contented eyes. "Come on, baby, just a couple more minutes."

Jenna laughed softly. "We have to get on the road before all the campers turn it into a parking lot. Don't worry, though. I have lots of that planned for the next three weeks." She shot him a wicked grin.

With a groan, he rolled off the bed. "Oh, OK. I'll remember that promise."

By the time they were on the highway, dogs sitting in the backseat and panting joyfully at the prospect of a road trip, the roads were just starting to get busy. Thankfully, they'd managed to miss the worst of it. When they reached the cabin, Jenna unpacked the truck while the dogs bounded around, stirring up birds and chasing squirrels. Danny filled the generator with fuel. It would provide power to the cabin and water pump so they didn't have to pump it by hand. He then chopped wood for the wood shed and brought an armful into the cabin for the stove. It was still pretty warm during the day but nights had the potential to get cold this close to the fall season.

They worked together to clear out the dust bunnies and stale air. They put away the groceries and their clothes, hung out clean towels and made the bed with fresh linens. When they were done, they ate a simple supper of scrambled eggs, beans, and toast on the front porch, washing it down with alcohol-free beer. Even though Danny didn't have a drinking problem, he could take it or leave it, so to support Jenna, he'd chosen to leave it.

Once their plates were cleared, Danny pulled out his old guitar and softly strummed as Jenna sat with eyes closed, listening the sounds of nature around her combined with the gentle sounds from Danny's guitar. The dogs slept peacefully at their feet. This was definitely her idea of heaven on earth. So much had happened over such a short period that she couldn't remember when she'd last been able to just sit and breath.

When the air cooled and the mosquitoes came out, Jenna and Danny went inside. Danny built a small fire in the woodstove and they both curled up on the old ratty sofa, Danny with his feet up on the equally old and ratty ottoman and Jenna laying the length of the sofa with her head in Danny's lap, both with a paperback, just enjoying being in one another's presence. The guardian angels stayed within range but out of sight. Mac, not wanting to distract Jenna, had also made himself scarce.

The cabin was completely dark except for the glow of the dying embers in the old woodstove when Danny woke Jenna, who had drifted off to sleep, her book resting on her chest. She sat up with an enormous yawn and followed him to the bedroom where they helped each other undress and crawled into the big iron bed covered in a thick feather duvet. Jenna loved this old bed. The mattress was so soft it felt like a full body hug as she nestled under the sheets and cuddled up tightly to Danny. She was overwhelmed with contentment and love for the man beside her. He was her heart.

They spent their days swimming and hiking and some just making love, slow and lazy, napping in between. They also found without all the noise of their busy city lives, they were able to talk again like they had when they were first dating. It surprised them both that, after almost eighteen years of marriage, there was still so much they didn't know about one another. Over the course of their vacation, they found they both harboured many mistaken assumptions and learned that, as was the tendency with people, many of their old wants and desires no longer held true. For many couples these types of discoveries pulled them apart, but for Jenna and Danny, it drew them even closer together. The only thing that was still hanging over Jenna's head was the knowledge that she was being unfair to Danny in not telling him about Mac and the angels.

They were two weeks into their vacation when she finally found the courage to tell him. They were sitting on the porch watching the sunset one evening after a long day of hiking through the forest trails picking berries for a dessert of mountain pies, when she finally broached the subject. Jenna was dreaming about what it might be like to live at the cabin permanently, when she remembered Danny had spent three months there not so long ago.

Without giving it much thought, she looked over at Danny and said, "Living out here must have been so peaceful?"

Danny gave her a strange look and said, "You do remember the circumstances, right? Peaceful isn't a word I would use. Painful is more appropriate."

Jenna felt the blood rush to her face, "I'm sorry, Danny, I wasn't thinking. I was only thinking about how wonderful these past two weeks have been." She was embarrassed by her thoughtless comment but angry that Danny hadn't taken it in the spirit it was intended. "But just for the record, it wasn't a picnic for me, either."

Then, seeing an opening to broach the subject of the her celestial side-kicks, she took a deep breath and said, "Look, Danny, I'm sorry. It was a terrible time for both of us but I think it really gave us the opportunity to discover how important our relationship is. It's so much more than petty misunderstandings and quarrels. If anything, I feel like it's brought us closer together and taught us how to be open and honest with each other."

Danny nodded his agreement.

Jenna continued. "Something else happened during that time that I didn't tell you about though because, to be honest, it's a little out there, and I'm honestly not sure how you'll react."

His body tensed noticeably as he braced for her confession. He knew there were still things she was keeping from him, but he also knew how hard it was for her to be completely open with anyone. She had been so self-contained for so long, the fact that she was even willing to try with him was enough to keep him engaged.

Jenna took another breath and pushed on. She told him about her life during the months they were separated and left nothing out, including the suicide attempt and Mac's intervention. When she was done, Danny just stared at her. His face was stony but the activity going on behind his eyes was palpable. After a few minutes, he opened his mouth then closed it again. He got up out of his chair and, shaking his head, started walking away. Jenna called out after him but he just held up his hand, signalling her to stop, and continued walking until she couldn't see him anymore.

Well, that went well, she thought to herself as she got up and went into the cabin. She listened for Danny's return as she cleaned up for bed. She wasn't worried about his safety—he was an avid woodsman and the dogs were with him—but she was afraid what she'd told him was a bridge too far. He was the kindest and most tolerant man she'd ever met, but she knew everyone had limits and she was afraid she'd reached his.

As she crawled into the big bed that night, it didn't feel warm or welcoming. It felt cold and empty. Hugging his pillow close to her so she could breathe in his scent, she cried herself to sleep, only to wake a few hours later to the sound of the old cabin door creaking open and the dogs' toenails clicking on the wooden floor as they all came into the cabin.

She'd left the bedroom door open so she would hear them when they got back. Before she could get out of bed to meet Danny, the two poodles pounced on the bed, tails wagging furiously as they licked her face. While she was fending off their puppy loving, Danny came in and pulled them, protesting, one by one, off the bed. Jenna propped herself up into a sitting position and Danny sat down on her side. To her surprise, his face was red and puffy, as though he'd spent hours crying.

Stroking the hair away from her face he looked down at her and said, "Jenna, I'm so sorry. I knew it was tough on you when I left but I had no idea how close I came to losing you. You always seem so strong and able to push through everything. Sometimes, I forget you're just human." He paused before speaking again. "I would never have forgiven myself, you know." Choking up, he fought to get himself under control. "As far as what or who you can see and talk to—or think you can see and talk to—I couldn't care less. I've always known you're special and I love you, end of story." That said, he leaned down and kissed her so gently she found her tears mingling with his. He undressed and crawled into bed beside her. He pulled her close and held her tightly, as though she could disappear at any moment. They both fell into an exhausted sleep.

Mac, Sam, and Danny's angel grinned at each other. They were pretty sure what the outcome would be, but humans had a tendency to be unpredictable. Jenna felt like the weight of the world had been lifted off her shoulders with Danny's full acceptance of her. She couldn't ever remember a time in her life when she'd felt so completely and unconditionally loved.

Back in the city, August soon became September and Jenna was back in the swing of things, juggling classes, art shows, and work on her paintings. Now that she had told Danny about Mac and the angels, he had a new understanding and appreciation for her work. They settled back into a life of kissing one another as they passed through a doorway and stealing rare moments for romance. They may not have had a lot of time together but they made the most of what they had, knowing that at the end of the year when Jenna graduated, things would slow down again.

Thanksgiving came and went. Halloween, too. Before Jenna knew it, it was the Christmas season. Cornucopias were being removed from department store shelves and Christmas decorations were replacing them. Jenna loved Christmas. It was her favourite time of year. As soon as the first snow fell she found herself humming Christmas carols. When her mother was alive it had been a festive occasion with rainbow candies in crystal candy bowls and boxes of chocolates brought out for the multitude of guests her parents entertained all through December. Every year there was someone at their Christmas dinner table who couldn't be with their own families for the season. Her mother even made sure to have a little gift under the tree for them. It was nothing big, just a box of candy or knitted slippers or mitts, but the gifts were always met with tremendous feeling.

Jenna had done her best to keep up the traditions after her mother died but had found it almost impossible. Either her dad wouldn't show up or he'd gobble down the food she'd worked so hard on and head right back out the door before gifts could be exchanged. Mac was no better, often opting to spend time with friends over the season instead of her. After the first couple of years she'd just given up and either stayed home, doing her best to pretend it was just another day, or, on rare occasions, she'd accepted invitations from her own friends' families. When she had her own family she was determined their Christmases would be as magical as her mother had made theirs.

When Olivia joined the family, she and Jenna agreed to take turns hosting one huge family Christmas. This year was Jenna's turn, both because Olivia hosted the year before and because Olivia's baby was almost due and she really needed to take it easy. She was due January 4, but everyone was hoping for a New Year's baby. Olivia was just tired of being pregnant. Her back ached constantly, and she couldn't tell the difference between her ankles and her knees, they were so swollen. And she was exhausted.

It was two weeks before Christmas and she was supposed to be helping Jenna, Brenna, Mackayla, and Julia with the Christmas baking but all she'd managed to do was take off her shoes and sit at the kitchen table with her feet up, sipping herbal tea. Jenna just laughed and said with all her other helpers there was no room in the kitchen anyway, so Olivia would just have to be the official taste tester. That suited Olivia just fine as she closed her eyes and took in the sounds of the cheerful chatter and laughter and Christmas carols playing in the background. She would have never believed she could find this kind of happiness again.

Sean, Danny, Brandon, and Ethan were all out at a tree farm just outside the city looking for the perfect Christmas tree. After the baking was done and the men had returned with the tree, they would have a dinner of take-out pizza and everyone would participate in decorating. It was Jenna and Olivia's tradition and the late-comers to the family could grumble all they wanted but the two women, who were closer than sisters, stood firm. In truth, the grumbling was more light-hearted teasing at how seriously the two took their Christmas traditions.

At the end of the day, when everyone was sitting in Jenna and Danny's living room with the fire crackling in the fireplace and the newly decorated tree shining so brightly that it could be seen in outer space, Olivia let out a soft sigh. She lovingly took in all these people she loved so much gathered together: her niece and nephew, her daughters, her soon-to-be husband, her sister- and brother-in-law. She found herself thinking about Mac.

"I hope you're out there somewhere, my love and that you've found the peace you were looking for," she whispered to herself. A tear slipped down her cheek. She wiped it away before anyone else noticed. Of course Sean did—his eyes never left his beautiful fiancée. But he just attributed the emotion to her pregnancy.

Jenna also sat back and took in the sight of her family chatting and laughing as they ate pizza and drank eggnog. But for her, there was so much more. For every person there was an angel and they were also chatting and laughing and communing. Her living room looked like it would burst at the seams with all the bodies mingling there. Then there was Mac, who sat at Olivia's feet and rested his head on her belly, chatting away to the baby dwelling there. She quietly got up, went into her studio, and grabbed a sketchpad. Then she sat back away from the others and rapidly sketched, a painting already taking form in her mind. She knew she had to capture this scene.

Danny, who'd watched her leave the room and come back with her pad, got up to look over her shoulder.

"Wow!" he said in amazement as the sketch started to come together. "It must be amazing to see the things you can see."

She looked up at him and smiled with eyes shining, full of all the love in the universe, and said, "Yes, my love, it really is."

Two weeks later as everyone sat around the huge dining table enjoying their Christmas dinner, Olivia got up to refill the sweet potatoes when she suddenly doubled over and gasped. The clatter of cutlery and sound of light banter came to an immediate stop as everyone at the table turned to look at her. Jenna and Sean were up and out of their seats at the exact same moment, rushing to her side as a pool of water appeared on the floor at Olivia's feet.

Sean panicked. "Oh my God! What do we do? The baby's not due for another week."

Jenna laughed then put her arm around Olivia's shoulder and slowly walked her to the half-bath, barking orders like a drill sergeant.

"Brenna! Go upstairs and get a pair of sweatpants and a hand towel! Sean, watch for contractions and start timing them. Mackayla, do you know where your mom's bag is for the hospital?" When Mackayla, wide-eyed and frightened looking, nodded yes, Jenna instructed Brandon to take his cousin home and get it and bring it back.

Brenna knocked on the bathroom door and handed the items through the crack Jenna provided. Jenna folded the towel to fit in the crotch of the sweat pants and helped a gasping Olivia get them on. Olivia was much shorter than Jenna so they had to be rolled up in order for her to walk without tripping. That done, Jenna called for Danny to come help guide Olivia to sit on the sofa. The contractions seemed to be coming much faster than they should for early labour.

Jenna took over timing them and sent Sean to call Olivia's obstetrician. When they gave the doctor the details, she told them to get her to the hospital immediately.

As Jenna helped Olivia sit up and start for the door, Olivia yelled, "Stop! Stop! I'm not going to make it! The baby's coming right now!"

Mac was standing beside Jenna now. She turned to look at him and he nodded that, yes, the baby was going to born right there, right now.

Fuck! Jenna thought to herself but outwardly remained calm as Sean completely melted down.

"OK, OK, let's get you lying back down." Gently, Jenna lay Olivia on the living room floor. "Danny, get me some quilts and towels. Just grab an armful, we need to get something clean under her. Sean, call 911, explain the situation—and Sean!" she barked, "calm down! Everyone else, stay out of the way!"

Nervous excitement filled the room as Jenna maneuvered Olivia onto clean blankets and helped her get out of the sweats she'd just helped her into, to find the baby had already crowned. Jenna felt a jolt of panic but she had two angels and Mac guiding her so she just took a deep breath and followed their instructions. Before long, a healthy baby boy was filling the room with angry screams.

Mackayla and Brandon made it back at the exact same time as the ambulance. Brandon put his arm around his cousin's shoulders and pulled her aside, giving the paramedics room to get into the house. Then followed closely behind. Mackayla grinned from ear to ear when she heard the cries of her new baby brother and saw her mother looking no worse for wear.

Jenna laughed as she saw it was Adam on duty. He took a minute to give her a big hug. As Olivia and baby were placed on a stretcher and loaded in the back of the ambulance, Jenna took the time to whisper to Mac, "So, brother, is he anyone we know?"

Mac laughed and said, "Nope, this little guy is brand new. It's his very first life experience and, boy, does he have a lot to learn.

Chapter 21

Graduation Day

Jenna sat at Olivia's breakfast nook looking down at the little bundle in her arms. William Noel Rafferty was three months old now and the happiest baby Jenna had ever seen. Mac leaned over her shoulder making goofy faces and cooing at him. Jenna rarely saw Mac anymore. He spent most of his time with the baby even though William Noel had his own guardian angel. Mac told Jenna he was just there to "show the kid the ropes, being his first time and all." Jenna just laughed and shook her head. Olivia raised an eyebrow in question.

It was already the end of March and, with the wedding only two-and-a-half months away, they needed to solidify plans. Since Jenna was Olivia's maid of honour, she'd taken it upon herself to ensure everything was moving accordingly. Thankfully, her courses were over. All she had left was to finish her practicum and hand in her thesis, so she wasn't spreading herself terribly thin. She didn't have to worry about the venue since it was taking place in Olivia's backyard. Still, she had to organize the rental of the flowered archway, chairs for guests, and a tent in case of rain. She had to get Olivia to select her flowers and order them. And she had to find a caterer.

It surprised everyone when Sean asked Danny to be his best man. Even though they'd become good friends over the past couple of years, everyone expected Sean to ask his younger brother Jake. But Jake was not known for his reliability, and Sean didn't want to risk anything going wrong, so he picked the one person he knew he would be able to count on and that was Danny. Jake would be a groomsman, along with Brandon and

Brenna would be a bridesmaid along with a cousin of Olivia's no one knew. Mackayla and Julia would be walking Olivia down the aisle. The doting grandparents on both sides would have the pleasure of sharing babysitting duties.

Jenna was glad they had at least that much figured out. It was going to be a very small wedding, with the wedding party making up almost half the guests. Olivia and Sean wouldn't have it any other way. The one thing Jenna didn't have to worry about was Olivia's dress. Olivia had picked it out months before and wouldn't let anyone see it, even Jenna. She wanted it to be a complete surprise.

Aside from the wedding planning, Jenna was also busy doing her practicum with Pamela and Rick Simmons. When they weren't running workshops, they each took appointments through the day. Together, they held group sessions two evenings a week. Jenna worked with them during those sessions, working on her thesis on the days in between. So far, she had a 3.8 average but her practicum was worth 5 percent of her grade and her thesis was worth 20 percent, so she was a long way from being home free.

With the importance of finishing her schooling and planning Olivia's wedding Jenna had stopped taking commissions and had postponed any further gallery showings until fall. Technically she'd be graduating the end of May and Olivia's wedding would be June 15, but she and Danny were looking forward to spending the rest of the summer in their little cabin in the woods. She did allow herself to work on one painting though. It was going to be Sean and Olivia's wedding present. She was very anxious that they like it. She was worried that it could be either received very well or very badly. Of course she was hoping for the former.

It was a style she'd never attempted before. Because Olivia loved the folk art of Mexico, Jenna was attempting to paint her version of the style with all the vibrant colours and movements. She had sketched out a family scene of Olivia and Sean with the girls sitting on the sofa gazing down at baby Noel. They'd named him William after Sean's dad, but in order to avoid confusion and in honour of the day he was born they called him by his middle name. The part Jenna wasn't sure would be received well was Mac painted into the clouds on the upper-right corner of the painting. If done right, you would barely notice him. She believed Olivia would be touched but it was Sean's reaction she was most worried about. still, she felt compelled to carry on with it.

It was midway through May by the time she'd finished. She was very pleased with how it had turned out but was still a bit concerned about Sean, so she decided to run it by Danny. He was in her studio looking at it for a long time before speaking. It looked like he was struggling for the right thing to say. Her heart fell. She'd worked so hard on the piece and Danny hated it. He didn't think she should give it to them.

"Jenna, it's amazing, and it's exactly the type of art Olivia loves." He paused. "I do see why you're concerned about how Sean will react, but I have to say, with all honesty, if he reacts badly, he's not the man we all believe him to be. Great job, baby!" Then he turned and kissed her.

She breathed an enormous sigh of relief and kissed him back with exuberance. The kiss had the potential to go much farther, but she had her second-last group session with the Simmons. She didn't have any time to lose, so reluctantly put her hand on Danny's chest and pushed away from him, her eyes still half closed, her breathing heavy.

"Sorry, lover, I have to get going. I'm on the home stretch, I can't fall apart now."

The mournful look he gave her made her laugh as she headed up the stairs to get ready.

That night there were several new faces in the group and the atmosphere felt off to Jenna. She felt like every nerve was strung as tightly as guitar strings. For the first time since she'd started working with the Simmons, Mac showed up.

She went to the bathroom so she could talk to him without anyone seeing her, first checking every stall. Then she turned to him and asked, "What's going on, Mac? Why are you here?"

"Honestly, Jen, I don't know. I was just told to be with you tonight, so here I am."

"Really?" she said, her voice wary. "I can feel something's not right but I just can't put my finger on it." She pondered, then looked him in the eye and asked again. "You have no idea what's going on?"

"I swear, Jenna. I have no more information than you do," he replied, hand where his heart used to be.

"Hummm?" Realizing she wasn't getting any more out of him she left the bathroom with him in tow and reentered the conference room where the group was just getting ready to start.

Most of the chairs around the square conference table were filled, with Pamela and Rick at the front and Jenna sitting back a bit since she was just there as an observer. Group always started with introductions, even if there were no new members. It was just a way of getting things started. Once everyone introduced themselves they were asked to share a bit about why they were there. As Jenna looked around the room at the familiar and not-so-familiar faces, she noticed a well-dressed woman close to her own age sitting beside a small child. Jenna had to do a double take. *What the fuck?* she thought. *Children aren't allowed in these sessions!* She was just about to say something to Pamela when Sam squeezed her shoulder and Mac motioned for her to stay silent.

Picking up her cell phone, Jenna pretended she had to take a call and left the room. Turning to Sam and Mac, she asked what was going on.

"That little boy isn't one of you, he's one of us," Mac said, as he pointed to himself and Sam.

Jenna stared at him, stunned. "What are you saying exactly?"

"He's living challenged, Jen, like me."

"Mac," her voice took on a warning tone, "I don't see ghosts! I see *a* ghost—right?" She said this between her teeth, trying to control their propensity to want to chatter.

"Well?" Mac's voice was cautious as he said, "I'm not entirely sure of that." Then he related what had happened in Lake Louise during the workshop where she first met the Simmons.

Jenna had just opened her mouth to offer her opinion on what Mac had just shared with her when Pamela came out to see if everything was all right.

Forcing a smile, Jenna assured her she was great and would be right in. She pretended to end the call. Going back to her seat, she studied the child sitting beside, who she assumed was his mother. The little boy looked confused as Jenna stared at him. Then he got out of his chair and came to stand beside Jenna.

"Can you see me?" he questioned.

Jenna tried nodding inconspicuously but it was Mac who answered for her. "Yes, she can see us both."

When Mac saw the boy, he immediately knew why Zadkiel had told him to be there that night. Mac knew the woman sitting beside the boy was his mother. Mac already knew the story before she even shared it. When it was her turn to talk, Jenna listened intently.

Her name was Eva and she had just been through a painful divorce from a man who had abused not only her but her son. He was a wealthy businessman worth close to a billion dollars. She hadn't expected to see a penny and honestly didn't care if she did. She'd just wanted to get herself and her son away from him, so when the court awarded $5 million plus child support and alimony, she had been stunned. He was furious, and had vowed to hunt her down and kill her.

Terrified for herself and her son, in December of 2004, she planned a trip to Indonesia. She'd always dreamed of going but had never had the opportunity and she felt it just might be far enough away from the monster she'd married. Of course no one predicted the earthquake or the tsunami that would hit the area that year. Even on the nineteenth floor of their hotel they could not escape the wall of water that washed over them. As the wave hit, Eva grabbed the doorframe and desperately held on with one arm while holding her son in the other. But she just hadn't been strong enough. They were both washed away. Eva's next memory was of waking up in a humanitarian camp. But her son's body was never recovered.

Mac could see the sorrow that had festered all these years. He could also see something that looked like a rope wrapped tightly around her hand. He followed the rope to its end where it was attached to the boy's ankle. He was unable to move on because he was held prisoner by his mother's unresolved guilt and grief.

It was then that he fully understood what Jenna's gift was and he could finally see the mark the other living challenged saw. Behind her left ear was a scar that resembled the eternity symbol. As she listened to Eva, it started to glow with an indigo light that only the living challenged could see. She would help this mother free her son. Mac didn't know how and he didn't know when, he just knew it, as surely as he knew he was coming close to completing his tasks here on earth. He shared with Jenna what he'd seen and told her he thought she would be the one to help Eva free her son. At the end of the group session, Jenna approached the Simmons to ask if it would be out of line for her to talk to Eva privately.

Neither Pamela nor Rick had any concerns with her request. Jenna had proven to be very empathetic and understanding in the time they'd worked with her. Not only that, but she had an uncanny way of cutting through the smoke and mirrors people tended to present and could find her way to the heart of the matter.

Taking Eva aside, Jenna explained who she was and why she was there. She also shared her own stories of loss and tragedy.

"Please don't misunderstand," Jenna said. "I'm not suggesting by any means that what I've suffered is in anyway comparable to what you've suffered. I couldn't imagine the grief of losing a child, especially in the manner you did." Eva nodded, tears coursing down her face.

Jenna wasn't sure how she was going explain to Eva that she was holding her son captive with the strength of her grief. As Eva was sharing her story, though, Jenna had started to sketch the little boy she saw. Having forgotten about it, and was holding it in her hands as she spoke to Eva.

When Eva looked down at her hands she saw the pad and grabbed it. She waved it in her face, asking where she got the sketch. Jenna explained it was her notepad and that she'd been the one to sketch it. Eva was showing signs of hysteria, so Jenna took her into the restroom and ran some cold water on a paper towel, then handed it to her. Eva took it and dabbed at her face. She took a deep breath, turned, and glared at Jenna.

"Explain that picture!" she demanded.

Without going into a lot of detail, Jenna explained that the picture had come to her as she was sitting listening to Eva's story. She explained that she was an artist who often saw things others didn't. As she was talking, the little boy, who was tied tightly to his mother, begged Jenna to tell her to let him go so he could move on.

Jenna didn't know how to do that without being completely honest, so she finally just said, "Look, this is going to sound insane, but I can see your son. He's standing right beside you. As a matter of fact, he's tied so tightly by your inability to move past his death that he can't move on. He's begging me to help you free him."

Eva stood staring at Jenna wordlessly. Jenna expected an angry tirade but she didn't expect Eva to quietly ask, "How do I do that?"

Jenna said, "I'm not sure. But we can figure it out together if you'll give me a chance."

Eva agreed and they set up a time to get together after Olivia's wedding.

Jenna finished her last session with the Simmons with rave reviews and, once her thesis was marked, she had a solid 3.9 grade point average. She graduated with her family cheering her on.

Next was the wedding, which went off without a hitch. Olivia looked stunning in a vintage dress of ivory lace that suited her to a tee.

The look on Sean's face as he watched her walk down the gravel pathway made everyone tear up. When the ceremony was over and it was time for the gift opening, Olivia announced that there was going to be a slight change. Before she and Sean opened their presents they had one of their own to present. They called Julia up to join them at the table overflowing with presents and gave her an envelope. Mackayla, looking like the cat that swallowed the canary, knew what was in the envelope and couldn't wait to see Julia's face.

Mac grinned as Julia tore open the envelope and began to read. A slow smile made its way across her face then she let out a "Whoop!" before running to Olivia and hugging her and then Sean tightly. As she cried tears of joy, Olivia announced the addition of her and Sean's daughter, Julia Ann Rafferty. Family and friends cheered and offered congratulations to the entire Rafferty family and Sean's parents hugged their new granddaughter. Olivia's parents had already accepted her as theirs—to them this was simply semantics.

When all the gifts were open, only one remained: Jenna's. Jenna had asked that they save hers for last. Her heart was in her throat as they tore the paper off and exposed the painting.

Olivia gasped and Mackayla exclaimed, "Look, there's daddy in the clouds."

Everyone waited with baited breath for Sean's response. With a big grin on his face, he hugged Jenna tightly and offered up a toast to Mackenzie Doyle, the reason he'd found Olivia.

Olivia hugged Jenna and said it was absolutely perfect!

Danny winked at Jenna.

With Jenna having graduated and Olivia's wedding behind them, life settled into a dull routine. Jenna started her own art therapy practice out of her home. Her first patient, of course, was Eva. The Raffertys were settling into wedded bliss. Life was back on track.

Mac wasn't surprised when he got called back up to the ether to meet with Zadkiel. Raphael was with him, both sitting on rocks overlooking an ocean.

"So, Mackenzie, it looks like you've accomplished what you were sent to earth to do. What did you learn?"

Mac stood there for a long time then said, "Well, I learned no man is an island, and despite common belief, no one enters the world alone and no one leaves it alone. To quote a pretty cool medic that I unfortunately couldn't help, 'No matter whether an action is positive or negative, every action is like a stone being tossed into a pond. The ripples it causes are far more reaching than any human can predict.'"

No sooner had he said this than Rita appeared to stand beside Zadkiel and Raphael. "You learned well, my son," she said then laughed at the look of confusion on Mac's face.

"Oh, Mac, I appreciate your attempt to get my life back on track, but I was gone long before you got there. However, I had a lesson of my own to impart and you took it to heart. Well done!"

Zadkiel cleared his throat, bringing Mac's attention back to him. "Now that you've completed your task, you can choose a body and a family. Which one appeals?" he asked, as he cleared the ocean scene away to show all the babies in utero.

Mac looked at the scene in front of him then back at Zadkiel and asked, "Can I just hang out with my family for a while? I feel like I can be of value to the new guy."

Zadkiel looked at Raphael and, after a few moments they both nodded their consent. Before Mac could blink, he was back with on earth with his family.

Jenna was sitting in her studio working on the sketch she'd made at Christmas when Mac got back.

"Hey, Mac, welcome back. You've been gone for a while." Then she looked beyond him and stopped mid-brush stroke as tears filled her eyes. "Hi Dad," she said. "It's been a long time."

About the Author

D. J. Callaghan is well equipped to write a book that tackles the difficult subjects of mental illness and loss. She has fought her own battles with these monsters and has lost numerous people to trauma. She wrote this book at the lowest point of her life, when she needed a story with a happy ending.

D. J. Callaghan lives in Edmonton, Alberta, with her husband and two fluffy standard poodles named Artimus and Black Jack Sparrow.